MASLOW'S BASEMENT

AIA PUBLISHING

DON THOMPSON

Maslow's Basement
Don Thompson
Copyright © 2023
Published by AIA Publishing, Australia
ABN: 32736122056
http://www.aiapublishing.com

ISBN: 978-1-922329-48-6

"Life is never made unbearable by circumstances, but only by lack of meaning and purpose."
Viktor Frankl

"The mystery of human existence lies not in just staying alive, but in finding something to live for."
Fyodor Dostoyevsky

"The two most important days in life are the day you are born and the day you discover the reason why."
Mark Twain

"If you ain't cruisin', you're bummin'."
Scott Fischer

One

I'm Roger Carrington, homeless CEO. That's not a Wall Street euphemism for a fired executive or a corporate leader taking a break between ventures to reconnect with family. No, I'm being much more literal. There's no family to reconnect with, anyway. No siblings, parents both dead, just an ex-wife ten years gone and two thousand miles distant.

I still have a corner office, though, doubling as the Residence—new construction on a prime piece of real estate on the northeast corner of a dirt lot under the I-5 in Seattle. A "coveted location," as my broker used to say. Good bones made from old shipping pallets I found nearby. I even have a view if I'm willing to drag my sorry ass five minutes down the road. Then I can see a small splash of blue, a single slice of Elliott Bay down the hill as Pine Street cuts through the ever-expanding forest of tall buildings on its way toward the water.

Those buildings, or smaller ones like them in Colorado, were my natural habitat for years. Now my habitat is considerably more natural, except for the wet whish and hum of traffic that serves as an unnecessary and unwanted alarm clock above me. On this gray drizzly morning in February, water drips from the edges of the overpass, setting up a muddy border around the camp I've begun to call home, separating it from what most people consider the real world.

A seagull banks in with a raucous cry and lands on the dirt a few yards away, keeping one beady eye on me until I turn up my palms as if to say, "Sorry pal, no scraps this morning." Then off he goes to try his luck elsewhere. I wonder if my hand movements scare him away, or if he attaches some meaning to them. I like to think he does.

At least he introduced himself. That's more than I can say for the humans living here. But I get it; I'm the new guy and won't be sticking around long if I can help it, so why should they bother with me? Hell, I don't even know if I want them to. It's probably better if I just keep my distance. But I do know their names, because I overheard some conversations through the thin cardboard walls of the Residence the other night. There's Mary, who lives in an army surplus tent across the way, Carlos, who has a shack something like mine and seems to spend most of his time on the nearby street corner in a yellow poncho trolling for money, and then there's Jimmy. Jimmy doesn't talk much, but when I heard a word or two yesterday, I could tell something wasn't right. His little lean-to, propped up against a concrete wall, could easily pass for a trash pile.

The rest of the space under our overpass is taken up with stored city equipment—a snowplow, a street sweeper, shipping containers, and scrap material. At least, I think it's scrap. If not, then I'm now a petty thief as well as a white-collar felon. My résumé grows, even here.

I crawl out of the Residence and bring my thinning, sixty-three-year-old frame to its full six-foot height, stretching each arm in turn toward the traffic above, working out the kinks. Yesterday, someone on the street asked me if I was Jeff Bridges, the actor. I guess my age and still-abundant long gray hair might have been a factor, and I took the rare compliment with silence and a smile, enjoying the fantasy and leaving the question dangling.

But back to reality. The sleeping conditions here aren't great, so I've scavenged enough clean rags and packing material to soften the ground a bit. Some folks have it a lot worse, like the doorway people downtown, or the addicts in their leaky tents on the sidewalk, or the old man I saw yesterday on the park bench covered with plastic trash bags against the rain. The overpass is like a hotel—well, maybe a motel—compared to their digs. And even prison seems almost luxurious in hindsight.

Life is a twisted path, and I've spent many hours revisiting mine, trying to understand how I got here, blaming anyone and anything but me. But I've finally come to the same inescapable conclusion that Margaritaville's Jimmy Buffet did: It's my own damn fault. That doesn't make things any easier, but it does free up the mind and simplify life. My executive to-do list, for example, is very concise:

1. Pee
2. Fill up water bottle
3. Find food

I walk a few yards away from the Residence, stand behind one of the massive concrete pillars holding up the freeway, and anoint it. *Pees be with you.* I smile and zip up. *And also with you*, I imagine it replying, a bit more spitefully than I think necessary. I mean, come on, I've given it a new raison d'**être**.

I check my water bottle, one of my few possessions remaining from the old days, and it's a little under half-empty. Its corporate logo seems to mock me, and I've almost thrown the damn thing away more than once, but it's made of high-grade stainless steel and will last forever. So I keep it and try to ignore the logo. I splash some of the water on my face and graying beard, rub it in with my hands, and dry off with my pulled-up T-shirt. I drink the rest.

The bottle goes into my daypack—another artifact from my ancient past—and I head across the lot, in front of Jimmy's drafty lean-to, past Mary's tent, and toward the street corner where Carlos is beginning his day. Mary sits just inside her tent, wrapped in a coarse wool blanket, and looks the other way as I pass. I approach the street corner and think, what the hell, I'm stuck with these folks for a while, so maybe I should at least try to be civil. I shout out to Carlos over the rising traffic noise, "Buenos días!"

He just rolls his eyes, shakes his head, and looks away toward the oncoming traffic. Maybe I shouldn't assume he speaks Spanish, or if he does, that he wants to hear it mangled by an old white guy like me. I probably offended him, but shit, give me a break. I walk on down toward the park.

On the way, I think about the little things that are becoming big red pins in the mental map of my diminished geography. The drinking fountain in the park. The public restrooms around town. The showers with decent water pressure down at the shelter on Yesler. The restaurants with the cleanest discards and the best times to check them. The guys to stay away from.

I pause at the park to fill up my water bottle and take in the scene: a winding path among old-growth trees, wet grass, the old man asleep on his bench, covered with black plastic trash bags against the droplets that still fall from the tree canopy long after a rain. I tried to talk with him yesterday but couldn't get anything more than a questioning stare from the brown wizened face under the tan cowboy hat, as if he were trying to remember me or gauge my intentions. Today I try again, but with the same sad results. He looks like a "Tex" to me, so that's what I decide to call him. Stereotypes be damned.

I walk on, passing nameless people in the street who seem in a serious hurry to get to their offices and begin their important days. They probably think they're impervious to ruin, infinitely distant from the likes of me, a different species. But they're wrong. We're all just two or three bad decisions or unfortunate events away from the edge. They avoid eye contact and I keep moving.

The high-end breakfast place on lower Pike might be good for a handout if I happen to catch the right busboy in the alley at the right time, so I pick up my pace and arrive at about nine, right after the early diners finish. The place reminds me of a favorite restaurant in Boulder where I once pitched venture capitalists and strategized with board members, but I try to push that memory aside as I approach the dumpster.

I can see someone on the other side of the big bin, just coming out the back door. I'm in luck; it's the same busboy I met a few days ago. I strain to remember his name and then it comes to me, just in time.

"Hey, Ernie, good to see you! Anything you want to get rid of this morning?"

"I don't know, man. Kenny almost fired me the other day for handing out stuff."

"Kenny?"

"Yeah, the shift manager."

I file away Kenny's name, having learned years ago in my corporate life that remembering and using names is a powerful thing, even when you don't actually give a rat's ass about the people behind them.

"So is Kenny working today?"

"No, but . . ."

"Look, Ernie, I really appreciated what you did for me the other day. Do you think you could just take a second to help me out one more time? Anything would be great. Day-old stuff, anything."

Ernie glances back toward the door. "Hold on. Let me see what I can do." Minutes later, he's back with a couple of stale cinnamon rolls and a leftover frittata.

"Thanks, buddy. Appreciate it."

Ernie nods and disappears back into the restaurant. I stuff the food into my backpack and move on down the road. My next stop is a pizza place down in SoDo called Tedesco's. I remember it from my young days in Seattle, but I'm surprised to see there's another spot just a few doors away with a new sign reading *Chicago Pies*.

I brush off my shirt and pants, run a hand through my long gray hair, and walk in the front door of Tedesco's. There are no customers.

"Excuse me," I ask the first person I see, a young man with dark hair, facial stubble, and a baseball cap. "Could I speak with the manager?"

"That would be me," he responds. "Actually, I'm the owner, Bart. And you are?"

"Roger," I say, extending my hand. I can feel Bart's eyes on my clothes and I wonder what he's thinking. I need to start things off right if I have any hope of making this a regular stop.

"Good to meet you, Bart," I continue. "Say, I was just noticing the new pizza place down the street. They giving you a run for your money?"

Bart laughs, nervously I think, looks to the side, then back at me. "What do you mean?"

"Well, no disrespect, but I just noticed they've got people waiting outside to get in and your place is empty. I'm a businessperson between gigs right now, and I'm just curious. I mean, you've been here for years, right?"

Bart doesn't respond right away, and I think I've lost him. But then, "Look, if you're hoping for a job, you've come to the wrong place. I'm not hiring. Obviously." Bart glances around the empty dining room.

"No, that's not it. I've been dealing with some challenges out of state for a while and came back here where I grew up to work on a new start. Things are moving slower than planned and I just need a little food to tide me over. Simple as that."

"Damn, I'm sorry, but I can't just give away stuff right now. You said you're a businessman, right? You've got to understand that. Maybe once I get out of this slump, okay? But not now."

"Sure," I say. "I get it. But just hear me out for a minute. How about I give you some free business advice and then I'll come back in a week or two. If things have improved, maybe you could give me a hand then. What do you say?"

"No disrespect to you either, but why should I listen to your advice? I mean . . ." Bart looks me up and down.

"Fair point. Still, just give me three minutes and maybe you'll change your mind."

Bart throws up his hands, points to a table, and invites me to sit.

"So how long has your place been in business?" I begin.

"Forty-five years, but I just bought it from the original owner two years ago."

"And how's it been going? Until recently, I mean."

"Good, actually. It helps to be right down here by the ballpark and football stadium. That's why I bought it. I used to clean up on game days and did okay in between. But now it's looking bleak. It didn't use to be that way."

"Before your competition set up shop down the street?"

"Right, but this area should be able to easily support two of us, no problem."

I nod and pretend to be thinking, but the situation is obvious.

"Okay Bart, here's the thing. Your customers are mostly sports fans, right?"

"Sure." Bart shrugs.

"Seattle sports fans, specifically," I continue. "They care about the Mariners and the Seahawks. They care about Seattle. By and large they don't give a crap about Chicago, but they've heard about their good pizza, so they give it a try. You've got to give them a reason to come back to you, so appeal to their hometown and team loyalties."

"By doing . . . ?"

"A few things. First, rename your place. Call it something like 'Home Team Pizza.' Then throw some unique Seattle items onto the menu. Like Geoduck Pizza, or Oysters on the Half Pie, or 12th Man Breadsticks, or I don't know, almost anything fun that ties you to Seattle or the teams. Differentiate yourself from the competition and become *the* Seattle sports pizza place. Invest in two or three high-quality screens and show the games. Attract the ticketless overflow crowd. Make it feel disloyal to eat Chicago pizza without actually saying that."

"Yeah, I don't know."

"Just think about it, okay? I'll check back in a few weeks to see how you're doing." I get up with a smile and head for the door empty-handed. But I've made a little investment. Now I'll just have to wait to see if it pays off.

It's hard on the ego, begging for food, but if I can strike a deal of some kind, that makes it easier. Asking for money feels completely different. I just can't do that, but I'll need a little cash for basic supplies from time to time and I don't know how I'm going to get it. I mull that over while walking back toward the heart of the city.

On the way, I pick up some day-old burritos at a food truck and make a new contact there. Now I've got more than enough food for today, and it won't keep, so what the hell. I decide to stop by the park on the way home and see if Tex wants something.

But when I arrive, Tex's bench is empty and a police car is pulling away. I think I see Tex in the back. Yeah, the guy's wearing a cowboy hat; it's him. They probably got him for loitering and are either taking him to jail or relocating him somewhere else in the city. I shake my head and move on toward the overpass. At least if he's in lockup for the night, he'll probably stay warm and get some food.

I'm still thinking about Tex and the extra food as I get to the overpass at dusk. Mary's tent is zipped up and Carlos is nowhere to be seen, but Jimmy is standing outside his hovel looking lost. I walk up to him while digging into my pack for a burrito.

"Hey Jimmy. My name's Roger."

"Get back! I can see what you're doing there."

Jimmy's eyes are flying between me and my pack as he

9

backs toward his shack.

"No, Jimmy, I've just got some extra food here and thought maybe you'd like some."

"How do you know my name? Did Jay-Jay tell you?"

"No, I just overheard someone using your name the other day. I live over there," I say, pointing to the Residence.

"Jay-Jay knows everything that goes on around here," Jimmy says.

I still hear fear in his voice, but Jimmy's shoulders have dropped a bit and he's taken a tentative step back toward me. He's looking at the burrito in my hand.

"Here," I say, slowly placing the burrito in its wrapper, along with one of the stale cinnamon rolls, on a nearby rock. "If you want this, you're welcome to it."

Jimmy nods. I take that as a thank-you and walk the last few steps home in the growing darkness.

Two

As I drift toward sleep under the white noise of overhead traffic, I avoid the present by revisiting the past. I'm lucky, I know. So many homeless folks around town hide from reality through chemistry instead. Meth, mostly, and recently P2P meth, which brings them to their mental knees in months, not years like the older ephedrine-based stuff. I'm starting to see it everywhere now.

I wonder if Jimmy is an addict, but I think he's probably just got some mental problems. We all have different kinds of anchors holding us down, and some of us have set our own; we just haven't found ways to get them off the bottom yet. I've heard activists talking about things like affordable housing, and that's great, but it's completely irrelevant if those anchors can't be weighed or cut loose. I'm learning firsthand that affordability is a very relative thing.

And so I revisit the past in an effort to understand my own firmly stuck anchor and find ways to free it. Or maybe I'm just avoiding the present. Whatever it is, I do this most nights, and the experience is like a lucid dream, one that sometimes lasts for over an hour and feels hauntingly real. I like to imagine if I can change the dream I can change the present—a kind of mental time machine without the nasty paradoxes.

Tonight, I drift back to my first days at Deep Learning Systems. The founders of DLS had come out of the University of Colorado two years earlier, and Jacob Hartman, a newly minted computer science PhD with a hard-driving analytical nature, was the natural leader of the bunch. He had decided that entrepreneurship looked better than a postdoc stint in some academic enclave and had convinced the others, Jennifer Dickinson and Wade Cantwell, to share the risks and potential rewards with him. Jennifer held MSEE and MBA degrees, and Wade had plowed through medical school, done a residency in psychiatry, then become enamored with the intersection between human and artificial intelligence. He set aside the potential of a lucrative psychiatry practice to pick up an MSCS degree, and was now looking forward to applying his combined background at DLS using AI techniques to help guide psychotherapy. The team worked out of Jake's basement in Boulder for the first two years, developing technology within the architectural framework laid out in Jake's dissertation, and combining their personal resources with a modest angel investment from someone on their advisory board.

I had flown from Seattle to Denver, after resigning from Microsoft Research a week earlier over a dispute about technology transfer, and was being recruited by the DLS board to provide a mature business perspective—to "put a little gray on the team," as one adviser described it. I took no offense at that, having accepted my late fifties with the confidence that came from a successful career in the mid to upper echelons of management in a variety of well-known tech firms ranging from AT&T to Sun Microsystems to Microsoft, with a couple of smaller stops in between. None of those management positions, however, would bring me much credibility with the bright young founders of Deep Learning Systems. For that, I would have to rely on my early AI work at Bell Labs following my PhD from the University of Colorado, and even that experience probably wouldn't earn me much more than an interested nod or two.

But as I met with the founders for the first time at a favorite breakfast spot just off the Pearl Street Mall, I was betting it would be enough to get me started. I knew my hiring would depend in large part on acceptance by the core team, but there was another important side to the question as well: I needed to determine whether this little start-up was right for me, whether it had the potential to become the financial success I needed to cap my career. I had spent much too freely on houses, cars, alimony, and a cash-draining but beloved boat. It was time to get serious about replenishing the coffers so I could maintain my lifestyle in retirement, which was looming not far down the road. I had to convince myself that the company's founders, their technology, the product concept, and the target market all added up to something that felt like a winner.

I walked into the café and immediately spotted three young people sipping coffee and quietly perusing menus at a table near the back of the small dining room—two men and a woman—all dressed in expensive-looking business suits. In Boulder, this was almost as shocking as encountering a ballerina wearing a tutu and pointe shoes on a wilderness trail. Still, I thought, *Okay, maybe they're just trying to impress me with their seriousness.*

"Hi, you must be the team from Deep Learning Systems," I said, smiling and extending my hand to the man nearest me.

I was met with a confused stare. "No, we're here for the International Corporate Law Conference. And you are?"

I was rescued at that moment by a tap on my shoulder and turned around to see a fit, young Black man dressed in dark jeans, a white T-shirt, and a loose green sweater.

"Over here," he said, laughing and nodding toward the other side of the room, near the fireplace. Still chuckling, with his hand on my shoulder, he guided me over to a table where the other two founders stood waiting for me, smiling. I suddenly felt twenty years older.

My guide introduced himself as Jake Hartman and the others followed, still looking amused at my mistake. Wade was a short young man with curly blond hair, a full reddish beard, and intense eyes, and Jennifer, who insisted on being called Jenny, had a pretty, bookish demeanor with glasses and long dark hair tied in a neat ponytail. I had a good laugh at myself and felt my age return to something nearer reality as I ordered the omelet special, and we all joined in small talk about the upslope snowstorm predicted for late the next day.

Soon the conversation turned to business. The three founders were clearly excited about their work and seemed to be watching my reactions closely as they described it. Jake's dissertation had taken a novel approach to the design of extremely fast, deeply layered neural networks—a form of artificial intelligence well suited to the analysis of images and natural language. Jenny's work involved the creation of an ultra-high-performance hardware platform for neural network execution built around parallel graphics processing hardware, and Wade was hoping to apply this powerful combination of technologies to increase the effectiveness of cognitive behavioral therapy. He intended to take advantage of existing patient–therapist transcripts and audio recordings, along with prognoses and actual outcomes, to provide advice to therapists.

The idea was to use natural language processing to identify which parts of a conversation between therapist and patient were most effective at treating disorders such as anxiety, depression, and PTSD, and then use this knowledge to guide therapists, either as a post-session learning tool or as an in-session real-time assistant. Wade described related work already done in the UK that had yielded a 53 percent patient recovery rate compared to the national average of 51 percent—a seemingly small percentage increase, but one representing tens of thousands of people. Another UK-based start-up had been touting a 73 percent recovery rate for generalized anxiety disorders, compared to the unassisted national average of 58 percent.

I was intrigued but hadn't yet heard anything that led me to believe there was a marketable product in the works, let alone a solid business plan. Wade's description of the intended application helped, but it left me with more questions. How would the technology be packaged for sale? Clearly, there was a large software component, but would there be a physical piece as well, incorporating Jenny's unique hardware work? Would the cognitive behavioral therapy community even accept such a product, let alone use it? Did the team and their advisers imagine a direct sales force? Practitioners would naturally be skeptical and would need convincing evidence of effectiveness and usability. There might be substantial cultural resistance to the use of artificial intelligence in this field. Was there a realistic revenue projection, or was this team going to present me with the usual wildly optimistic "hockey stick" graph soaring into the stratosphere soon after product launch?

Over the next two hours, and several coffee refills, I pressed them on these and other questions. Jake handed me a copy of their business plan and used it to illustrate and support many of the team's answers, most of which I found encouraging. The first target market segment would be online talk therapy (with later expansion to in-person sessions), and the primary competitive edge would be real-time advice provided to the therapist during sessions in addition to post-session analysis. Wade stressed the importance of positioning the product as a tool for therapists and not a replacement for their skills. Patients would interact only with the human therapist, not with the technology. All this, he admitted, would require some nuanced marketing, a talent they currently lacked.

Jenny described a cloud-based approach to the product that placed her specialized hardware and the team's software in large third-party data centers, eliminating physical product shipment to customers and allowing it to be sold as a subscription service accessed via broadband internet connections. I suggested they consider Microsoft's then-emerging Azure platform, with its scalability and guaranteed up-time, and the team seemed receptive.

Naturally, there were several holes in the business plan, but none that seemed fatal. And in a way, this was what I had hoped to see, as it reinforced the need for the kind of leadership I felt I could bring to the fledgling company. I liked the recurring revenue model implied by the subscription scheme, and while there seemed to be some competition brewing in this market, the team had yet to identify anything to rival their novel technology in terms of its real-time performance and low costs. Their recognition of *some* competition, though, was what I wanted to see. I knew that a lack of emerging competition often implied a lack of market altogether.

The team's revenue projections, however, were considerably lower and slower than I expected. I'd thought I would have to warn them about overoptimism, but it seemed I would need to do the opposite. The market appeared poised to take off, and they needed to move more quickly to meet demand and establish dominance. They were clearly enamored with the early stages of their unique technology but seemed reluctant to share this with an expanded development team as early as I thought necessary. I would need to push hard on this point but without bruising egos or alienating the team. And to accelerate progress, we would need to attract a solid round of equity investment as soon as possible. I began to see that as my top priority—if I took the job. At the same time, I didn't want to do anything that would result in a premature product which might damage the company's credibility and lead to failure.

On the other side of our discussion that morning, I found myself being thoroughly vetted by the team, something I expected and found encouraging. These people cared deeply about their venture, and they wanted to be certain about bringing in the right kind of leadership. I detected some natural pushback when I commented on the technology, relying on my aging PhD and high-level experience at Microsoft Research. They wanted to be sure that a new CEO would provide solid, knowledgeable leadership without micromanaging the technical team.

We wrapped up our discussions as the restaurant was beginning to prepare for the lunch crowd. By that time, I was all but certain I wanted the challenge, but I wasn't sure the founders were convinced about me. That is, until the last few minutes, when Jake mentioned something about ice-climbing plans for the coming weekend. I'd never done any technical ice-climbing, but I had lots of rock-climbing tales to tell, and I shared one of them about a route up Mt. Baker, north of Seattle. As a much younger man, I'd preferred solo climbing, as risky as it was, and I'd be surprised if this wasn't the credential that tipped the scales and won the approval of the founders. But winning the board's approval would prove to be another matter.

Three

The morning after that long breakfast meeting, I got a call from Stan Gorman, the chair of the company's advisory board, inviting me to dinner that evening in Gold Hill, a historic former mining town up in the mountains ten miles west of Boulder. Stan was a graying, slightly overweight, middle-aged professor in the Leeds School of Business at my alma mater, the University of Colorado, and was known to— if not liked by—every entrepreneur up and down the Front Range. Years ago, I had considered hiring him as a consultant for a strategic planning effort at Microsoft, but I felt the cultural fit was wrong and never even interviewed him. Now the tables were turned, and Stan was in a position to hire me. Or not.

"So what do you think of our three founders?" he asked, as we started up Sunshine Canyon in his black trail-ready Jeep Wrangler. A loaded question if I'd ever heard one.

"Sharp, motivated. Excited about their technology, as they should be," I said. "A little naive when it comes to getting a start-up off the ground fast enough to grab market share. Maybe a little guarded about their ownership. Filling out the team with equally competent and driven developers might challenge their egos a bit."

"Uh-huh."

I couldn't read Stan's reaction, and I thought I smelled alcohol on his breath as he turned toward me. Did he agree with my assessment of the team, or was he just acknowledging my statement? He focused on the road ahead as the pavement ended.

The remaining part of the route up the mountain was a classic Colorado twisty no-guardrails gravel road with precipitous drop-offs into a rocky canyon on one side. Stan's jeep was handling it well, and I had lots of experience with this kind of road, but my foot jumped to an imaginary brake pedal more than once as we narrowly recovered from skids around unguarded curves. Being in the passenger seat was a far different experience from being in control.

The dimming of the evening sky and the predicted snowstorm made our situation feel even more perilous as we went along, and when we arrived at the Gold Hill Inn and stepped out of the jeep, I was surprised to find my legs shaking. My steady old rock-climbing mentality seemed to have all but evaporated with the years. I was also feeling the altitude. Stan seemed completely unfazed by any of this, and I did my best to appear the same. Still, I couldn't help but wonder how our trip down the mountain later that night would feel in total darkness and falling snow.

The warm glow of a rustic fireplace greeted us as we entered the inn's dining room, and I slowly felt my blood pressure return to normal. Nestled beneath the Continental Divide, the inn felt remote, warm, and inviting. Boulder had managed to retain most of its charm, but it had also become a busy, high-energy entrepreneurial town in the last decade, and being just a few miles away, in this old mining town in the Rocky Mountains, was a nice reminder of the old days.

Even so, I knew I needed to pull some of Boulder's entrepreneurial energy up the mountain with me if I was to get what I wanted that night. Earlier in the day, after a follow-up conference call with the founders and brief meetings with the other board members, I had decided that I wanted to pursue this new venture and develop DLS into a real company, with the goal of taking it public and reaping a chunk of the financial rewards. I was very early in the game, and those rewards could be significant if I kept a level head and made rational, impersonal business decisions like those which had gotten me this far in my career.

In a gesture that I took to be a good omen, Stan ordered a bottle of DeLille Cellars D2, one of my favorite Bordeaux-style blends from Washington State, and the waiter poured us each a glass after Stan tasted and approved it. We ordered our entrées and the waiter disappeared.

"To a fruitful discussion," Stan toasted.

"A fruitful discussion," I echoed, clinking glasses.

"So you've given me your initial impression of our fledgling team," Stan continued. "What about the product concept? Is this something you could get behind?"

"Absolutely. I think it's well differentiated from the nascent competition, thanks mostly to the unique hardware-augmented design of the deep learning system. And the cloud-based subscription model is a winner, in my view."

"Hmm, you sure about the subscription model?" Stan asked. "I've been trying to change their young minds on that one."

"Yeah, I'm convinced. You sacrifice some revenue up front, but the recurring cash flow from a larger set of smaller customers can be a huge stabilizing factor. And we can still push for an earlier revenue start."

"Okay, now we're talking about something near and dear to me. With Jake's current plan, we're years away from any substantial revenue, let alone profitability. I want to see us divert some engineering resources to fix that."

I distinctly remember my alarm at Stan's words as I tried to hide my concern. "What did you have in mind?" I asked.

"With the technology we have today, and a few months of new work, we could come out with a talk therapy app like you're starting to see out there. You know, one of those apps on your phone that can hold a decent text conversation with you, provide a little empathy, maybe even help people think through their problems? With our technology, we could make one that feels a lot more real than the others you hear about, and start bringing in some revenue right away. Once that happens, we can return to the main product focus."

I couldn't believe what I was hearing, and "Big Red Flag" didn't begin to describe my alarm at that moment. But still, I kept as cool as possible, seeing enormous potential in the company and not wanting to jeopardize my opportunity.

"I, uh, share your desire to accelerate things, but respectfully, I don't think that's the way to do it."

"Why not?" Stan asked. "It would only be a temporary placeholder and could decrease the amount of shareholder dilution that I—*we* would suffer from a large venture round."

"Stan, there are several apps like that out there today, and they're all disappointing. They're toys. I've tried using a few out of sheer curiosity. If we threw another one into the market with the extra bit of engineering you propose, even if it worked somewhat better than the others, we'd look like fools. It could seriously damage our credibility within our actual target market. And beyond that, the basic technology your team is developing has enormous potential for other applications down the road. In my opinion, we need to keep focused on that core strength."

"I guess we'll have to agree to disagree on that for now," said Stan.

"Okay, as long as you understand I'd continue to push back if I were to join the company," I added, deciding that taking this stand was fundamental.

"Let's move on. What are we missing?" Stan asked, as he held his glass up to the light of the fireplace, looked through its dark ruby contents, and then back at me. Obviously, he was asking about things he'd already formed strong opinions about. I'd been on the hiring end of interviews for years and now had to consciously adjust to the subordinate position, tamping down some mild annoyance.

I allowed myself a small chuckle. "What are you missing? Well, about 90 percent of the company, I'd say. You're going to need an engineering team at least five or six times the size of your current one, including a few folks with cloud-based deployment experience." I noticed Stan wince at my last remark. "You'll need a marketing guru and a small team of smart businesspeople under them, and you'll need those first, before even thinking about a sales team. Then I'd recommend a dedicated test group, separate from the development team for objectivity, and a support organization, well-trained and field-ready. Oh, and one HR person to start with."

"Anything else?"

I had to laugh again. "Money. Lots of it. You're going to need a solid round of venture funding to support this kind of buildup. But you know that already."

"What about sales strategy? How do you see us getting to our target customers?"

"I've given that some thought," I said. "And I'd recommend borrowing an approach from the pharmaceutical companies. You'll need sales reps who have credibility with both therapists and administrators—people who can connect with the staff like the drug reps do. People with psychology backgrounds, even advanced degrees, if you can find them."

The entrées came and the conversation slowed as we enjoyed our roast elk and wild boar. But then, seemingly out of nowhere, came Stan's next comment. "Roger, here's the thing. You've never done this before, and that concerns me."

"Beg your pardon?"

"You've never run a start-up before."

I took another sip of wine and noticed that Stan's glass was already empty. I filled it for him. "You're right, in a literal sense. But you've seen my CV. I've started and run product groups twice the size DLS will ever be, all within major corporations."

"Ah, but that's the difference," Stan countered. "Those large corporations have nearly unlimited resources, established infrastructure, strong branding and huge existing market presence. You won't have any of that to build on."

"A fair point," I said. "But I've seen firsthand what those components look like after they've been refined by fire over decades; I've seen serious mistakes made too—some by me— in exploiting those key resources, and I know how to avoid those mistakes. I also know when to recruit critical expertise I don't personally have. I have absolutely no problem hiring people smarter than me."

Stan nodded. "One more thing. If it became necessary

down the line, would you have any problem firing one or more of the founders, or even lobbying to oust a board member?"

I wondered about the background of the question but didn't hesitate. "None at all. I've had plenty of experience terminating employees and avoiding legal complications. I've found that the key's not to get too personally involved with the team while still earning their respect. Everyone has a sell-by date."

Stan had finished his second large glass of wine, while my first was still half full. He flagged down the waiter. "Could we have two generous pours of your best cognac to finish off here?"

I was getting concerned but knew I couldn't refuse the gesture. I could see freezing rain turning to snow outside the window and knew the road down the mountain would be treacherous, especially with an intoxicated driver.

The table was cleared and the cognacs arrived. Fielding an increasingly disjointed set of questions about my venture capital contacts in the Bay Area, I pretended to sip at my drink while Stan's disappeared alarmingly fast. He ordered a second glass, and I politely refused, holding a hand over my barely touched first one. Finally, Stan seemed ready to call it a night, requested the check, and paid it.

"Let's head on down the mountain," Stan said as he stood up with a wobble. "I'll talk with the rest of the board in the morning and then give you a call at the hotel. How's that sound?"

"Sounds like a plan," I said, watching Stan's slow progress toward the door. He fumbled for his keys and shuffled over ice on his way to the driver's side of the jeep.

"Hey, Stan," I said. "Why don't you let me take the wheel? You're looking a little shaky there."

"I'm fine. Just need to find the damn key. Okay, there you are, you little bastard."

I made my decision knowing it could kill any progress I'd made toward landing the job. But better it than me. "Give me the keys, Stan."

"You watch yourself, Roger." He was slurring his words now. "You think you can order me out of my own jam dee— my own damn jeep?"

"No, just out of the driver's seat. Come on. Hand them over. I'm not letting you kill us both tonight."

Stan snorted, ignored me, and opened the driver's door to get in. But he misjudged his step as he pivoted to enter the vehicle and slipped on the icy pavement. I helped him stand, apparently uninjured, and walked him over to the passenger side, stuffing him into the jeep and fastening his seat belt.

"You just shot yourself in the fucking foot," he mumbled. "You can be a real son of a bitch, you know that?"

"Yeah, when I need to be."

As I backed out of the parking space in front of the inn, I heard Stan snoring and took a deep breath with the expectation of a tedious but quiet trip down the mountain.

I crawled down the road, adding the jeep's off-road lights when I could, and shutting them off when reflections from the falling snow blinded me. The world had turned white, and the edges of the road were hidden by new snow, making it difficult to see the drop-offs. But I'd been on this road and others like it in my Colorado past and knew how to handle it. In fact, I was glad for the distraction, as it let me avoid thinking too much about the probable loss of a job I wanted.

Back in Boulder, I woke Stan enough to get his address in Table Mesa, then hauled him up to his door, tossed his keys in after him, and took an Uber back to the hotel.

~

The next morning, I woke to a sunny day and the sound of snowplows. That was just like Boulder in late December, I remembered: a raging storm one day with sun and melting snow the next. My flight back to Seattle, out of DIA, wasn't until the middle of the afternoon, so I settled in for a leisurely breakfast at the hotel, having convinced myself that I'd made a good decision the night before and that finding a new opportunity would be no problem. Still, I had my phone out on the table while I read through my free copy of the *Boulder Camera*. The call would come eventually, and I'd need to accept my fate as gracefully as I could. I liked the idea of running a start-up in Colorado, even if it wasn't this one, and I didn't want to burn any more bridges than I already had. Boulder was still a small town with lots of crosstalk.

I finished breakfast at around 11:00 and there'd still been no call. I shrugged, packed my bags, and left for the airport. DIA was known for its long security lines, and I didn't want to miss my flight. I turned in the car, took the shuttle to the main terminal, and plodded my way through security. Then, just as I was waiting for first-class boarding to be called at the gate, my phone's ringtone startled me. I moved a few feet away from the podium and answered the call.

"Roger Carrington?" asked the voice on the other end.

"Speaking."

"This is Kavi Singh from the board of Deep Learning Systems."

"Yes, hello, Dr. Singh."

"Roger, I've been asked by the board to follow up after your meetings with our team."

"An unenviable task, I imagine," I said, stepping farther

away from the crowd at the gate.

"I'm sorry?"

"Things got a little, uh, animated, during my meeting with Stan last night, so I wasn't entirely clear about the outcome."

"Okay, well, regardless, the entire board voted this morning, and we're prepared to offer you a key position at the company. We'd like to send you the formal offer. Are you still interested?"

It took me a second to recover, as I wasn't expecting this result. But now, I noticed, my role was being vaguely described as "a key position," and not specifically as Chief Executive Officer. That would have to be dealt with, probably along with other terms, but there was no harm in keeping my options open.

"Yes, I'm still interested."

"Excellent. I'll email the offer before end of business today."

Four

My flight into SeaTac arrived at about six, and the email from Kavi Singh hadn't yet appeared. I checked my spam folder. Nothing there either. I decided to let it go for the night and allow myself time to cool down before reacting to whatever might be in the letter. I needed employment but didn't have to take this particular job, and getting a little mental distance from the last couple of days wouldn't be a bad idea. If I wasn't genuinely willing to walk away from the opportunity, I'd do a lousy job negotiating.

The heated seat and steering wheel in my new BMW M5 provided their expected comforts as I drove home to Kirkland in a cold rain. I had purchased the car as a sort of consolation prize just before leaving Microsoft and financed it to conserve cash, something I found embarrassing but grudgingly prudent, given the uncertainty of my employment going forward. Sitting in the dealership, filling out the loan application under the watchful eyes of a sales manager half my age had been humiliating, and I still felt the sting of it.

I also felt a familiar but blessedly transient pang of guilt as I exited the 405 and had to stop briefly at the top of the off-ramp next to a rain-soaked, middle-aged woman standing on the side of the road with a sign reading "Anything Will Help." I stared straight ahead as if she didn't exist and moved on when the light changed. *You can't give money to people like that; they'll just spend it on drugs or booze.*

The gate to the parking garage under my condo on Lake Washington opened as it sensed the car's RFID chip, and I pulled into my reserved spot—warm, safe, and dry. I rolled my luggage into the elevator and rose to the top floor, where my home spanned the width of the building and had a stunning view across the lake toward Seattle. I paused and let the scene take me away from the last few days before brewing a cup of coffee and settling in. Light from the full moon broke through the clouds and sparkled off the wind-chopped water below. Did I really want to leave this place to take an all-consuming job at a risky start-up where everyone was a quarter century younger? No. And yes. If all went well and the company succeeded, I could keep the condo and the boat tied to the dock below, maintaining a spot for occasional getaways and later retirement. If things didn't go well, it might be hard to recover at my age and find a new opportunity that could support the kind of retirement I wanted.

I knew I was living beyond my means but had always assumed that the next venture would keep the dream alive. And so far it had, but just barely. Now my income was gone, but the expenses continued, and they were substantial. Dividends from my stock portfolio would partially cover things, but I'd also be eating into my modest capital base at a worrying rate. If I kept the condo, the boat, cars, with property tax and insurance on everything, not to mention alimony, loan payments, and all other living expenses, I probably had three years at best, and much less if the stock market took a dive. It was a frightening but motivating challenge.

The feeling reminded me of my solo climbing days. I was never a true free-climber, ascending a rock face without any protection at all, but when a climbing buddy wasn't available, I often risked practice climbs alone, placing protection points and clipping my rope into them along the way like a lead climber but without followers, then "cleaning the rock" while rappelling back down. The trick was not to get too far up the rock before placing the next chock or nut. A fall would take me twice the distance from the last protection point, assuming it held, and I was always tempted to risk a little more exposure when a safe spot was right in front of me but a more interesting one was another ten feet up. Climbing solo like this allowed me to take risks without having to consider any other climbers on the rope below me. The adrenaline rush was amazing, but the risk multiplied with every additional foot.

Now the risk wasn't physical; it was financial, and much less fun. I could probably mend some relationships and crawl my way back into a stable job with Microsoft, or maybe land one with Google or Amazon, but this little company in Boulder, barely worth anything at the moment, could become my winning ticket if I played it right. And the adrenaline rush would be phenomenal.

My phone vibrated and I checked the inbox. There it was, the offer from DLS. I considered staying with my decision to wait until morning, but the temptation was too great. I read through the offer, losing enthusiasm with each sentence. The salary was meager, as expected, and the signing bonus was ordinary. But I was more curious about the equity position, and that was well below anything I would consider. They were offering me 2 percent of the company, and I'd already decided that my lower limit would be five, with future performance-based increases beyond that. But the job description was the most demoralizing and amorphous part of the whole thing: *Director of Corporate Strategy.* A staff position? What the hell was that? It was insulting, to say the least. At best, it sounded like a move by the board to appease Stan while maintaining balance. As far as I was concerned, the position would be CEO or nothing.

I wondered how much input had come from the founders, how much was from the board, and how much came specifically from Stan. I considered firing back an immediate rejection but thought better of such a knee-jerk reaction and decided to sleep on it, if sleep would come at all.

Five

Sleep was choppy, and my half-awake attempts at formulating a response to the offer during the night turned out to have little value in the light of day. I reread the offer two more times over breakfast and once again came close to blasting out an angry rejection. But in the end, my more rational side prevailed, and I wrote:

Dear DLS board members,

Thank you for the offer to join your company and for hosting me during the last few days. I believe Deep Learning Systems has outstanding potential, based primarily on the well-differentiated intellectual property at its core, the product concept, and the emerging market.

But unfortunately, I found your offer unacceptable in two fundamental ways: the role itself and the associated equity stake.

I believe I am exceptionally well positioned to take your company from its present embryonic state to a successful public offering or an equally lucrative buyout in the span of three to five years, and I would welcome the opportunity to do exactly that as your CEO with a reasonable ownership percentage. But I cannot accept your offer as it currently stands.

If you would like to discuss more acceptable terms, I am open and motivated to do so.

Sincerely,
Roger Carrington

I hit Send and decided that getting away for a day or two would be better than sitting around the condo waiting for a response and pondering my fate. What would be, would be. I packed up a few essentials and headed down to the dock.

There, resting in the morning's calm water, side-tied to the dock, was the one possession I treasured above all the rest: my forty-eight-foot American Tug, *Independence*. She was a capable vessel, with a dark blue hull and white superstructure, suitable for long cruises up the Inside Passage to Alaska or down south to Oregon, California, and beyond. But today she would take me on a quick trip to a local destination: an anchorage in Quartermaster Harbor, an inlet of beautiful Vashon Island in the sound between Seattle and Tacoma.

The weather had calmed overnight, and the new day was overcast, with a hint of orange winter sun leaking under the clouds low in the southeast. The forecast looked good for the day but warned of deteriorating conditions beginning late the next day. With careful timing and a little luck, I would be off the water by then.

I checked all the vessel's systems, fired up her six-hundred-horsepower diesel engine, and moved her slowly away from the dock out into the cold, deep water of Lake Washington. My route took me past UW's Husky Stadium and through the locks marking the boundary between the lake's fresh water and Puget Sound's salt. Once outside the locks, the wind picked up, producing a light chop on the sound as I cruised down Elliott Bay alongside the Emerald City itself.

The pilothouse of *Independence* was the one place where I felt completely satisfied with life, and I savored the feeling as I made the turn, an hour later, into Quartermaster Harbor. Once in the treelined inlet, the wind dropped, the water turned to glass, and I brought the vessel's speed down to a crawl in the no-wake zone.

Finally at anchor in the harbor, far removed from the events of the last few days, I vowed to keep my phone off until the next morning. Whatever was happening in the minds of the people in Boulder, whatever decisions they might make, all that was beyond my control now. If things went well, I would have plenty of control later.

~

The next morning, I arrived back at the dock just as NOAA Weather Radio was warning of gale force winds beginning earlier than originally expected. My short trip had achieved its distractive purpose, and I was once again ready to deal with the reality of my situation. I was ready to negotiate, if there was enough headroom, but I was also ready to walk away and keep my eyes open for another opportunity if this one didn't pan out.

Back at the condo, I occupied myself with new research on AI and neural networks as they were being applied to the analysis of natural language, but I also delved into the history of the basic technology. I had forgotten that the earliest work stretched as far back as 1943, when neurophysiologist Warren McCulloch and mathematician Walter Pitts were using simple electrical circuits in a primitive attempt to model neurons in the brain. Work continued, on and off, into the 1970s and 1980s until optimism peaked with Japan's Fifth Generation efforts. But interest faded again until just a few years ago, when much faster hardware became available and software techniques were further refined. Applications like IBM's Watson and various game-playing systems began to capture the public imagination, and AI technology began to take advantage of creative new hardware/software trade-offs. I immediately thought of Jenny Dickinson's work with high-speed specialized hardware at DLS, and my hopes for the company grew stronger. This could be a winner if they could get product to market quickly enough to head off the competition but without sacrificing quality.

The call came at 5:30 that evening. I'd been expecting an email instead, so had to adjust to a real-time approach at the last second. I also hadn't expected this particular caller.

"Roger, this is Stan."

"Oh, right. Hello, Stan. I was expecting Kavi, so you kind of took me by surprise."

"Kavi? Smart guy, but too soft. That's why I wanted to get to you first."

"Okay . . ."

I put the call on speaker and opened my laptop to take notes, expecting new offer details.

"I'll be totally honest with you, Richard—uh, Roger. You

seem more like a Richard. Anyone ever call you that?"

"No, I don't think so." This conversation was beginning to remind me of the one at the end of our meeting in Gold Hill, and I pushed my laptop to the side.

"Well, maybe they should," Stan continued. "Never mind. I called to tell you I opposed the board's revised offer today. But I only have one fucking vote, even though I'm the chairman, so there you go. You're gonna get the offer, and if you take it, I'm gonna have to work with you, and I will because I believe in this company. And I might come around to believing in you too, eventually, but you're gonna have to earn that. You know what I'm talkin' about?"

"I have a rough idea."

"I've got a big stake in this company, and I'm gonna do whatever it takes to keep it, including getting your ass fired if necessary, okay?"

I heard liquid pouring in the background and didn't respond.

"So we'll be fine as long as I have your support and you have mine," Stan continued.

"And that means?"

"You give me public credit for my leadership and a little discretion about certain other things. You do that and we both get what we want. You okay with that?"

"I can work with that," I said, choosing my words carefully.

"Cheers," said Stan. The phone went dead.

I stared out the window across the lake and pondered my situation. "Everyone has a sell-by date," I'd said a few days ago. But everyone also has a selling *price*. I'd have to think more about mine.

The long-awaited email arrived at about ten that night, and the offer had changed substantially. Apparently, the majority of the board had more confidence in my ability to lead the company to its next stage, because the position was now CEO, but with a provisional sell-by date. The employment contract was for one year, with an option for another three if I was able to secure a Series A round of venture funding by the end of the first year, and if the board and the three founders voted unanimously to retain me. The offer was sweetened with a stock grant of four percent with options for another three. There were other perks as well, but this was enough to make me weigh the substantial upside potential against the downside of working with someone who not only had the power to vote me out after a year but also had the potential to drag the company down and ruin the upside for everyone. Over the next twelve months, if I accepted the offer, I would either need to "earn" Stan's vote without compromising on my fundamental positions or carefully engineer his departure. Either way would work for me.

After some perfunctory soul-searching, I decided my price had been met. I accepted the offer.

Six

The memory of that decision years ago seems both vivid and foreign as I wake to the rising sound of overhead traffic in the world I now inhabit. I long for the pride I felt so viscerally then, even as I regret much of what followed.

I crawl out of the Residence to a brutally cold winter morning and pay a visit to my favorite freeway pillar. It's always there for me and is probably the most consistent, stable, and solid thing in my life right now. I even find myself telling it things about my past that I won't reveal to the humans around me. Sad, right? Maybe, but also helpful, possibly even therapeutic. I finish my morning ritual, make my usual closing remark, and turn to leave.

And also with you.

I raise a half smile and walk into the frigid morning, thinking it might be time to try and connect with my little community, or at least make a deal with them. I've been thinking about this for a while and have decided there might be room for a food-for-money trade. Carlos and Mary seem to be okay begging for money, and I can't face doing that myself—not in this context—but I am getting better at my hunter-gatherer role. I've seen Carlos doing his thing in his yellow poncho on the street corner and noticed Mary at the park once, making a halfhearted attempt with the tourists who sometimes wandered over that way. But the small amount of money they collect probably doesn't go very far for food, especially at the local 7-Eleven. And I have no idea how Jimmy eats at all.

With the first step of a deal in mind, I leave the overpass and head into town. I'm wearing my thin cotton-lined jacket, and the wind is cutting through it easily, so I take an alternate route using the leeward sides of tall buildings as a shield when I can. That helps, but I'm still starting to lose feeling in my hands and arms. I ignore this and move on.

My first two stops yield two old breakfast sandwiches, a burger with fries on the side, and even a large Caesar salad. I consider going a little farther south to try my luck at the Mexican food truck, but a freezing rain has started. I turn around, deciding I've collected enough of a food offering to try for a deal, and I've got at least a two-mile walk ahead of me. Normally I wouldn't be concerned, but this is different. Must be an arctic front blasting through.

A half hour later I've lost all feeling in my fingers, and my ears are stinging with the freezing rain. I wipe my nose and find that my mustache has grown icicles. I walk on, hard against the wind, my lungs beginning to hurt. I adjust course, again trying to use the buildings as windbreaks. There's a recessed doorway ahead with no one in it, so I duck in, shivering and hoping for a few moments of shelter. I wrap my arms tightly around my soaked chest and try to conserve some body heat. Sleep is tempting, but an old memory tells me it's a bad idea. People in parkas and long overcoats walk by, eyes straight ahead except for the quick side-glances I'm coming to expect. Do they care at all? Are they afraid of me? Hah! Like I could do anything to them, even if I wanted to. I'm starting to want to.

The door behind me opens abruptly and slams me in the back.

"Hey! Get the hell off my doorstep, you filthy loser!" I don't even turn to look at the man. I've got no leverage here, and I know it. I get up stiffly and move on down the street against the howling wind. On the next block, I find another recessed entryway that looks more promising. The door is chained, so I settle in. My eyes close, and I tell myself it's just for a few minutes of peace, a temporary escape from the world. But there's a sound, a car horn, and it jolts me awake. A black SUV has stopped, and someone is waving, apparently trying to get my attention. The passenger-side window rolls down, and I think, *Shit, not again.* But the person is smiling and seems insistent, so I get up painfully and walk to the curb.

"Here," a man says, and hands me a hooded down jacket with the store tags still attached. "Looks like you could use this more than I can right now."

I'm stunned. Not just by this person's generosity and kindness but also by the hard realization that I am no longer a shrewd dealmaker, let alone a CEO. I am homeless and I look it. I'm now part of another world, a lower caste. And I'm in trouble.

"Thank you, sir. Thank you." I barely recognize my own voice. The man nods, the window rolls up, and the car moves on. I walk back to the doorway, incredulous, grateful, confused. The price tag on the jacket tells me it was more expensive than anything I would have purchased for myself, even when I *was* myself. Why did the man do this? He knew he couldn't expect anything from me in return, now or in the future. I mean, hell, even when I gave Jimmy that little bit of stale food the other day, I was thinking of it as a sort of investment, hoping it would help me get in with the overpass group so I could make a deal with them later.

I take my old jacket off, put on the new one, hood up, and begin to feel human again. The promise of warmth and protection from the wind is almost overwhelming as I continue my journey home, expecting to blend in with others on the street in my new disguise. But I'm surprised to notice more side-eyes and even the occasional frown.

Then I understand. In my hurry, I've left the tags on the jacket, and these people are convinced I've stolen it. I don't look like someone who simply forgot about the tags after a recent purchase. I duck into the next doorway and rip them off.

I walk the two miles back to the park and am not surprised to find the old man I've named Tex there, stretched out on his bench. I knew he'd be back. This is his home, and no matter how many times they chase him away, he'll always return. I get it, and it makes me smile for the first time in hours. I know what I need to do.

"Hey, Tex. I brought you something." I pull the burger out of my pack and show him. "It's cold by now but still fresh. Want some fries with that?"

He doesn't seem to get the fast-food joke or say no, so I take his silence as a yes.

Tex lifts his head and props himself up on an elbow. He raises the brim of his cowboy hat slightly and stares at me with questioning eyes. His wizened brown face convinces me that he was once a hardworking ranch hand. Maybe even a ranch owner. In any case, he's seen a lot of sun and wind. Under his plastic bag rain shield, he's wearing a heavy denim jacket over several layers of shirts. He seems warm enough for now. I hand him the burger and a bag of fries.

Tex looks down at the food, then up at me with a bit of light in his yellowed eyes and the barest hint of a smile. I return the smile and head for home.

Back at the overpass, I realize I don't have enough food left to be convincing about a trade, let alone a permanent deal, so I postpone my plan and head for the Residence. But as I'm about to pass Mary's tent, I notice her sitting just inside the entrance, wrapped in her ratty old army blanket with knees pulled up to her chest, staring straight ahead and smoking a cigarette. I wave to her. She doesn't move, even between puffs, and I imagine she's trying to trap as much warm air as possible under that blanket. But she's also ignoring me. I can handle active indifference from people out in the real world because I've been there and understand their awkward attempts at guilt-avoidance. But coming from someone where I am now? That just hurts.

I arrive at the Residence and immediately wolf down everything remaining in my pack. I hang my old cotton jacket on a nail to dry and settle in for the night. The new coat feels like a warm sleeping bag and I expect to drift off easily, but instead I'm reminded of the many times I ignored homeless people standing on cold and rainy off-ramps while I sat wrapped in the leather luxury of a heated car impatiently waiting for the light to turn. I expect the guilt to pass as it always did then, mere seconds after the green light released me. But there's no green light here.

In the few seconds it takes me to walk back to Mary's tent, I start and finish an argument with myself. *What's she done for me? If she was an employee, would I reward this kind of behavior? No. But shit, man, you don't know what's in her head or what she's been through.*

I approach Mary's tent head-on so she can't avoid me this time. "Hey, I'm Roger from, you know, right over there." I glance toward the Residence.

Mary's eyes meet mine for an instant and then they're looking through me again. I remove my new jacket and hold it out to her, feeling the icy breeze. "Here. It's too small for me."

She doesn't reach for it. "What do you want?" she asks.

Her question pisses me off as I stand there freezing, and I think about walking away. I consider demanding help with my plan to organize our food/cash situation, but then surprise myself. "Nothing," I say. "You looked cold."

Mary hesitates and seems to be struggling. Finally, she reaches out and accepts the gift. "Thank you," she says.

I nod, smile, and return to the Residence.

Seven

I'd like to say I slept well last night, wrapped in the warmth of a satisfied conscience. But that would be a lie. I can't count the times I woke in the cold, berating myself for making such a stupid, emotional, and impractical choice. I mean, hell, when it comes right down to it, we're each responsible for our own survival, right? Isn't that why flight attendants always say to put on your own oxygen mask first? Wasn't Ayn Rand right?

Okay, I know the mask thing is a bit more subtle and a lot less self-centered than that. And as much of a capitalist as I am at heart, I can't go as far as Rand does. I guess I've become as much a philosophical mess as a physical one.

As I peer outside the Residence this morning, I see the frost that covered the dirt last night is gone, replaced by mud. That's okay. I'll take it, because it means the arctic air has passed and we're back to more typical Seattle weather. My seagull stands in a cracked-ice puddle a few feet away and looks hungry, so I find a few pieces of stale cinnamon roll and toss them out. He gobbles them down and flaps away, crapping all over the Residence on his way out.

And also with you, my friend. I flip him the bird. I allow myself a smile and finish up my morning routine. I know he doesn't intend any offense; at least, I like to think not. My old cotton jacket is nearly dry, so I put it on and head out into the world.

Carlos is already at his corner, working the traffic. He looks over at me, raises his chin and smiles. I wonder what's changed.

"Hey, how's it going this morning?" I shout.

"Not bad. Made a few bucks already and only been flipped off once."

"The guy in the white Mercedes?"

"That's the one."

"Asshole."

"Yeah."

I wave and continue on down the street. It takes the better part of an hour to walk to the shelter on Yesler but the effort is well worth it. I never want to live in a place like that, much preferring the independence and privacy of the Residence, but it offers one of the crucial things that life at the overpass does not: a shower.

Because I'm not a resident of the shelter, getting into a shower stall requires trading work for water, and even then it's not always possible. But today it is. I spend the morning cleaning toilets, earning my seven minutes of timed bliss under a cascade of hot water. There in that ancient shower stall, even with its ongoing battle between mildew and chlorine bleach, I find the closest thing to paradise I've known in a while. The world outside disappears and I'm enveloped in peace. I can't believe I once rushed through this deeply transformative experience every day before work.

My seven minutes are up, and I reluctantly leave paradise to dry off. I wash my underwear, socks and shirt in a rusted old sink and finish off everything with a hairdryer. The world feels new as I reenter it. I talk my way into a few day-old burritos at the Mexican food truck, eat one, and stuff the others into my pack. The other restaurants aren't in a giving mood today.

But my luck changes as I walk by the Pike Place Market. There, on the sidewalk, is something that looks like a credit card. My mind races through the problems with identity theft from the perspectives of both the cardholder and the thief. It's a pain in the ass for one, and a limited opportunity for the other. Even if the thief can manage to quickly make a few purchases without showing other ID, the bank's fraud-detection algorithms will soon notice an unusual pattern, place a hold on the account, and alert the cardholder. Good times will quickly end for the thief. I know. I've been the cardholder. But maybe now I'm the thief.

I pick up the treasure and sigh. It's just a Starbucks card. I notice an astonishingly beautiful young woman texting on her phone nearby and decide to be honest; a warped form of altruism, I admit.

"Excuse me, miss, is this yours? I found it here on the sidewalk." The woman looks up from her phone, and I see an immediate transformation in her pretty face as her smile vanishes, replaced by a flash of alarm. She pulls her handbag close and darts away. She'll meet a friend for lunch, I imagine, and will tell her all about the disturbing experience she had today with a creepy old man down by the market. I look at the card again, shrug, and decide to keep it.

I step into the "original" Starbucks shop across from the market, knowing this is a misnomer, as the very first

Starbucks café was actually located over on Western Avenue. I'm guessing I'm the only one here, including the barista, who remembers the old place or even knows it once existed. I feel a part of history, a tattered old monochrome ghost materializing in the present. Can anyone here even see me?

Apparently, the barista can. "Can I get something started for you, sir?"

"Yes, I'd like a double tall mocha, with whip," I say, hoping the card isn't a dud and planning my exit in case it is.

"Anything else for you today?"

"Can you tell me how much is left on my card?"

The barista takes the card, scans it, and returns it with a smile. "You have $187.57 remaining after the mocha."

I try to hide my elation as I casually order two lemon scones and a prepackaged turkey sandwich. I thank the barista and step away from the counter to await my coffee, feeling almost like a member of society again.

My last stop on the way home is the park, and I'm pleased to see Tex sitting up on his bench, awake for once, his tan cowboy hat looking like a natural body part. I sit on the other end of the bench and rummage through my pack, looking for something to leave with him today, finally deciding on half of the fresh turkey sandwich. I pull it out and lay it on the bench next to him, complete with a Starbucks napkin. He looks down at the food, then back up at me. There's that familiar questioning stare, but this time I think I see something more in his eyes. He reaches up and tips his hat. I smile and leave him to his meal.

Back at the overpass, I notice Mary sitting inside her tent, reading a paperback and wearing her new down jacket. She looks up from the book and motions for me to come over. She has built an awning from an old blue tarp, and it forms a kind of outdoor living space at the front of her tent, where she joins me now. I wonder why she's created this space, as we don't need protection from the rain here under the freeway, but I guess it might just be her way of marking her territory. We sit on the ground facing each other a few feet apart, and she smiles—sadly, I think. She puts her book down and I'm surprised to see it's a Steinbeck novel: *Of Mice and Men*.

"How's it going?" I ask, not sure how to begin a conversation with this woman who, until yesterday, has actively ignored me.

"Okay. Guess I've been better."

Mary's voice is raspy and she reminds me, in more ways than one, of Janis Joplin.

"Oh?" I ask.

"Yeah. My mother died yesterday."

"Damn. I'm sorry. Were you close?" I ask.

"No, but still."

I nod and stare off toward the downtown office buildings. "Yeah, still. I get it. Your father?"

"I haven't seen him since I was five or six. He's long gone."

"Any brothers or sisters?"

"A brother. That's how I heard. He drops off a note every now and then, sometimes with a few bucks. Hands an envelope to Carlos from his car." Mary rolls her eyes.

"He doesn't just give it to you directly? Stop and talk for a minute? Get you the hell out of here?"

"He stopped by my tent once last year. But his wife, the bitch, made him promise never to do that again."

"And he just follows orders?"

"I know, right? But he's always been like that. She's got him by the balls."

"What's his name?"

49

"Tim."

I'm thinking, *Wow, if this Tim guy has a car, he's probably got enough money to get his sister out of here—at least lend her a room or couch at his place.*

"But why the hell doesn't he just . . . ?"

Mary seems to read my mind. "Not gonna happen as long as the bitch is breathing. What about you? Any friends out there?"

"Hah! Not anymore. Actually, I'm not sure I ever had any. Business partners, employees, board members, but nobody I'd call a real friend. Well, maybe Claire. She was my admin assistant."

"Uh-oh."

"No, it wasn't like that," I say. "Well, okay, it sort of was. But she was the only one I could talk to honestly about the business. She was a good listener, and smart. She knew how to pull ideas out of me, and she had her own as well. I miss her."

Mary takes off her wool cap, runs a hand through her hair, and puts it back on. She glances at my left hand. "Ever been married?"

"Once, years ago. It didn't last long. I just wasn't around much—always confused urgent things with important things. You know what I mean?"

"Not really, no." Mary says, looking puzzled.

"Well, it doesn't matter. It's all in the past." I get up on one knee, thinking it might be a good time to finish the conversation and move on, but Mary seems to want more.

"The past, yeah. I try not to think too much about that," she says. She wraps her arms around her knees and glances around the encampment. "It's too depressing. You ever wish you could change something back then? Something that would make all this go away?"

50

I sit back down, feeling an odd but not unwelcome sense of identification with this poor woman.

"All the time." I pause before deciding to continue. "I made a stupid mistake at a company I was running, and over half the employees lost their jobs because of me. Ended up in prison for it."

"Damn. So you lost a lot of money?"

"Everything. Money, cars, houses, boat, reputation. Nobody'll hire a felon."

"You were kind of a shithead, sounds like."

I laugh at Mary's directness. "Yeah, kind of a shithead. Still am, I guess. The good thing is I can't do much damage here."

Mary smiles. "Well, that's something. Want a cigarette? I found a full pack yesterday down by the park."

"Thanks, but that's one good thing I managed to do—kicked the habit a long time ago. Have you tried?"

"Nah. I can't do that," says Mary. "It's my one and only pleasure in life. Well, that and reading." She glances down at the Steinbeck novel. "And besides, maybe it'll kill me. Sometimes I think sooner'd be better than later."

"You don't really mean that."

"Yeah, I do. Some of the time. Maybe most of the time. I mean, look at me. Look at us, living in the fucking basement of Maslow's pyramid!"

"*Abraham* Maslow . . . ?"

"I was a psych major at UW for a while."

"What?"

"I know. Hard to believe, right?"

"What happened?" I ask.

"You don't wanna know."

"Actually, yeah, I do."

"Hmm. Maybe another day."

I take my cue. "Okay, before I go, I'm curious about something, or someone, around here."

"Okay . . ."

"Jimmy mentioned a person named Jay-Jay the other day. Who's that?"

Mary laughs. "Oh, that's just his imaginary adviser, I guess you'd say. Jimmy's schizophrenic. Harmless, but seriously schizophrenic."

"Ah, okay. That fits."

I get up to leave, Mary thanks me for the jacket again, and I drop off a burrito for Jimmy on my way back to the Residence.

Eight

Isettle in for the night, satisfied with the day. What a strange feeling. Not bad, just surprising. I could never have imagined a day even remotely like this when I was running DLS, let alone felt good about it. What specific objectives had I met today? How had I directly impacted the bottom line? Who had I influenced? Was I on track with my exit strategy? I can't check any of those boxes today, at least not in any conventional way.

But I certainly did during my first year at DLS. I was flying fast and high then. By the end of that year, my list of accomplishments looked like this:

- ✓ Closed a Series A round of venture funding for twenty million
- ✓ Gave successful interviews with the *Wall Street Journal* and *Forbes*
- ✓ Established strategic partnerships with both UCSD and the Cleveland Clinic

✓ Promoted Jake Hartman to VP, Engineering
✓ Formalized Jennifer Dickinson's role as Manager, Platform Development
✓ Formalized Wade Cantwell's role as Manager, Application Development
✓ Filed a patent on Jennifer's unique hardware acceleration design
✓ Set comp plans for founders and new hires
✓ Provided budget for ten new software developers and three hardware engineers
✓ Hired Stella Lujan as VP of Marketing and provided budget for five more hires
✓ Hired Claire Daniels as my administrative assistant
✓ Renewed my employment contract

I had also begun to explore ways to reduce Stan's influence, although that would never appear on any list, and success was far from certain. With lots of help from Stella, our newly hired VP of Marketing, I had convinced everyone on the board—apart from my nemesis—that avoiding the short-term revenue temptation to market a therapy chatbot, and instead focusing all resources on our serious longer-term mission, would lead to the best combination of credibility, profitability and sustainability. Market research had supported our approach, and Stan, under great pressure from the rest of the board, had reluctantly agreed and voted to retain me.

I'd purchased a well-equipped Range Rover to blend with the high end of Boulder culture and was smiling as I pulled it into the company parking lot on a beautiful spring day. The trees were just beginning to bud, and I could hear Boulder Creek chattering over its rock bed as it flowed past our building. The tasteful *Deep Learning Systems* sign above the large glass doors made me nod with satisfaction. *But this is only the beginning, and nothing is guaranteed*, I had to remind myself.

"Good morning, Dr. Carrington," our new receptionist said as I passed by the front desk on the way to my corner office.

"Good morning, Amy. And it's just Roger," I said with a smile, a nod to Boulder's informal culture.

Claire Daniels, an administrative assistant I'd hired just a few weeks before, was already hard at work in her office next to mine. "Morning, Roger. I'll be right in," she said, reaching for her coffee.

"No hurry. I'm gonna grab a cup and be right back."

Claire was sitting at the small conference table in my office, tapping something into her iPad, when I returned with my coffee.

"So, it looks like a busy Monday," she said, glancing at the tablet. "You've got Senior Staff at nine, your regular one-on-one with Stella at ten-thirty, a lunch meeting with Dr. Davidson and Wade at the European Café, and then Jenny wants a few minutes at three. Dinner with Kavi at the Greenbrier caps it all off at seven."

"What's his agenda? Any clues?" I asked.

"Kavi? He wasn't very forthcoming, but my best guess is something about the board. He was kind of grumpy Friday after the board meeting, and that's just not like him."

"Right, okay. What's the status on our spot at the AI conference in June?"

"We're in. Just got off the phone with the conference coordinator before you arrived, and we've got a seat on the neural net panel for Jenny and a featured talk for Jake early the second morning. Wade leads a roundtable on the last day. Stella deserves all the credit for getting this started, so you might want to mention something when you meet this morning. She's such a positive force around here."

The morning flew by and my lunch with Sheryl Davidson and Wade was productive. Dr. Davidson was in the Denver area for a conference, and we were taking advantage of her presence to tie up a few loose ends and celebrate our partnership. She was the chair of the Psychology department at UCSD's Revelle College and had been working with Wade for the past several months on the technical details of a partnership, and now the university had agreed to accept a small stake in the company in exchange for access to an extensive database of cognitive behavioral therapy transcripts and recordings, part of a long-term longitudinal study, all tagged with outcomes. These, along with a similar database from the Cleveland Clinic's Neurological Institute, would form the primary training and testing sets for the DLS neural network. All transcripts and recordings would be anonymized using our natural language processing capabilities to change patient names, therapist names, names of places, and other potentially identifying information. An encrypted file would tie the anonymized data to real patients and could only be accessed by the appropriate therapist. The same system would ultimately be used by our regular customers and had passed all the tests required for HIPAA privacy compliance.

That evening, fresh off a productive day and still full of energy, I arrived at the Greenbrier to find Kavi moping over a martini. It was an incongruous sight—this handsome, turbaned Punjabi Sikh with a dark beard and a PhD after his name, hovering over his very western drink.

"Guess," he said in response to my questioning look.

I sat down. "Stan?"

Kavi nodded. "We're so close to breaking through to the next stage, Roger. So close. And that . . . that guy . . . puts his own investment in the company ahead of everything else, including the company itself, in my opinion. It doesn't make any sense. It's self-defeating."

I thought Kavi was going to call Stan an asshole, which would have been perfectly appropriate, but he never swore, even now, when his level of frustration was the highest I'd seen from this normally calm and rational man. I flagged down a waiter, ordered a glass of Malbec and turned back to Kavi. "Talk to me."

"He still wants you out. Even after this past year's results."

"Nothing new there," I said.

"He's been trying to convince the board to invalidate your new employment contract."

"What? Is anyone even listening to that crap?"

"Not seriously, but it's a major distraction."

"And how could they even do that?" I asked.

"Only one way. They could claim incompetence and buy you out."

"That's insane."

Kavi just nodded.

"It's still about his accelerated revenue scheme with that toy app, isn't it?" I asked. "I thought we'd gotten beyond that long ago."

"Stan seems stuck on the idea, Roger. He's convinced we can't get to a public offering quickly enough otherwise, that we won't be able to reach profitability fast enough, or ever. He won't be able to personally cash out when he wants to. That's the real issue."

"He does understand he'd be cheapening the company's image, probably beyond repair, right?"

"I don't know. I think he believes that our base technology would set us apart, that we would somehow avoid that trap."

"He's delusional."

"Maybe. And there's some personal animosity involved."

"No shit."

Kavi smiled for the first time that night.

As we worked our way through dinner, the conversation shifted to more mundane topics like comp plans and cash flow. But my mind was still spinning in the background.

They could claim incompetence and buy you out.

At our current valuation and my vesting status, a buyout wouldn't get me very far. And I needed to get far this time. Even with this year's increase, my salary and bonus weren't nearly enough to cover expenses across two homes, cars, boat, alimony, and other long-term debt, and I couldn't bring myself to sell anything. As a result, my investment portfolio was shrinking by the month.

In that moment, I was struck by something painful that should have been obvious for a while: in at least one significant way, I wasn't all that different from Stan.

~

They could claim incompetence and buy you out.

That seemed like a big stretch as I thought about it while driving to work the next day, especially given the progress I'd made in the last twelve months. But even if it didn't come to that, Kavi was right: the distraction alone could derail us.

I arrived before anyone else and started a pot of coffee. Returning to my office, I noticed with satisfaction that Claire had just walked in and was also beginning her day early. *I made a good hire on this one,* I thought, and invited her into my office for a chat.

"Did you want to take a quick look at the schedule for today?" she asked, sitting down at the conference table with her iPad.

I sat across from her and noticed, not for the first time, how pretty her mid-thirties face was when she brushed her dark brown hair back over one slim shoulder and smiled. And her dress looked both professional and alluring at the same time.

No, don't go there, you idiot. You absolutely cannot go there.

"Later," I said. "I want to talk about something else first."

"Okay, shoot," she said.

"The rumor mill. As much as I'd like to think people would come directly to me with concerns, it's just a fact of life in an organization like ours that they won't often do that. Things can fester until they get out of hand. I'll try to be more encouraging about people dropping in for a chat, but you could play an important role too. I'd like you to keep an ear to the ground and let me know if you pick up anything I should get ahead of. Would you be willing to check in with me on that from time to time?"

"You want me to be a kind of intra-company spy." Claire was smiling with an amused sparkle in her eyes.

"Well, I wouldn't quite put it that way . . ."

"Sure, no problem." Her smile faded into seriousness. "Is there something you're specifically concerned about right now?"

"Not really, no. Just a precaution."

Claire and I finished up our discussion and I took advantage of the half hour before my first meeting to continue thinking about Stan, the board, and my future.

They could claim incompetence and buy you out.

Of course! *That's the right tactic*, I realized. *Just the wrong target.*

"Claire!" I called through the office wall.

She appeared in the doorway. "Yes?"

"Would you please dig out all the incorporation documents for me? Particularly the info on equity positions?"

"You got it."

Minutes later I was studying Stan's stake in the company and putting together a simple spreadsheet. If I could convince the rest of the board to split an investment with me, we could buy Stan out and increase our own holdings. Claiming incompetence would be the easy part.

The biggest problem was that my share of the buyout money would wipe out over two-thirds of my meager personal portfolio. The risk was enormous, but the reward could be too. What was the worst-case scenario? Failing at the coup attempt wasn't it. I'd almost certainly lose my job, but I'd still have my portfolio. No, the worst case would be if I succeeded in ousting Stan but then failed to make the company succeed. Then I'd lose almost everything and have to start over at a time in life that would make it difficult, to say the least. The best case? I'd pull it off, nominate a sympathetic chair, bring the company public, and walk away with tens, maybe hundreds of millions.

I felt like a rock climber again, eyeing two potential protection points: one easily accessible to my left, but leading up a boring overused route, and the other in a crack twenty feet up an overhang to my right, but with a nice shot from there to the summit—a route for the record books. The adrenaline rush could be amazing. I chose the adrenaline.

Nine

That year at DLS was proving to be less like an adrenaline rush and more like a steady climb, but the rush was about to come. We had succeeded in filling out the engineering and marketing teams and were actively searching for a Sales VP. At the same time, Jenny's group had successfully deployed her massively parallel acceleration hardware at an Azure server site, and Wade was putting his neural network through rigorous training using the UCSD-provided data. Jake's leadership of the overall engineering team had been outstanding, and his growing reputation in the academic and tech communities had endeared him to Marketing.

But we were still over a year away from initial product release, and the pressure for revenue was getting intense as we burned through cash at a rapid pace. Our biggest challenges now were careful testing and intensive planning for a major marketing campaign. Our target customers were younger, innovative psychotherapists in small- to medium-sized practices, with one exception. We also needed at least one well-known university or institute to adopt, actively use, and publicly champion our approach. Credibility in the field was key.

In the midst of all this slow but steady progress, however, one thing moved ahead much faster than I expected.

~

"Got a minute?" Claire asked through my partially open office door.

"Always. What's up?" I motioned to a guest chair in front of my desk.

"Rumblings you should know about."

"Okay . . ."

Claire closed the door and sat down. "I happened to overhear a phone conversation between Stan Gorman and someone at CU while Stan was here yesterday for the final Sales VP interviews. In fact, the candidate you approved this morning, Bob Macintosh? He was in the room with Stan at the time. I was just walking by the conference room and couldn't help but hear, so I parked myself outside for a minute. Stan can be awfully loud sometimes."

"Yes he can. Especially when he's . . . Never mind. What did you pick up?"

"Well, he was talking to someone named Cliff, and he asked if this Cliff person was at his office at the university today. So I'm guessing he meant CU."

"And?"

"And he was asking Cliff if he'd be interested in a business consulting gig here. I think he called it a 'strategic review.'"

"Did he say anything else?"

"I don't think so. No, wait, there was something at the

end of the conversation. I couldn't hear everything, but it sounded like he was pushing for action before the board meeting next month."

"Aha. Makes sense, unfortunately."

Claire looked up with concern. "What does all this mean? Did you already know about this?"

"No, I didn't, but I have a pretty good idea what it means."

"Is your job on the line?" Claire asked.

"Why would you ask that?"

"You know, two and two? The chair is trying to bring in a consultant behind the CEO's back. That's not usually a good sign."

"Right. It's not. But it's a very useful sign, so thank you."

"Useful how?"

"Useful because it forces a decision."

"Roger, why are you being so evasive with me? Maybe I can help. Talk to me!"

I didn't answer.

"Don't you trust me?"

"It's not that. It's just that I'm not certain I can protect you—your job—if I get you involved any further."

"Come on, Roger. That's bullshit and you know it. You don't trust me."

"Look, Claire. I'm just trying to deal with this news in real time."

"Okay, let me tell you exactly how I see my situation," Claire said, pinning me with her normally soft brown eyes. "I'm not worried about my job, so let's just take that off the table. I'm damn good at what I do, and I can always find work. That's not a problem. If someone else comes in to take your place, I'll quit anyway, even if the new CEO wants to keep me on."

"Really? Why would you do that?"

"Because I want to work for *you*, not some random CEO who just drops in for the money. I think you've got the best interests of the company and its employees at heart. You've brought us this far."

"Claire, I hate to disappoint, but I *am* in it for the money. I'm not some perfect, altruistic angel. This is my ticket to a decent retirement."

Claire was silent.

"But at the same time," I continued, "if I'm successful, everyone else here will benefit right along with me. That's how it works."

"Okay, I get that. So please trust me and tell me what I can do."

It took me a few seconds to decide, and I could see both pain and eagerness on Claire's pretty face as she waited. Then it became clear to me. I had a much better chance of succeeding with Claire by my side than if I continued to keep my plans from her. I couldn't do this alone. I needed her under-the-radar intelligence-gathering, but I also wanted her smart and assertive presence as a sounding board. I valued her pushback; it made me think more clearly. And Stan's apparent willingness to let Bob Macintosh in on his scheme told me the time for action had come. I might even be too late, I worried, because the Macintosh alliance probably wasn't the only one Stan was pursuing.

"Okay, I want your help, Claire. In fact, I need it. But you need to understand that once we start down this path, our fates are probably linked. This will be risky for you."

"I think I've already made my position very clear on that." Claire was smiling again, with the same conspiratorial flash in her eyes I'd noticed when I first asked her to keep her ear to the ground.

"Yes, you have. Thank you."

Over the next half hour, I reviewed everything with Claire: Stan's dogged, short-sighted attempts to accelerate our revenue stream, which required moving me out of the way; the personal animus between Stan and me, beginning with my first interview long ago; my trust in Kavi as a sympathetic and powerful board member; and even Stan's alcoholism, which I felt was a threat to the stability of the company. I described my alignment with both Engineering and Marketing as an offset to the schism that Stan was now apparently trying to create between me and the future sales team. I could see Claire taking all this in and processing it. She never needed to take notes, and I often wondered if she might have an eidetic memory.

When I finished, Claire was nodding. "This all makes sense now."

"How's that?"

"You know Janine, Stella's new assistant over in Marketing?"

I nodded.

"Well, she and I had coffee together the other day and she mentioned something that just seemed a little odd, but I didn't think much of it at the time. She said she'd been on loan to Stan to schedule Sales VP interviews, mostly offsite lunches. Were you aware of those?"

"Sure, I was in the loop, but just for the final three like I requested."

"Right, but here's the weird thing. Janine said a few of the earlier meetings didn't end up being with Sales candidates at all."

"Who were they with, then?"

"Apparently with other board members. One-on-ones. Janine saw them meeting in the parking lot before leaving together. And like I said, I didn't think much of it at the time. I mean, he *is* the chairman of the board, and he knows all those guys beyond just their roles here, so why wouldn't he go out to lunch with them? At least, that's how I saw it at the time."

"Maybe he was just looking for an excuse to have a few drinks in the middle of the day," I said, only partly joking.

"Maybe. Probably, from what you've told me. But Janine said those lunches still showed up on Stan's calendar as being with Sales candidates, not board members."

"He probably just didn't take the time to change the calendar entries or tell Janine. Or he forgot."

"Hmm. But why would this have happened several times?"

"You think he's trying to hide his lobbying efforts."

"Yeah, now that you've given me more background, that's exactly what I think."

I stood up and stretched each arm toward the ceiling in turn, trying to relieve the lower back pain that had been plaguing me recently. "I've got a plan. Let's get some more coffee, and I'll fill you in."

~

Back in my office, coffee cups refilled, I told Claire everything I'd learned from Kavi about Stan's plan to remove me for incompetence via an equity buyout.

"But that's insane," Claire said. "Incompetence?"

"Well, it might sound crazy on the surface, but listen. Stan actually has a semi-reasonable business case, and that's what makes this dangerous. We're getting to the point where revenue is essential. Our burn rate is too high without it, and we'll be forced into a second round of financing in about a year if we can't begin selling product fairly soon."

"But isn't a second round kind of common for a start-up like ours?"

"Yes, absolutely. It's almost a certainty for most. But it comes with a price. All shareholders get diluted in the process. And I think Stan is attempting to avoid that for purely personal reasons, and is trying to convince others. He wants to cash out at a decent valuation as soon as he possibly can, and the only way to practically do that is to take the company public or get us acquired. Both require either profitability or a very strong near-term case for it. And, of course, product sales are key in any case."

"And your plan doesn't get us there?" Claire asked.

"Oh, it gets us there. Just maybe not as quickly, at least in Stan's mind."

"I'm sorry, but why go with yours then?"

"Because the alternative might look attractive in the short term—early sales of a cheap derivative product targeting a mass market, making our balance sheet temporarily look good, but it would be a major distraction, delaying or even killing our longer-term prospects, making it unlikely we'd ever achieve the kind of serious value I'm after. With our technology and the academic and clinical partnerships we're developing, we're well on the way to creating a tool for psychotherapists that can provide them with real-time guidance in addition to post-session learning opportunities, all based on thousands of hours of clinical experience that demonstrates the effectiveness of delivering the right words, the right questions, the right observations *at the right time* in the therapeutic process, based on a patient's specific diagnosis and personal history.

"If we attempt to accelerate revenue by employing bits of our technology in yet another cheap personal chatbot that barely passes the Turing Test, we'll damage the brand we're trying to build. Sure, we might pull in a few million dollars in the short run, making our cash flow situation temporarily look good, and we might even be able to convince ourselves it's a necessary stepping stone, but we'd be deluding ourselves. We'd be giving up on the real DLS vision, squandering our current technological advantage. We'd almost certainly never become the multihundred-million or even billion-dollar company I'm driving toward, if we survive at all."

"Sounds like you've got a strong case."

"Well, I've been convinced of that from the beginning. But we're dealing with Stan here—the biggest individual shareholder and a guy who's desperate for a near-term jackpot for reasons none of us completely understands. And that kind of desperation can be contagious."

"So what's the plan?"

"We remove Stan using the same tools he's planning to use against me. With a little more evidence, claiming incompetence should be easy. A buyout will be financially painful for me and the board in the short run, but it's the best path I can see."

"How can I help?" Claire asked.

I gave Claire two assignments: go to lunch with Janine and see what else she knows, and find out who Cliff is. Learn as much as possible about his marching orders.

Ten

A week later, Claire was back in my office with a smile that told me she had news.

"Two things," she said in response to my raised eyebrows. "First, from Janine. Stan never bothered to join the others in the early Sales interviews, and yet he voted no on all of them. The three finalists were all people Stan knows, and two of them, including Bob Macintosh, were his students a few years ago. It looks like he handpicked them."

"All right, not the most transparent process in the world, but not particularly damning either. And hell, I signed off on Macintosh myself. He was clearly the strongest candidate. What's your second thing?"

"This one's a lot more interesting. I have a good friend who's an admin over at the Leeds School of Business at CU, and she tells me that our friend Cliff is an Assistant Professor there, Cliff Hutzinger."

"Okay, not surprising . . ."

"Right, but here's the good part. Hutzinger is being

considered for tenure, and according to my friend, Stan is the only member of the twelve-person tenure committee who's holding out. They require a unanimous vote and Stan has been dragging his feet for weeks. Why would he do that if he thinks highly enough of the man to hire him as a special consultant on a critical issue? I can think of one possible reason."

I nodded. "Because Stan wants leverage on the guy."

"Exactly. Hutzinger gives the board a report in line with Stan's views, and if he does a good enough job with that, he gets tenure."

"If true, that's extortion."

"Yep. So what do you want to do now?" Claire asked with an eager smile.

"I think we play along for a while. If Stan proposes this consulting thing to the board and I oppose it, I'll look defensive and weak. So instead, I'll embrace it with confidence, give it my full support and wait for the results. Then, if things go as expected and Hutzinger advises against my strategy, I'll fight it vigorously while you use your contact at CU to see if that tenure vote goes through. If it does, I think we'll have more than enough ammunition to move against Stan."

"And if it doesn't?"

"Then I just continue to fight on the merits. That's a fight I think I can win, but it probably won't be the last if Stan is allowed to stick around."

"What else can I do for now?" Claire asked.

"Stay in touch with your friend at CU, but be careful. We don't want those conversations to leak. Can you trust her?"

"Absolutely."

"Good. I'd also like your help putting together a kick-ass presentation for the board next week. I'll work with Jake and Stella on theirs, making sure we're all in sync, and I'd welcome your help on those as well."

"Great."

"And Claire?"

"Yes?"

"Well done."

~

A few days later, we were ready. Without revealing the threat of a biased outside consultant, I had prepared the engineering and marketing teams for a contentious board meeting. It's not easy to strike a constructive balance between fear and resolve when motivating people, but with Claire's help, I was confident I had done just that. We needed everyone to viscerally understand that our company was at a critical inflection point while also strongly believing in our winning strategy.

I had asked Jake and Stella to invite their key managers to attend the board meeting with them, not as presenters but as detail backup. I had also cleared the way for Claire to be present, ostensibly as my notetaker. In reality, I wanted her to see firsthand what we were up against. Notes or not, I knew she would remember important details and nuances that might escape my notice.

Claire, Jake, Stella, and I sat at the table with the five board members, along with our brand-new VP of Sales, Bob Macintosh, while our Engineering and Marketing managers sat in chairs around the periphery of the room. We were ready.

Stan opened the meeting at nine o'clock with the usual greetings and formalities, and I marveled at how smooth, congenial, and professional he could be when sober. He described the main purpose of the meeting as a critical update for the board as they considered the company's possible need for a Series B round of financing. To that end, his agenda included presentations from me, Jake, Stella, and even brand-new Bob. This would take us up to lunch at the Flagstaff House, to be followed by a wrap-up session at three-thirty.

I rose, strode to the podium, and smiled, surveying the room. Unlike this kind of high-level gathering at other companies in my past, this group was not simply a collection of older white males like me. To be sure, it was decidedly tilted in that direction, but there was Kavi in his turban nodding confidently toward me; Stella and Jake, both accomplished people of color ready to present their progress; and young Jenny Dickinson, the brightest female engineer I had ever encountered, and absolutely critical to our product's success. And then there was Claire, admittedly in a traditional female role, but with far more insight and influence than anyone here understood.

"Welcome," I began. "Thank you all for being here this morning and for your ongoing efforts to make Deep Learning Systems the leading AI-based psychotherapy assistance system in the world. That's not hyperbole. That's exactly how I foresee it, and exactly how our leaders here are creating it. I think you'll be more than pleased with what you hear from them today. But first, let me set the stage with an overview."

I began with a year-to-date corporate budget summary, admitting to a 2-percent overage due to extra spending on cloud deployment, but pointing out that this also implied lower capital equipment expenditures going forward. In effect, I claimed, this was an investment in our future financial stability. Having dispensed with the semi-bad news, I announced that we were two weeks ahead of schedule in product development, and then teased significant advances in strategic partnerships that Stella would cover in her upcoming presentation. I closed with an enthusiastic welcome to Bob Macintosh along with expectations for his success in implementing our subscription-based sales model. I glanced at Stan during those last remarks, but any discomfort he might have felt was well disguised.

Jake went next. To applause from the room, he announced Wade's completion of the first major round of neural network training against a large number of UCSD transcripts and audio recordings during the past week. Even better, he mentioned with a smile toward Wade, the team had used the results to adjust the network's vast array of parameters and had gotten some astoundingly good results against the test data from the Cleveland Clinic. And none of this, Jake pointed out, would have been possible without Jenny's innovative hardware. Jake finished with details expressed in several compelling charts, and then handed the meeting off to Stella.

"Good morning!" Stella said, her bright eyes shining with confident enthusiasm. "As Jake mentioned a moment ago, our strategic partnerships with UCSD and the Cleveland Clinic are both starting to pay off. Both organizations have provided thousands of data sets in exchange for minor stakes in the company, and to date, we've used the training set from UCSD and the testing set from the clinic in an effort to introduce some variability in the data and reduce bias. Wade's next step will be to reverse the situation: training sets from the clinic and testing sets from UCSD. And so far, as you've seen, the results are more than encouraging."

Stella waited as more applause broke out in the room, then continued. "And here's some new information that came in this morning, just before I walked into this meeting. I have to apologize to Roger for blindsiding him on this, but I'm quite sure he won't mind a bit when he hears the news. If all goes as expected with beta testing this year, and with lots of expert help from Wade, UCSD's Psychiatry Residency Program has agreed to become our first real user, and a highly visible one at that! Roger and I have been discussing this possibility, but I, at least, didn't expect it to happen this early in the game. So, you might ask, how does this prestigious customer fit with our strategy of attracting a broad set of small- to medium-sized practices with a subscription service model? As Roger and I have discussed, our strategy is significantly strengthened by landing one or two large, visible, and respected customers as 'credibility anchors' before switching gears to sell to the larger market. Roger, may I share your analogy that convinced me of this?"

"Sure," I said, feeling a surge of confidence and pride in my team. "By all means!"

"Roger calls this the 'Tesla Strategy.' Remember when that company first started selling its cars to a very limited but influential segment of the market? Do you remember what those all-electric vehicles were? They weren't geeky Prius-like things targeted at a broad middle market. No, they were sleek, super-fast, all-electric, head-turning roadsters. They lost money for the company, but they bought it some serious credibility. They created not just buzz but confidence that Tesla could produce a great product. But the high-end sports car market wasn't Tesla's real target. They wanted the mass market, and that's what they're now tapping, more successfully than any other EV maker in the country.

"So our strategy is to land one, maybe two highly visible customers up front as our 'credibility anchors' and then switch our focus to the much broader market with an affordable subscription model. We've got UCSD, and we're working on the Cleveland Clinic."

In the midst of more applause around the conference table, Stan stood and waited for the noise to subside. "Thank you, Stella and Jake, for those informative presentations. I think now would be a good time for a break before we hear from Bob and then head out to lunch."

I noticed the departure from Stan's agenda and motioned to Stella to join me outside the conference room. "Well done, Stella. So great that your news arrived in time for the meeting. Had you been pushing them recently?"

"Maybe a little," Stella said with a wink.

"So I want to give you a heads-up about something I think Stan will do in the wrap-up session after lunch. He cut you off before you were done with your presentation, right?"

"Yes, I had some detail about our upcoming middle-market promotional plans and some positive leads from Jake's speech at the recent AI conference, but that's okay. I'll include all that in my quarterly report. No problem."

"Good," I said. "So here's the thing. In the wrap-up session I expect Stan to propose an 'independent' consultant to assess our current long-term strategy. Stan apparently wants to spring this on us in front of the board, but unknown to him, I got wind of it last week. My message to you, as it will be to the rest of the executive staff, is not to spend any worry time on this. If Stan proposes this today, even though I think it's entirely unnecessary and maybe even hostile, my plan is to embrace it enthusiastically, to exude confidence that any such review will support our existing plan. And your announcement today made that much easier."

"Still, should I be concerned?" Stella asked.

"No. Absolutely not. We have an overwhelming case for our strategy, and we should be able to easily convince any objective consultant."

"Are you implying that this consultant might not be entirely objective?"

"I don't know. But even if he isn't, I've got a solid plan to deal with the situation. Trust me."

After the break, Bob Macintosh gave a brief, nearly content-free presentation in which he expressed gratitude for being a part of our company and confidence about his ability to hire a killer sales force to help us realize our shared goals. I was impressed with his polished style, though, and felt that he could be a real asset if not turned to the dark side.

Lunch at the Flagstaff House was excellent, but with a price tag that didn't seem to match Stan's apparent concerns about our cash position. I had watched Stan's alcohol intake, and while it might have put most mere mortals under the table, it wasn't particularly excessive for him. Even so, back in the conference room at three o'clock, Stan seemed a little looser, and I wondered if he had imbibed a bit more, somewhere out of sight. He remained silent and smiled serenely during an extended Q&A session in which the board peppered me and my team with questions about our timeline and tactical details. He looked like he had fallen asleep with his eyes open. But then he made his move.

"There's one more item I want to, uh, put on the table before we adjourn this afternoon," he said. "I think everyone here would agree that our engineering and marketing teams have made great progress since last quarter's meeting. And I think we owe it to them, and to ourselves, to do everything we can to ensure that their good work leads to the kind of financial results we all expect."

I turned to the side and whispered to Claire, "Here it comes."

"So to that end," Stan continued, "I'd like to propose that we bring in a seasoned expert to evaluate our strategy and help us fine-tune it."

Fine-tune it, my ass! I wanted to say but didn't.

"And the expert I have in mind," Stan said, "is Dr. Clifford Hutzinger from CU. He's a professor and accomplished researcher who focuses on early-stage start-ups, and I think he's just the person we need to validate our approach. But before we vote on this, I'd like to ask Roger to give us his perspective. So, Roger, would you be willing to devote a few hours of staff time to this in the coming weeks?"

"Absolutely," I said. "I believe every business plan can benefit from outside expert opinion, and now's a perfect time for this. My staff and I would be proud to explain our strategy and get some fine-tuning. Yes, I'd support this move as long as the funding comes from the board's discretionary pot."

The proposal passed with a single opposing vote. Kavi shot me a questioning glance as he cast that vote.

Eleven

Those were the good old days, I'm thinking as I emerge from the Residence to a rare sunny day in Seattle. Why don't we ever understand that when we're in them?

My seagull is already in place, waiting for a morning snack, both feet in a puddle. I search for something, anything, but come up empty-handed.

"I'm sorry, buddy. We're out of stock right now. Would you like us to back-order for you?"

The bird raises his head and produces three classic gull cries.

"But you know what?" I continue. "I just thought of something. There is one thing I can give you, even though you probably won't appreciate it. Since you're around a lot, you need a name. See that tent over there?"

The gull glances in the direction of Mary's home—I swear he does.

"Okay, that tent belongs to a lady named Mary, and she is the inspiration for your new name. Welcome to the overpass, Maslow."

Another three cries and Maslow takes flight. This time he craps all over Mary's tent on the way out.

The morning feels full of promise, and I decide it's a good day to check in with my potential business partner, Bart, down at the pizza place.

On my way down to SoDo, I stop by the park to fill my water bottle and check on my speechless friend, Tex. He's there on his bench as usual, and he tips his cowboy hat to me as I pass. *Major progress*, I think.

I pick up a few day-old burritos from the Mexican food truck on my way south, stuff them into a plastic bag in my daypack, and continue on. The whole journey takes about an hour, and as I reach Tedesco's Pizza, I notice that it's not Tedesco's anymore. It's Home Team Pizza. *Major progress again*, I think.

I walk in the front door to a very different scene than I remember from last time. At least half the tables are full, and a cook twirls dough in the kitchen behind a new counter. A technician is installing two large screens on opposite walls of the dining room. I walk up to the counter and speak to a young man waiting to take orders. He looks to be in his early twenties and has short, spiky blond hair. He's squinting as he looks up at me.

"Is Bart here today?" I ask.

The young man takes another long look at me and says, "Sorry, but we're not hiring, if that's what you're after."

"No, that's not it," I say. "I just want to have a quick word with your boss."

"Do you, like, have an appointment or something?" he asks, his squint now turning to something more like a smirk as he glances at my ratty jacket.

"No, no appointment. Didn't think I'd need one. I mean, come on, you're not a frickin' law firm!"

"You're gonna have to leave, like, now."

"I'm not going anywhere until I see your boss."

"I'll give you thirty seconds to get your ass out that door before I call the cops!"

"Jeffrey, what the hell's going on out there?" I hear Bart yell as he appears through a door in the back.

"This old guy is causing trouble and—"

"Hey, Roger!" Bart smiles broadly as he recognizes me and comes out to shake my hand. "Great to see you! I was wondering when you'd be back."

Jeffrey stands behind the counter with his mouth open. I flash him a smile and turn back to Bart. "I was in the neighborhood and thought I'd drop by to see how the place is doing."

"Great, I'm glad you did. Come on back to my office and let's talk for a few minutes. Want a Coke or something?"

"Sure."

"Jeffrey, get Roger a large Coke. He's my business consultant and the whole reason I could hire you, so bring the drink back to my office along with an apology."

Bart motions to a metal folding chair in the tiny office. "Here, have a seat." He sits behind his vintage gray metal desk and props his feet up on it. A faded old photo of Bart standing next to Edgar Martinez at a Mariners game adorns the otherwise bare wall behind him.

"So you've made some changes around here," I say. "And you've got some real live customers out there!"

A knock on the door interrupts us, and Jeffrey appears with a large Coke and a generous slice of pizza on a paper plate. He places them both on the edge of Bart's desk in front of me.

"Just in case you're hungry," he says as he turns to leave, then whirls back around. "Oh, and sorry, man."

"Apology accepted, Jeffrey. Just remember, things aren't always as they first seem."

Jeffrey nods and makes his exit.

"He's not a bad kid, actually," Bart says. "A hard worker."

"Just trying to do his job, I'm sure. I get that. Still, a slightly more nuanced approach might be in order, don't you think?"

"Absolutely. I'll have a talk with him later. So hey, I want to thank you for your advice a while back. As you can see, I took it, and business is already a lot better and will probably just go up from here once I get those screens installed and finish updating the dining room. You should see the new menu too. How did you come up with all those ideas on the spot, anyway?"

"Experience, I guess. I've seen a lot of ups and downs in business."

"Well, this is definitely an up for me, and I want to do whatever I can to make it one for you too."

"Thanks, Bart. I appreciate that."

"So here's what I'm thinking," Bart continues, removing his feet from the desktop and sitting up straight in his chair. "I'd like to create a job for you. It wouldn't be much at first, but maybe it would help."

"What kind of a job did you have in mind?" I ask, expecting something like dishwasher or maybe waiter.

"Adviser, I guess you'd call it. I can't pay much right now, and it would be very part-time, but I'd value more of your ongoing thinking about this business."

I'm surprised, to say the least, and wonder where this

offer is coming from. Is Bart just feeling guilty about my situation? Is this simple charity, or is he seriously wanting more guidance? And beyond Bart's motivation, and despite my need for money, I honestly don't think hiring me makes any business sense. I've already put him on a good path. There isn't much more I can do, and I wouldn't feel good about pretending there is. If I were his adviser right now, I'd tell him not to hire me.

And besides, he would run right into my criminal record if he did a background check, which, as his adviser, I would always recommend doing in a case like this. And there would be other complications as well.

"Bart, I can't tell you how much I appreciate this, but I don't think we should go down that path. You've got a lot of new expenses right now, with your renovations and all, and I've already given you everything you need to succeed, anyway. But I have another thought, if you're open to hearing about it."

"Fire away," Bart says, leaning back with hands linked behind his head.

"I live with three other folks who have even more problems than I do right now. We're all homeless, as I'm sure you've guessed, and some are reasonably good at panhandling for money—which I can't bring myself to do—but I'm good at gathering food. So I'm looking for ways to bring in a bit more of that on a regular basis in exchange for a cut of their money. I've got longer-term plans, much bigger ones, but right now this is the best I can do."

"I have to admit, you've got me a little confused, Roger. You just don't fit my image of a homeless guy other than, sorry, your clothes and all. Someday I want to hear about your bigger plans, but it sounds like you're not ready to talk about that yet."

"Right," I say, not having the slightest idea what those plans might actually be.

"Okay, so what about this: three days a week—let's say Mondays, Wednesdays, and Fridays—you come by, and I'll make sure there are four personal-size pies waiting for you, with salads. And I might have a question or two about the business from time to time. How does that sound?"

"Sounds perfect. One more thing just occurred to me, though. When your business gets to the point where you need another waiter, or even a dishwasher, I've got someone in mind who'd do a great job for you. The only problem is, you might need to ignore his immigration status and deal with him on a cash basis. Do you think that might be a possibility?"

Bart smiles. "Between you and me, it wouldn't be the first time. Sure, I think we could work something out."

Twelve

I leave the restaurant with four pizzas folded into my pack and notice that Bart has included a thick roll of dollar bills in a plastic bag along with the food. Feeling wealthy and satisfied with the day's progress, I decide to stop by a little bookshop in Pioneer Square that I've noticed several times before but never visited.

I immediately like the place. It smells Seattle-salty-damp with a hint of creosote and has a creaky wood floor, like parts of Pike Place Market, and every dark wood-paneled wall is covered with floor-to-ceiling bookshelves. Most of the books look like they're used, some thoroughly. Two comfortable-looking chairs with small side tables and reading lamps straddle a closed door at the end of the long, narrow space. An attractive, middle-aged woman in a peasant dress, with long gray hair, sits behind the sales counter next to an ornately beaded lamp and looks up from her book as I walk further into the shop. I notice an espresso machine behind her, along with a regular coffeepot.

"Could I have a drip coffee, please? Black?" I ask, thinking I might stay a while and should probably pay something for the privilege.

She glances at me again, then turns to pour the coffee.

"Oh, and where would I find something by John Steinbeck?" That earns me a smile.

"About two-thirds down, on the left side, under Fiction. There's also one of his under Nonfiction, I believe."

I nod, pay for the coffee, and take it with me on my search. Not being much of a fiction reader myself, I'm not aware of Steinbeck's range and am surprised to find so much by him. The only novels I've heard of are *The Grapes of Wrath* and *Of Mice and Men*, but here on the shelf in front of me are many more. For no reason other than the sound of the title, I pick up *Sweet Thursday* and take it back to one of the reading chairs.

Flipping through the pages, I smile. There's a guy in the book named "Joseph and Mary," and that is enough to send me back to page one. Over the next several hours, I live in Steinbeck's world near Monterey, seeing life through the eyes of an oceanographer, a prostitute, several conniving but soft-hearted drunks, and a wide range of people in between, all trying to come to grips with life in their own ways. It rings true.

I'm nearly finished with the book when I'm surprised by the sound of rain on the sidewalk outside and look up to discover it's almost five o'clock, and the weather has taken a dramatic turn. I wait for a lull in the showers and then get up to go home. I want to get some food to Tex before dark.

I place my book in front of the woman at the counter and reach into my pocket to pay for it. But she looks up at me with sympathetic eyes and says the book's free.

"It's too tattered to sell," she says.

I thank her, stuff the book into my pack and head into the wet world.

It takes me about forty-five minutes to make my way back as far as the park, and I arrive as the sky is darkening with the hour and the weather. One of the burritos is for Tex, and I look forward to his confused but grateful smile. I remember every smile, but he acts like each encounter is brand-new and unexpected, out of the blue, a lucky break.

But today it's my turn to be surprised, and not happily. As I approach the edge of the park, I see familiar blue lights flashing through the rain against the dark background of evergreens, and I worry that the police are once again trying to make Tex move on. Don't they know he'll just be back in a day or two? This is his home.

Coming closer, though, I see that the flashing lights are coming not from a police car but from a black van. Closer still, I can read the lettering on the side: *Seattle Coroner*.

I'm not particularly prone to emotion, but this gets to me. My throat tightens, and I find it hard to swallow as two men carefully move a covered body from the park bench into the back of the van. A small crowd watches silently from a distance.

Tex had a story, and like everyone else's, his has a beginning, a middle, and an end. And here is the end, the only part I really know anything about. What about the rest of his story? Has it all been about survival, or did the man do something interesting with his life and pick up a few unique bits of wisdom along the way? Did he make a difference in the world, or is his legacy nothing more than a freed-up park bench, now available for someone with a similar fate?

I wait for the van to leave and the crowd to disperse, then

slowly approach the bench. A tan cowboy hat sits there alone, and two black trash bags lie purposeless on the ground, now reduced to the status of trash themselves. I pick up the hat, place it carefully on my head against the rain, and make my way home.

~

"Hey, Rog, what's with the new hat?" Mary asks as I try to make my way past her tent unnoticed.

I touch the brim and shrug. "Found it at the park just now."

"Huh. Looks a lot like the one that old guy on the bench wears."

I sigh. "Yeah, well, it is. He's dead."

"Shit. What happened?"

I shrug again. "I don't know. Probably no one does. I think he just reached the end of the line." I take a few more steps toward the far side of the overpass.

"Damn. You wanna talk about it?" Mary asks.

I glance toward the Residence thinking, *No, definitely not,* but then look back at Mary and give in. "Sure."

I sling the pack off my shoulders, remove the hat, and duck under Mary's blue awning. Fighting some newly flared-up back pain, I sit cross-legged with her flickering camp stove between us and the hat in my lap. Mary's brown hair falls out of her blue wool cap and looks like it needs a good brushing. No, a serious wash. I'm tempted to mention the shower down on Yesler but think better of it. Mary's slowly becoming a friend, something rare in my old life, and I don't want to screw that up.

"So damn," Mary continues. "How'd you find out?"

"I got to the park right when the coroner was loading him into the van. I was stopping by to leave him something to eat, but then, well . . ."

"I'm sorry, Rog. You knew him, right?"

"Not really. Just tried to help a little now and then. I called him Tex. No idea what his real name was. He never spoke, but sometimes he'd smile in a confused sort of way, and that kept me coming back. I guess I hoped maybe I'd make a connection someday."

Mary's eyes softened. "Sounds like you did, even if it was buried down deep somewhere."

"Maybe. But why should I even care? Why should any of us try to understand anyone else? Most of the time I don't even understand myself," I say, shaking my head.

"Yeah, who does? But there it is and here we are."

I raise my eyebrows at that. "Hmm, I guess. Oh, that reminds me, I've got a few things for you." I unzip my pack and pull out a burrito, a pizza, and a book. "Here you go."

Mary picks up the novel and eagerly scans the back cover. She doesn't even glance at the food.

"I know you like Steinbeck," I say.

Mary's broad smile confirms that. "*Sweet Thursday* is one of my old favorites, but I don't have a copy anymore. Haven't read it in probably twenty years. Totally made my day."

"I'm glad, but curious. Why Steinbeck? Why do you like his stuff so much?"

"I don't know. Maybe because so many of his characters are down-and-out. Some are so out they don't even know it. That's kind of comforting. Sick, right?"

"No. Not at all."

Mary stares into the camp stove flame as dusk turns to dark, and neither of us speaks for what seems like minutes. A small teapot sitting above the flame starts to boil.

Eventually I break the silence. "Hey, could I ask a favor?"

"Sure, anything."

"Could you hand out the rest of this food tonight? There's much more than I can eat, and it won't stay good for long."

"No problem. I'll take care of it."

"Thanks. I just don't feel like talking with anyone else right now."

"Like I said, no problem. Go get some sleep. And hey, thanks for the book."

I tear off half a pizza for myself, hand over the rest of the food, put my hat on, and walk the remaining fifty feet back to the Residence. I eat the pizza as slowly as I can, trying to stretch out dinnertime and avoid too much thinking about the uncertainties of life. And the certainty of death.

Thirteen

It's another clear morning, and I join it after a dreamless night. Tex is still very much on my mind, and I'm oddly grateful to have him there. While the thought of his empty bench makes me vow never to accept the same fate, the feel of his hat on my head gives me a strange but welcome sense of hope. And yes, I admit, I just plain like the way it looks.

My freeway pillar is as accommodating as ever, and Maslow is nowhere to be seen, so I decide to jump right in and begin my day of foraging. But glancing across the encampment, I notice that Jimmy's hovel is looking even worse than usual, and I feel I should check in with him before heading out.

"Hey, Jimmy!" I shout, ten yards away from his lean-to. "You around?" I know he is; he's never not around, but I don't want to surprise him.

The ripped cardboard flap that serves as his door opens a few inches, and I see part of his face through the crack. Jimmy is around twenty-five years old, I'd guess, and has a sparse beard and stringy blond hair hanging down to his shoulders. I can see he's wearing his ancient Seattle Sonics cap and probably has on his usual Seahawks sweatshirt and ripped jeans. I don't think I've ever seen him without the cap.

Jimmy opens the door a little further and nods. Unlike old Tex, he never smiles, not even in a confused way. I take the nod as an invitation to approach his shelter.

"So, Jimmy," I say, glancing toward his damaged door and front wall. "I'll check around for some dry corrugated cardboard while I'm out today. Looks like you could use some."

"Yeah."

"And while I'm at it, you need some food too?" I ask.

"Yeah, but not those burritos, okay? I just have to put 'em down there." Jimmy nods toward a partly covered hole in the dirt a few feet away.

"What the hell?" I say, staring at the hole.

"I can't eat those anymore."

"So you've been burying the damn things?"

"Yeah."

"What a waste! Why?"

"They're trying to kill us."

"The burritos?"

"No. Well, sort of. The cops."

"With poison burritos?"

"Yeah."

"I don't think so, Jimmy."

"Wait . . . Are you in on it too?"

"No, Jimmy. I would never do anything like that."

"You sure?"

"I'm sure. Who told you about this?"

"Jay-Jay."

"Ah, right. Okay."

"The cops want us out."

"That's probably true, but I don't think they'd—"

"Oh yeah. Jay-Jay told me. You didn't hear?"

"No, I didn't get the word. But why bury them?"

"Can't let the seagulls get 'em."

"Because they'd die too?"

"Duh. And I have to piss on 'em."

"The seagulls?"

"No, the burritos."

"Okay . . . Why?"

"Otherwise the birds would dig 'em up."

"Right. Makes sense."

"Uh-huh."

"Okay, Jimmy, no more burritos. But listen, I'm not gonna let anyone get to you, okay? You can stop worrying about that. I've got good connections."

"I hope you're right. I'll tell Jay-Jay."

"You do that, buddy. Pizza okay?"

"Pizza's good."

Jimmy backs into his shelter like a hermit crab retreating into its shell. I get it. Even without schizophrenia, it's tempting to hide away from a hostile world. Living here, it's hard *not* to feel that way. Still, the whole thing with Jay-Jay is batshit crazy. But then again, I've got my freeway pillar and Maslow, so who am I to judge?

I pass Carlos in his yellow poncho on my way downtown. It's not raining, but I guess the color must help him be seen. He's busy with a guy in a BMW who's rolled down his window and seems to be searching his wallet, so I just smile and keep moving. The driver is probably flipping through twenties, tens, and fives, looking for a few ones to get rid of. I used to be that guy, except I wouldn't have stopped in the first place.

The empty bench at the park makes the place seem

quieter than usual this morning, not that Tex ever made a sound when he was here. His two old trash bags are still on the ground in front of the bench, and the sight of them brings back unwelcome feelings, so I pick them up and stuff them into a nearby trashcan before filling my water bottle and heading out to the street.

Encouraged by yesterday's results at Home Team Pizza, I decide that today might be a good one for the breakfast place on lower Pike. There's no similar deal to be made there, because they're successful already, but still, nurturing connections doesn't hurt, and I'll probably come away with some decent food. I need a special offering tonight if I'm going to convince my overpass family to adopt my plan. I'm feeling confident and comfortable in my new hat as I approach the restaurant from the back.

Someone is taking a smoke break in the alley by the dumpster, but as I get closer I can see it's Kenny, the shift manager, not the busboy. I consider ducking around the corner and coming back after lunchtime, but he's seen me and it's too late. He crushes his cigarette under a shoe and turns to head back in. He'll lay down the law with the staff, shutting down any hope for leftovers in the next few days, so I've got to take a shot now.

"Hey, Kenny, hold up a sec!" I'm glad I remembered his name.

"Can't. House is full. No time."

"No, come on, Kenny. It'll only take a minute. I've got some hungry folks back home, and I bet you're gonna toss out enough this morning to feed them for days."

"Fuck off and get a job!"

"Really? That's how you deal with your guilt?"

"Your name's Roger, right?"

"Right."

"Fuck off, Roger."

Kenny flips me off and returns to his important responsibilities, whatever those are. At least he's unequivocal and clear in his guidance; I'll give him that. Not bad traits in a manager, although I'd suggest adding a touch of empathy to the mix.

I should cut him a little slack. There's no way for Kenny to know it's nearly impossible for me to find the kind of work that will get me out from under the overpass. No one wants to hire a convicted felon, even a white-collar one. And one without a mailing address or phone number is even less likely to find the sort of employment that will buy him that address and phone. It's like what my software engineers called a resource deadlock and what everyone else calls a Catch-22.

Feeling a bit deflated, I decide to try the Mexican food truck next, reminding myself to avoid the burritos this time. But that's also a bust. The Health Department is inspecting them today, and they're in no position to welcome me. I get it. They've got to try and keep their B rating at very least, and my presence wouldn't help. I keep my distance and move on.

It's Tuesday, not a pizza day, so Home Team is out too. I touch the brim of my hat, as if that could bring me a shot of magic confidence, then kick myself for the stupid thought. I look around and see a McDonald's and a donut shop on the next block. McDonald's franchise owners tend to stick to corporate guidelines, so it probably isn't worth the humiliation it would cost me to make an attempt there. But the donut shop? It looks like a mom-and-pop place, so maybe.

I enter the small shop, doff my hat, and pretend to peruse the chalkboard menu on the wall. I'm starving, and the smell of the place is enticing: fresh coffee, hot fried dough, sugar.

The young woman behind the counter finishes with the customer in front of me and smiles.

"Can I help you, sir?" she asks.

"Yes, thank you. Great shop you have here. Very attractive."

The woman smiles again, but this time I notice her eyes straying to the front door behind me. She's obviously hoping another customer will come along so she's not alone with me. Something occurs to me that might help relieve the tension.

"My name's Roger, and I'm a volunteer working to feed the homeless here in Seattle. And as I'm sure you can imagine, some of those folks can get very depressed, so I try to bring them something special now and then. Something to raise their spirits a bit. And, well, a good donut does that better than almost anything I know."

I've got her attention again and she seems more relaxed.

"So I'm wondering if you might be willing to contribute a dozen or so to the cause? Even day-olds would be welcome."

"Let me see what I can do," she says. "Hold on a sec. I'll be right back."

"Thank you so much." I nod and back away from the counter because I imagine she's concerned about the contents of her tip jar. I would be, if I were in her shoes.

A new customer walks in just as the woman reappears with a bag. She smiles again as she hands it to me, and I glance at her name tag.

"Thank you, Susie. You've made a real difference today." She has, at least for me. I put my hat back on, tip it to her with my best smile, and walk out the door.

I haven't actually lied about being a volunteer, I assure myself. *After all, I don't have to be doing this, and I'm definitely not getting paid for it, so hey, that's what I am: a volunteer. I can live with that.*

Back out on the street and a block away, I look in the bag. There's a nice assortment of goodies, and they still seem reasonably fresh. I pull out an apple fritter and devour it on the spot. I feel elevated, and not just from the sugar.

Fourteen

It's early afternoon as I arrive back at the overpass with the bag of donuts, a flattened cardboard box for Jimmy, and a new identity.

I'm ready to try for a deal, to organize my crew, and I'm wondering how one schedules a meeting in this world. But I'm saved the trouble, because everyone's already sitting together under Mary's blue awning. Carlos waves me over.

I duck under the tarp and sit next to Jimmy, handing him the cardboard. He nods and accepts the gift. I notice everyone staring at the bag I'm holding, so I rip it down the middle and spread out the contents in the center of the group. "Dig in," I say.

"See, this is exactly what I was talkin' about," Carlos says to the group as he picks up a maple bar and takes a bite. "Anybody have a problem movin' ahead?" he asks. I look around the group with confusion as Mary and Jimmy both shake their heads solemnly.

"Okay then. So, Roger," Carlos begins. "We been talkin'

the last few days."

"Oh?" I say, removing my hat and wondering if I'm about to get ejected from the community.

"Yeah. And we want to ask you something."

"Sure, go ahead."

"You been good to us, bringin' in food every now and then. You didn't have to do that, but you did. You could've just kept it all for yourself, but you didn't. And then there's the whole thing with Mary's coat. And cardboard for Jimmy."

Carlos stops for a second, smiling. "And you're makin' the rest of us feel like shit, man!"

I laugh, still not sure where this is headed.

"So," Carlos continues, "we want to see if maybe you'd be interested in some kind of deal. You know, balance things out a little."

"I'm just grateful to be here under this overpass with you guys," I say.

"I call bullshit on that," says Mary with a grin.

"No, it's true," I say. "Sure, I'd rather be in a nice hotel downtown, or a house up on Queen Anne, but like you said the other day, 'There it is and here we are.'"

"Well, we're all glad you're here," Carlos says. "So here's what we been thinkin'. Mary and I aren't too bad at makin' money—mostly me if we're bein' honest, right, Mary?" It's Carlos's turn to grin now.

"Jimmy, you help keep us safe. And Roger, you don't seem all that good with money, but you're great at bringin' in the grub and other stuff. So how about we all focus on what we're good at and then share it all around at the end of each day?"

Mary and Jimmy are both nodding, and I like what I'm hearing, even though the money comment stings.

"So what does that mean, exactly?" I ask.

"We're puttin' you on salary, man!"

So much for being a volunteer, I think. *But okay, nobody out there needs to know about the "salary."*

"And on top of that," Carlos continues, "we want you to be president of our little country right here in the middle of frickin' Seattle!"

Wow, I laugh to myself. *From nothing to volunteer to president in one day. Not bad.*

"Thanks, everybody. I'm honored, but I can't accept your whole offer. I'm fine with everything except being president. I think that should go to Carlos, at least for the first term. Then maybe we should hold an election every year or so after that. All in favor?"

After a few moments of hesitation and glancing around the group, everyone raises their hands.

"Good," I say. "Motion passed. Carlos, it's your meeting."

Fifteen

Before we separate for the night, Carlos brings another motion to the floor.

"So, Mary, you read a lot of books, right?"

"I guess, yeah. Why?"

"Well, some of the rest of us don't read all that much. I was thinkin' maybe you could read to us every now and then. A little entertainment, you know. Something to look forward to. Maybe like every other night?"

"You mean instead of me begging for money?" Mary asks. "I hate that shit."

"I know. That's prob'ly why you're so piss-poor at it. But we need more than just me out there. Maybe not on reading days, though. What d'ya think? With Roger bringin' in the food, we don't need as much money. I think we'd be good."

Mary glances back into her tent. "Yeah, I guess I could do that. I'm gonna need more books, though."

"Got you covered there," I say. "So are you making a formal motion here, Mr. President?"

"Yeah, if that's what it takes."

"Okay, I second that motion," I say. "Sounds like a great idea."

Carlos nods in silence.

"So, Carlos, now you call for a vote. Just say 'Motion seconded. All in favor?'"

"All in favor?"

All hands go up.

"Great!" says Carlos. Then, apparently remembering something I said earlier, "Motion passed!"

⁓

It's been a good day, and the first one that feels something like progress to me. Maybe we're inching up the pyramid, from Maslow's basement to the first floor. Still, in the back of my mind something's bothering me. I've felt this kind of progress before, back in my corporate days, just before things went south.

Back then, product development was on target, strategic partnerships were blossoming, HIPAA compliance was in hand, and the market looked promising. But then there was Stan—our company's Achilles' heel, our turd in the punchbowl, our unforced error. To me, all these metaphors fit.

But apparently not to everyone. Dr. Clifford Hutzinger presented his findings at a special board meeting called by Stan for that purpose, and his presentation was well received by the majority. He skillfully used our own product schedule and sales projections to argue that our plan, while viable, would be incompatible with an IPO or buyout in the near term. Unfortunately, our early partnerships, as important as they were for our "Tesla Strategy," wouldn't be providing any significant revenue for the next couple of years, and this too provided fodder for Hutzinger's argument.

On the one hand, I sympathized with his general position because I was still very concerned about my own personal finances and wanted my shares to pay off as soon as possible. But on the other hand, I was also convinced that any substantial payoff, not to mention the company's essential credibility, would almost certainly be put in jeopardy if we gave in to this kind of short-term revenue temptation. To realize the full potential of DLS, we would need to stick to our plan, avoid distractions, and take the slightly longer path.

I laid out this argument in detail and added what I thought might be a sweetener: Once we established our reputation and had a solid initial customer base, we could explore the idea of a phone-based app, but not a half-assed therapy chatbot. Our app would indeed converse with its users but then, using the power of our back-end neural net system, it would help guide them into therapy with qualified human practitioners specific to their needs. Therapists interested in referrals from this system would pay a small recurring fee to be included in our database and would be asked to contribute anonymized patient transcripts or recordings to be used as new training data for our neural net. Those who were already full DLS customers who also wanted referrals from the app would be spared the additional fees.

But as convincing as I felt my argument was, greed won the day. At least, that's how I saw it at the time. If it hadn't been for Stan's influence, we wouldn't have wasted a second discussing a regressive short-term approach, but now it seemed we were about to adopt one. As an executive board member, I wasn't considered part of the core advisory group and was asked to step out of the conference room for the remainder of the meeting. Not a subtle message.

I ran into Claire in the hallway and could tell she understood at once. Why else would I be leaving the meeting on my own?

"Tomorrow might be a good time to visit your friend at CU," I said.

Sixteen

"**I** was the lone dissenting vote." Kavi slowly shook his head as he sat next to me at the bar of Hotel Boulderado and gazed up toward the ornate ceiling. "I can't believe everyone is buying into this . . . into this nonsense."

"I think the word you're looking for is 'bullshit,' Kavi."

"They're going to force you out, Roger, and there's very little I can do about it."

"I've got something in the works, but it means things could get a little nasty," I said.

"Oh?"

I described Stan's possible extortion of Cliff Hutzinger. "We should have some proof in the next day or two."

Kavi was still shaking his head. "That's helpful. But it's circumstantial evidence—not ironclad proof of wrongdoing."

"Then there's Stan's drinking," I added. "You've seen it; I know you have. Given the amount of influence Stan has with the board, that's a huge destabilizing factor."

"Agreed. But it's still not enough. You know how loyal the

board is to him. We need something more. How committed are Engineering and Marketing to our original strategy?"

"Very. It was basically Jake's idea from the beginning. I just fleshed it out and ran with it. And Stella—you can probably tell from her board presentation—she's all in. She's making it happen as we speak."

"Okay then. I think our way forward is clear. Scary, but clear."

"An ultimatum?"

"Basically, yes. We're at an existential tipping point, Roger. Are you ready to risk the whole company? Are the founders ready to risk it?"

"I think so."

Kavi looked me squarely in the eye. "You need to be sure. Once you can answer that question with an unequivocal yes, let's talk again. But it must be soon, my friend. Very soon."

~

"How did things go over at CU?" I asked Claire as we sat down for our morning meeting the next day.

"Dr. Hutzinger's tenure was approved late yesterday."

"Aha, just as we thought. Good work, Claire. Well done."

"Thanks. So what's next?"

"I need to meet with Jake and Stella ASAP. Can you set that up for this morning?"

"On it. What should I tell them it's about?"

"Tell them . . . Tell them it's a special strategy meeting. With just the two of them; no direct reports this time. My office."

"That'll get their attention."

"I hope so. Things are going to get a little crazy here for a while, so buckle up."

Claire smiled. "I'll be right next door if you need anything."

~

Jake and Stella looked at me expectantly as we settled in around the small conference table in my office, coffees in hand.

"Let me get right to it," I said, and briefed them on Stan's proposal.

"What would it take for each of your teams to switch from our current strategy to this temporary approach, with the goal of turning our cash flow positive long enough to land more funding at a higher valuation or even go for an IPO?"

"You're joking, right?" Jake said. Stella was wide-eyed and silent.

"No joke. What would it take?"

"Seriously? You're actually considering this?" Stella asked.

"I didn't say that."

"Okay, hypothetically?" Jake said, standing up and moving to my whiteboard. "Here's one way to look at it. I'll use a scale of 0 to 9, where 0 means no change and 9 means a total restart from scratch. Our core software wouldn't change much, except a few tweaks on the front end. But the target user and the user experience would be totally different. We'd need new software on both IOS and Android phones and new app developers for that." He wrote $\Delta SW = 6.5$ on the board.

"Jenny's specialized hardware design would remain mostly unchanged," Jake continued, "but we'd need to scale its implementation way back. Hosting it in full parallel form in the cloud is expensive, and we expected that cost to be offset by the standard product pricing Stella has put in place. That kind of performance just wouldn't be needed in the cheap app scenario, which doesn't involve real-time neural net-generated advice—just simple conversation. We'd have to scale it way down in order to make any money." Jake wrote $\Delta HW = 2$.

"Any ballpark guess at the delay to our current plans?" I asked.

"I'd need a day or two to get you a real estimate, but ballpark? Don't quote me on this: probably around six to nine months." He wrote $\Delta T \sim 9M$. "I think we'd still be able to keep about 80 percent of engineering on plan."

"And here's another thing," Jake continued. "I'm sure you've thought about this, but a chatbot? Really? Do you know what that would do to our credibility?"

I just nodded and turned to my Marketing VP. "Stella?" I said.

"Well, this would mean starting over from scratch in Marketing. We'd be looking at completely different target customers. Advertising changes dramatically. Our web and social media presence gets a reset. Trade show and conference plans get altered or delayed. Using Jake's scale, I'd give the whole thing an eight. Marketing could probably react in a little under Jake's timeframe, so engineering would still be the critical path.

"But this is crazy," Stella continued. "So why are you even asking?"

"I'll explain in a minute, but first I'd like your perspective on the potential credibility impact that Jake brings up."

"Potential? I'd say it's more like a certainty," Stella said. "There must be eight or ten chatbots right now that claim to offer some degree of AI-based counseling or companionship. And with most of them, you could do just about as well talking with Alexa or Siri. None of them seems to have any grasp of real in-depth talk therapy, and some are just plain embarrassing, possibly even dangerous. We've designed our powerful neural net approach as an adviser to actual therapists, not a replacement for them. If we put something out there like Stan seems to want, that would be corporate suicide. I could see an app, somewhere down the line, that helps direct patients to real therapists using our system, but not this."

I nodded and turned to Jake, who was still standing at the whiteboard, his eyes flashing with anger.

"Okay," he said. "Your turn. What the hell's going on here? Did that damn consultant relight Stan Gorman's fuse on this stuff?"

"Yes, and it's burning fast."

"But this is insane!"

"Of course it is, and that's why we need to work together to put out the fire in the next few days. There's some background I need to give you."

Jake rejoined Stella and me at the table, and I filled them in on Cliff Hutzinger's findings and the board's reaction. When I finished, they were both shaking their heads in disbelief.

"And two more important details," I said, deciding that full disclosure couldn't wait. "The board knows exactly where I stand on this, and with the exception of one important member, they want to fire me. They can't make this kind of fundamental change in strategy without a CEO who will agree and execute, and that CEO is definitely not me."

"Shit!" Jake said, slamming a fist down on the table. "I can't believe it's come to this. This is insane."

"Second that," Stella added. "There's got to be something we can do."

"There is. But now we're getting into some very sensitive stuff, so I need your assurance that what I'm about to tell you won't go anywhere beyond this room. Not inside the company. Not with family or friends. Not anywhere. Do I have your word on this?"

"Yes," they said in unison.

"Okay. There's very strong evidence that Cliff Hutzinger was pressured into producing his results. Actually, 'pressure' isn't the right word. It's flat-out extortion."

"Why? How?" Stella asked.

"Stan knew he was going nowhere with this whole thing and decided he needed a highly credible outsider to do an independent assessment that would make the case for him. Cliff Hutzinger filled that credibility gap nicely. The only problem was that Stan couldn't be sure Cliff would reach the conclusion he wanted, and a generous consulting fee wasn't enough to push him over the edge. So Stan found another lever to pull. Cliff was being considered for tenure at the university, and Stan is on the approval committee. Tenure approval requires a unanimous vote, and Stan threatened to vote no unless Cliff came through for him. In fact, he held up the committee for weeks. Well, Cliff came through with flying colors at the board meeting, and his tenure was approved yesterday. He's now a full professor with a guaranteed position. That's worth a hell of a lot more than a consulting fee."

"Unbelievable," Jake said. "So can we use that to get out of this mess and back to work?"

Stella held up a hand and interrupted. "Can you prove any of this, Roger?"

"Not conclusively, and that's a problem. The evidence is purely circumstantial. But still, it's one important tool in our kit."

"And the other tools?" Stella asked.

"Here's where it gets tough," I said. "I know where you both stand on the big issue. But I don't know if you feel strongly enough to bet your jobs and the entire company on that stance. Jake, you're the original founder and the architect of our product. DLS wouldn't exist without you and couldn't make it going forward in your absence. And Stella, your contributions to our marketing strategy have been outstanding, and now your execution of the plan is essential to our future. The bottom line is that the company fails without the two of you, and I think the same argument can easily be made about Wade and Jenny. I'm expendable, but only if replaced by someone equally dedicated to our strategy, and that's not the kind of replacement the board has in mind."

"I'm in," Jake said without hesitation. He glanced toward Stella.

"Absolutely. No question," she said, nodding vigorously.

"Excellent," I said. "So, just to be clear, what we're talking about here is this: We expose Stan's scheme to the board and invalidate Cliff's conclusions. Then, if that's not enough to get Stan ousted and restore our strategy, we issue an ultimatum. Either Stan leaves and the strategy is restored, or the three of us walk out together, along with anyone else who'll follow. Are we agreed?"

"For me, it's a no-brainer," Jake said. "Stan's alternate strategy is a road to failure. It serves nobody but him, and I'm not sure it even does that very well."

"Agreed, yes," Stella said. "But what about the other member of your executive team? What about Macintosh? Do we need him in on this?"

"No, there's no leverage for us there. And besides, he'll come around once we get through this."

I felt lighter and more confident as Jake and Stella left my office. Now all we had to do was execute.

Seventeen

"Claire, do you think you could dig up anything more concrete on the tenure thing at CU? Something I can use if Stan denies it all?"

"Maybe. I don't want to get my friend in any trouble over there. Let me think about it and I'll get back to you soon."

"Okay, great. Anything would help. And also, I want to brainstorm with you about ways I can arrange a meeting with all the board members except Stan without tipping my hand. They can't know he won't be there until they arrive."

"Intrigue. I love it. Sure, when do you want to get together on this?"

"My schedule's packed for the rest of the day, as you know. How about we talk over burgers at the West End Tavern after work tonight? My treat. Well, actually, the company's treat."

"Uh . . . sure. That should work. What time?"

"Meet you there at seven?"

"Okay, see you then."

After Claire left my office, I began to second-guess myself.

Should I have asked her to meet about this over dinner? Would she take that the wrong way? Did I want her to? Damn. *You cannot go down that road, man. She works for you, and the ethics are crystal clear. But it's just a business meeting over burgers, right? So don't get all tied up in knots.*

The rest of the day was filled with back-to-back meetings, leaving no more time for introspection. When I finally checked my watch, it was six-thirty, and the only people left in the building were Jake, Jenny, Wade, and a few of their engineers. They were working hard to meet an upcoming beta milestone, and I smiled at the thought of their dedication. Some would probably stay all night.

Driving west on Pearl Street, I marveled at Boulder's mountains looming ahead. As many times as I'd seen the Flatirons, whether from the road below, from a trail at their base, or from inches away when climbing the massive rock faces themselves, I never failed to appreciate their dangerous beauty. These near-vertical formations defined the eastern boundary of the Rocky Mountains and made a dramatic transition between the forested Front Range and the midwestern plains stretching all the way into Nebraska, Kansas, and beyond. From my very first days in Boulder as a young CU student, I had always seen the Flatirons as symbols of transition and challenge.

Now, as I parked the Range Rover and walked a half block to the West End Tavern, the imposing dark silhouette of the mountains against the last light of evening confronted me again. Approaching the door to the tavern, I kept one wary eye on that enormous mass of rock as if it might suddenly fall, burying the whole town and me with it.

But warm lighting, enticing smells from the grill, and muted sounds of conversation in the tavern coaxed me out of that dark mindset as I scanned the room for Claire. I was a few minutes early and she hadn't arrived yet, so I took a table for two in a back corner of the room and ordered a beer. As usual, the tavern's clientele was an eclectic set. Over at the bar, the largest group looked like young, hyperactive tech people, while a loner nursing a drink at the end of the bar—older, deeply tanned, and sporting a cowboy hat—might just as easily have come from a ranch on the plains or the boardroom of a local company. A sharply dressed collection of men and women at the largest table in the place just had to be lawyers, and three guys wearing Boulder Fire-Rescue jackets were chowing down on burgers and cokes at a table near the door. Several other groups and a few couples chatted away at tables near me.

This is good, I thought. *A very public, unintimate setting. Perfect for an informal but professional dinner meeting with my admin. Shouldn't be a problem at all.*

Shouldn't have been, but was. At least for me. I looked up to see Claire enter the front door and speak to the hostess, who pointed her in my direction. She smiled brightly, waved, and walked toward me, wearing a short green skirt over black leggings. She removed a black jacket as she walked, revealing a white top, cut lower than I'd ever seen at the office. *Is this her normal after-work look? And does she always walk like that, and I just haven't noticed before?*

I stood and greeted her. "Hey, Claire, thanks for taking the time to meet tonight. I really appreciate it."

"No problem. What's good here?" she asked after sitting down, adjusting her skirt, and glancing at the menu.

"Well, burgers, definitely, and the fries are excellent," I answered with a nervous laugh. "Would you like a beer or something?"

"Sure, why not. It's after hours, right?" Claire looked up from the menu with the same conspiratorial grin I'd seen many times in the office, but now it seemed to carry new significance. Her lips were a deeper red, and her brown eyes sparkled, reflecting the light of the small flickering candle in the center of our table.

Our waiter brought the beer, and Claire began our meeting with a toast. "To DLS and its delivery from evil!"

"Delivery from evil!" I echoed, trying to shut down a guilt-ridden flashback from a long-ago church service.

"I have news," Claire announced after a sip from her glass.

"Do tell," I said, eyebrows raised. *Do tell? What the hell was that?*

"You were busy in meetings and there wasn't much left to do for the day, so I left work early and dropped in on Annie, my friend at CU."

"Oh?"

"Yes, and she told me the minutes of the tenure committee are public; something about the fact that CU is a state school. So I was able to get them online, just like anyone else could if they knew it was possible. I wonder if Stan knows. Anyway, I now have the voting records from the last three monthly meetings concerning Dr. Hutzinger and one other professor."

"And?"

"On Hutzinger, all members except Stan voted yes in the first two meetings. Stan abstained, citing the need for more investigation. University policy only allows one more meeting after that before Hutzinger would have to wait for next year's cycle to try again, and that third meeting, as you know, happened the day after Hutzinger's board presentation. That time, the record shows Stan voting yes."

"Excellent! And you have actual hard copy of all this?"

"I do, and there's more. This is even more damning, but, unfortunately, we can't use it directly because it would implicate Annie. It turns out that Stan and Cliff had been emailing back and forth on an unrelated topic, cc'ing Annie as Stan's assistant. Well, apparently Stan forgot about the cc line and started using that same email thread to discuss Cliff's consulting contract with DLS. Big mistake. The last email he sent said, 'You support me at the DLS board meeting, and tenure is yours.'"

"The smoking gun," I said. "Outstanding."

"But one we can't use directly," Claire reminded me.

"Okay, but it gives me a lot more confidence in our plan. And if it ever came down to a lawsuit, we could get a subpoena and access the emails that way, without involving Annie at all. Even the threat of that could work well for us. Amazing work, Claire. Thank you."

"You're welcome," she said, smiling broadly. "Just doing my job."

"But doing it exceptionally well," I said, locking eyes with hers for a few intense seconds.

A waiter interrupted, bringing our food and shifting the mood. Over dinner, we chatted easily about Boulder's natural beauty, favorite hiking trails, other good restaurants, and equally innocuous subjects. Then, after the plates were cleared and coffee ordered, we got back to work.

"So my idea," I said, "is to expose Stan's corruption to the rest of the board without him being present, effectively invalidating Hutzinger's conclusions and setting the stage for Stan's removal as chair. To further strengthen the case, I want to have Jake and Stella there to present their very convincing rationale for staying with our current strategy. The plan is to come out of that meeting with a vote removing Stan and replacing him with Kavi."

"Got it. Dr. Singh would be a huge improvement over Stan in every way imaginable. So it seems the only issue for now is how to carefully orchestrate that meeting, right?"

Claire's long brown hair framed her face as she leaned forward with both elbows on the table, hands clasped under her chin, smiling at me.

God, she's beautiful, I thought. *And so damn smart. Smarter than me in many ways.*

"Right," I said. "I'm thinking about a direct approach. Contacting Stan before the meeting, revealing what we've got on him, giving him an off-ramp, a chance to save a little face. I'll tell him we came across the public tenure information during due diligence on Hutzinger, making sure to keep Annie out of it. Then we'll call a meeting with the others, avoiding all the cloak-and-dagger stuff. It's a lot simpler, but I'm worried it's not bulletproof."

Claire sat up straight again and brushed her hair back. "I think you're right to be worried. It won't work," she said, shaking her head.

Okay, that incisiveness is exactly what I need right now, I thought. *She's amazing.*

Claire continued. "No matter how convincing your warnings or threats, Stan won't just pack up and go away. He's devious, especially when he's had a few, and we both know he'll have had a few at that point. He'll find a way to derail the whole thing ahead of your meeting. He'll do whatever it takes, including outright lying, maybe even blackmailing a board member, to consolidate his power and toss you aside. Don't give him that chance."

"So . . . ideas?" I asked.

Claire smiled and touched my hand across the table. I felt

a pleasant electric jolt as she slid her hand away and hoped she couldn't feel me twitch in response.

"I'm no genius here, Roger, just lucky. There's a super-simple solution."

"Really?"

"Really. It turns out that Stan's wife has convinced him to finally take a vacation. They're heading down to Cabo for a week starting Friday. So while he's away . . ."

Claire's conspiratorial smile was back, and I felt another electric jolt. But not in my hand this time. *Come on, man, focus!*

"That is just incredible," I said. "How did you find out?"

"Annie."

"Of course. I should have guessed. But how do we make sure that none of the other board members reach out to Stan in Mexico before the meeting?"

"Got that covered too. As I'm sure you can imagine, Annie is not at all happy working for Stan. She hasn't been for a while and plans to look for another job soon, so she's willing to help us out a little more. It turns out that Stan is basically inept when it comes to doing anything online, so Annie does virtually everything for him, including managing his mobile phone account, so that gave me an idea, and Annie agreed.

"All the rest of our board members are here in town next week for a Technology Incubator Conference at the Hyatt. So once we pick a date and time for what we'll announce as a 'mandatory emergency board meeting,' none of them will have an excuse not to attend. We'll hold our meeting at the Hyatt right after the last conference session that same day."

"Sound's great, but what does that have to do with Stan's phone?" I interrupted.

"Sorry, got a little ahead of myself. Minutes before we contact the board members, Annie will disable Stan's international calling option, making voice and internet communication impossible. She'll re-enable it after the meeting, when the vote is complete and the damage done. Being on vacation, Stan probably won't notice the short gap in service, but even if he does, it'll be easy to blame it on a glitch of some kind. Oh, and I'll have Annie temporarily disable voicemail too. We don't need to worry about Stan emailing from a hotel computer either. He doesn't know how and refuses to learn."

"Talk about devious!" I said, laughing and pointing across the table. Claire and I hashed out a few more details, then adjourned our meeting.

"Walk you to your car?" I asked.

"Not necessary, but sure, that'd be nice."

Claire's car was less than two blocks away, and the time went by much more quickly than I wanted. I stood by as she unlocked her car door.

"Thank you," I said. "I can't tell you how much more optimistic I feel about all this."

"I'm glad," Claire said. She looked up at me with soft eyes as we stood together, silent for longer than I could stand.

"Great meeting," I finally said. "I should get going."

"Right," Claire said. "Me too. We got a lot done tonight. Maybe we should do this again soon."

That left me speechless. I smiled, turned, and walked back to my car. The evening was over, but that smile lasted long into the night.

Eighteen

The next morning, Claire slid sideways into my office, a finger on her lower lip, her brow knitted. She was a few minutes late for our regular meeting.

"Roger, I'm so embarrassed about something I said last night, at the car . . . and it kept me up all night. I'm sorry if I—"

I cut her off with a broad smile and a wave of my hand. "I have absolutely no idea what you're talking about. But here's a cup of coffee, all ready to go. Two creams, one sugar. Thought you might need it."

"Thank you. I, uh . . ."

"All your ideas and suggestions were excellent last night, Claire. All of them."

~

On Tuesday of the following week, we were ready. Claire had reserved a meeting room for seven o'clock at the Hyatt, alerted Annie to disable Stan's international phone service and voicemail, sent out the mandatory meeting notice, and coordinated with Jake and Stella on their presentations. Claire would attend the meeting to record the official minutes.

I spent two hours with Kavi over lunch, briefing him on the plan and securing his agreement to take over as chairman of the board if the vote went as expected. He seemed only mildly surprised at the further proof of Stan's treachery. Now we would engage in a bit of that ourselves.

Claire, Jake, Stella, and I arrived at the hotel at six-thirty and checked on the meeting room. A *Deep Learning Systems* sign stood outside on a silver stand, and a large hi-res screen was up and running inside, ready for my team's presentations. Expecting hungry attendees coming directly from the conference, Claire had requested a selection of hot and cold hors d'oeuvres, which we found attractively arranged on a side table. The large, dark cherry conference table dominating the center of the room was surrounded by ten low-backed leather chairs.

Kavi had taken the initiative to ensure everyone had gotten the meeting invitation and would attend, so at a few minutes after seven all board members were present, taking advantage of the food and trying to hide worried curiosity behind small talk.

"Let's all have a seat and get started," I said, choosing a chair at one end of the table and waiting for the group to settle. "So I'm sure you're wondering why Stan isn't here to open the meeting tonight. Let me get right to the point."

To a stunned audience, I laid out the details of Stan's extortion of Cliff Hutzinger, displaying the public records of his tenure committee votes and alluding to further proof of intent. When I finished, I looked around the room and wasn't sure I had reached everyone. I continued carefully.

"Now, like all of you, I'm grateful for Stan's initial investment and his early-stage involvement. But it's been clear to me for a while—and I know I'm not alone in this—that Stan's personal motivations for an early payout have clouded his professional judgment. And now, I submit, he has shown us that he is entirely unfit to continue on this board, let alone lead it."

I let that statement sink in, then, hearing no pushback, I continued. "There's also an elephant that's been living in the boardroom for some time now, and I think we have a responsibility to confront it, especially in light of current developments. As I'm sure you've all noticed, Stan has a serious problem with alcohol. Now, I don't presume to understand the reasons behind Stan's behavior, nor do I believe it's our job to judge him personally. But it *is* our job to protect this company from unstable leadership."

"Are you proposing to insert yourself as chair?" interrupted a clearly suspicious member seated next to Kavi.

"Absolutely not, John. As CEO, I'm totally committed to driving this company toward operational success, and I have no desire to add anything to my role which might distract from that. And I'm also a believer in the general wisdom of separating executive and advisory functions. But yes, we do need to address the question of board leadership, and I'll have a nomination for you in a few minutes. But right now, it should be clear to all of us that the counter-strategy Dr. Hutzinger proposed in his presentation last week was heavily biased, to put it politely. So if you'll bear with me for just a little longer, I'd like to turn the floor over to Jake and Stella to help us understand why we need to retain our current plan."

As expected, my two VPs did a superb job. Jake skillfully dismantled Hutzinger's arguments, citing specific technical issues and related schedule impacts. Then Stella reviewed the current marketing plan and outlined the deep changes and delays that would result from Stan's plan, pointing out that even if everything else about his plan was workable, the engineering and marketing time to implement it would erase almost all the early revenue benefits. Finally, she addressed the credibility problem created by proposed changes, claiming this could easily destroy the company's ability to attract our ultimate customer base. Her talk garnered several nods around the table.

"Does anyone have questions or concerns about staying the course?" I asked after Stella sat down.

There were a few minor questions, but general agreement seemed well within reach. I thanked Jake and Stella, excusing them from the rest of the meeting. Claire remained, diligently taking notes even though I knew she would be able to recreate the entire meeting from memory.

"And now," I said, "I move that we dismiss Stan Gorman for cause, resolving that he is no longer competent to lead this board or participate as a voting member."

I hoped that someone other than Kavi would second the motion, but no one did.

"Hold on, Roger," came a voice from the other end of the table. It was John Kingston, a Senior VP at Google and the same board member who had questioned me moments earlier. "You're moving a bit too fast for my comfort here, and I daresay one or two others might agree."

There were several nods around the table.

"Don't get me wrong," John continued. "You and your team have convinced me about our strategy, and you've been very persuasive about Stan. I don't substantially disagree with you on either count, and I doubt whether anyone else does either."

Again, more nods.

"That said," John continued, "I think we owe it to Stan to hear him out, to let him defend himself if he can. Then we can hold a vote. Not now. And honestly, Roger? I think your little stunt today was unwarranted and borderline unethical."

"Fair enough," I said, trying to project calm rationality even as I felt heat rising up my neck and face. "I'll schedule a meeting for next week after Stan gets back into town."

Nineteen

"Do you have a few minutes to debrief?" I asked Claire after everyone else had left the meeting room. I knew I could count on her for some perspective.

"Yes. That didn't end quite like we hoped, did it?"

I was about to answer when we were interrupted by a hotel worker who walked in and began cleaning and resetting the room for another meeting.

"What do you say we go back down to the lobby and talk there?" I suggested.

Getting off the elevator, I scanned the lobby and noticed a quiet lounge at the far end.

"You okay with the bar?" I asked.

"Sure."

Claire and I sat across from each other in comfortable club chairs with a low table between us. There was only one other small group in the place, and it looked like they were getting ready to leave. The lights were low.

"You're awfully quiet," I said.

"Yes, I'm sorry. I feel partly responsible for the way things turned out tonight. You wanted to avoid the cloak-and-dagger stuff, as you called it last week, and I sort of pushed in the opposite direction. And now look where we are. I shouldn't have done that."

"No, don't second-guess yourself."

A waitress approached and asked if there was anything she could get for us. We quickly scanned the wine list.

"Claire?" I asked, glancing up at her.

"Just coffee, thanks. No, wait, might as well. Could I have a glass of the Pinot Gris?" She pointed to a line on the list.

"The Rutherford Cab," I said. "Thank you."

The waitress disappeared and I turned back to Claire. Her eyes were wet, and she looked to the side as I turned toward her. "Seriously, don't doubt yourself. Maybe we lost the first battle, but we haven't lost the war. It's just going to take a little longer."

"Uh-huh."

"And anyway, I'm still convinced your plan was better." The wine arrived and I proposed a toast: "To burying the devil!" That brought a little laugh from Claire as we clinked glasses.

"To burying him!" she said. "I guess we'll never know what would've happened if you'd talked with Stan first, like you wanted to."

"Honestly, I think we'd probably be in worse shape now."

"How's that?"

"Well, regardless of what Stan might have decided to do, the rest of the board would have felt blindsided. I'd much rather have all of them on our side, feeling informed in advance of a critical vote. I think that's what we achieved tonight. Sure, the vote is delayed, but we laid all the essential groundwork."

"There's still chaos ahead, when Stan gets back," Claire

said. She was regaining her composure and I was glad to see her shifting back into planning mode.

"No doubt," I said. "Any thoughts on how to minimize that? How to get to a vote without too much bloodshed?"

"Actually, yes. If you still trust me." A sad smile formed on Claire's lips.

"Of course," I said. "More than ever."

She smiled more brightly and took a sip of wine before speaking. "We need to ensure that the next person Stan hears from is you, not one of the board members. It would be ideal if you could talk with him face-to-face, but I don't think we've got that luxury. We can't guarantee that one of the board members won't get to him first when he returns from Mexico."

"Right," I said. "We've got much better control over who reaches him by phone."

"Exactly," Claire's conspiratorial smile was back. "We don't tell Annie to re-enable international calling until the moment you're ready to call."

"And maybe we should wait a couple of days for that," I suggested. "Because if anyone's going to try reaching him, they're likely to do it soon, probably even tonight, or tomorrow at the latest. We'll leave the blackout in place for a while in case anyone tries. Then, after my call, things could go one of two ways: either Stan decides to save face and resigns quietly, not admitting any guilt, or he fights like hell, despite all odds."

Claire nodded in agreement. "If it weren't for one particular thing, I'd expect option two. That's more in line with who the man is."

"And that one thing?" I asked.

"If we expose what he did on the university tenure

committee, he'd almost certainly lose his *own* tenure. He'd probably never work in academia again."

"Of course. He'd lose on both ends," I said. "He'd be done."

"We just need to make sure he understands that."

"Yes."

We locked eyes across our little table for several excruciating moments, her soft brown ones meeting my intense green ones until her softness won, and I had to look away.

"I think I know what we both want right now," Claire whispered, shifting in her chair so her gaze met mine again. One of her legs brushed mine under the table.

"You're not talking about work anymore . . ." I reached out to touch the hand she offered.

"No, definitely not."

Claire's inviting eyes were all I could see now.

"I didn't think so." I slowly moved my hand up her arm, along the side of her neck, then behind her neck, pulling her gently toward me across the low table. She opened her mouth almost imperceptibly as our eyes locked, and we moved closer still.

Our waitress rescued us at that moment, though neither of us wanted saving. "Would you two like anything more tonight?"

We immediately dissolved into laughter, confusing the poor waitress and breaking the spell. In a way, we *were* rescued that night, but walking right up to that erotic boundary and living there on the edge for just a moment without crossing? That was intoxicating. We instantly became addicts of the edge.

Twenty

"What is it about boundaries and edges, Maslow?" I ask my seagull friend as he stands within the confines of his little puddle outside the Residence. He cocks his head to one side, eyeing me for clues about breakfast.

"I don't know about you, my friend, but humans are strange. We hold seriously contradictory shit in our heads all the time and hardly ever notice the conflicts, or at least don't admit it. The small intersection between all that stuff—the comfortable place—that's where we live most of the time. We only seem to go to the edges when we're strong enough, weak enough, or get pushed there by big events. You following me?"

Maslow raises his head and emits three piercing cries.

"And sometimes just because it feels so damn good!" I add, tossing out two stale pizza crusts. Maslow gobbles down the first piece and flies away with the second one. Would he ever consider sharing a treasure like that with a gull friend? I don't think so. But if he did, he probably wouldn't spend even a millisecond agonizing over the choice.

I can't believe I'm spending any time thinking about this stuff as hunger gnaws away at my gut. I've tried to crawl up and out of the basement a few times, and I've made some good efforts—I'll give myself that much—but life on the street drags me back down every time. My version of *Eat, Pray, Love* has become *Eat, Pee, Live.*

I put on Tex's hat—my hat—and pay a visit to my freeway pillar. I zip up, tip the hat to my tall concrete friend, and walk into the world. *Pees be with you.*

And also with you.

I'm going to try again today, I think, so I head downtown with the idea of first picking up a little artificial pride from Starbucks across from the market. The balance on my card says I'm still welcome there.

Standing in front of the place, I run a hand through my dirty hair, button up my jacket to hide my stained shirt, and walk through the door of the only club that will take me now. The smell of roasted coffee and the promise of fresh food draws me to the barista's counter.

My Starbucks card buys me a double tall mocha with a lemon scone, and I look around for a place to sit. The room is packed, but there's one chair across a small table from a short, plump, balding man with a sour, stubbly face. His dark green shirt is faded, untucked, and noticeably fraying around the collar. A small scar extends from the side of one eye, giving him an unbalanced look. Despite all that, or maybe because of it, I decide to take the seat. Besides, anything beats trying to eat breakfast on a cold drizzly street at rush hour.

"You mind?" I ask the man, nodding toward the empty chair. He looks up from his phone and shrugs. I take that as an invitation and sit down across from him.

I don't expect a conversation and don't even want one,

so I'm happy with the silence as my table partner returns to texting. The scone is satisfying and the hot mocha sprinkled with cinnamon reminds me of a long-ago vacation in Thailand, but I'm jerked back to reality minutes later as the man across from me puts down his phone and clears his throat to speak.

"You know you stink, right?"

I look up, stunned.

"You need a shower if you're gonna hang out here," he says.

Without warning, my inner fifth grader emerges. "Okay, well, *you* look like shit. How'd they even let you in the door?"

The man scowls at me and I'm thinking, *Great, here comes a fight. I'll never be allowed back in here.* But then, to my surprise, the scowl slowly, very slowly, transforms into an amused grin.

"Charlie Duncan," says the man, extending his hand.

I laugh, shake my head, then his hand. "Roger Carrington."

"So where you from, Roger?"

"Seattle. You?"

"Same now. New Jersey before. You got a story; I can tell," says Charlie.

I nod and take a sip from my coffee. "Looks like you've seen some life yourself. And how do you even have a phone? Sorry, but it just doesn't fit, you know, the rest of you."

"I'm a lawyer."

"Bullshit."

"You're a direct SOB, Roger. I like that. And you're partly right too. I was a defense attorney in Newark for a few years— public defender, actually. Then I lost my license in the state for showing up drunk in court one too many times."

"And now?"

"I came out west trying to escape everything, and that's

one thing I managed to do exceptionally well. Escaped a bad job, a bad marriage, and good money." Charlie's amused smile reappears.

"I get it."

"You look like you do. So what's the deal?"

I pause before responding, trying to ignore the implied insult. *Why should I tell this guy anything? But hell, what've I got to lose?*

"I was the CEO of a high-tech company in Colorado."

"You're shittin' me."

"Nope. It's true. But I panicked, made a stupid mistake, and ended up in prison. Lost everything."

"Damn! And now?"

"Now I'm here chewing away at the balance of a Starbucks card I found on the street and talking to some guy who says he's a lawyer."

Charlie smirks. "Come on, man. What's next for you?"

"I don't know. I'm working on some ideas."

"Hmm, smells a little like horseshit to me. Anyway, I gotta go. Meeting a guy about getting my law license for Washington State. Maybe I'll see you around."

"Yeah, maybe."

I watch Charlie walk out, then, seeing no one looking my way, I turn to take a quick sniff of my left armpit. At least he was telling the truth about that. I get up and begin the long trek down to the shelter on Yesler.

~

After showering, washing my clothes in the sink, and drying them as thoroughly as possible with a hair dryer whose short cord is securely fastened to the wall, I head down to SoDo.

It's pizza day, and I need to do my job.

Bart isn't in, but Jeffrey has today's allotment ready and waiting. I thank him, stuff the pies and salads into my pack, skip the donut shop, and head back toward Pioneer Square to look for another book for Mary.

"Hi, good to see you!" says the familiar gray-haired woman behind the counter at the bookshop as I walk in. "Black coffee again?"

I think about my recent double-caffeination at Starbucks but can't resist the offer. It's almost overwhelmingly nice to be remembered. "Thank you, I'd like that. My name's Roger, by the way."

"Denise," she says. "Glad you decided to come by again."

I take my coffee back to the Steinbeck shelf and look through the available choices. Then, just when I'm about to pick *East of Eden*, I notice a book containing all six of Steinbeck's shortest novels. Perfect for Mary's group readings after *Sweet Thursday* is done. I pull the volume off the shelf and take it with me back to the counter.

"Oh, that one's in good condition," says Denise with a sad smile. "I'm sorry, but I can't give it away."

"Not to worry. Money is no object, as long as we're talking less than five bucks."

"Sold!" says my new friend.

I pull five bills out of the plastic bag that Bart included with his first pizza allotment a week ago and gladly hand them over.

"So you must be a real Steinbeck fan," says Denise as she slides the book back across the counter to me.

"I'm not sure yet. Maybe. I'm a volunteer trying to help the homeless in our community and one of my clients is definitely a John Steinbeck fan. She's reading his books to folks in her little encampment."

"That is absolutely fantastic! What's the name of the volunteer organization you work for?"

It shouldn't surprise me, but her question does just that, and it takes me a moment to recover enough to advance my lie one step further. *I need a name right now. Damn, what's a good name?*

"It's called Stairway," I say. "The idea is to help people climb up and out of basic survival mode."

"That's wonderful! Strange I haven't heard of that particular group, though. I try to keep up with things like that."

"No, I'd be surprised if you'd heard of us. We're a brand-new nonprofit I'm just getting started in Seattle."

I walk out of the store berating myself. *Mary's right. I'm still a shithead, lying like that. But I don't know, maybe calling it a lie is a little harsh. I mean, that's how any start-up begins, right? It's all fiction at first.*

Twenty-One

As the sun dips behind the Kitsap Peninsula and slowly turns the Emerald City from green to gold, everyone gathers at Mary's tent. I distribute the day's food, and we all eat dinner together. Although I will always value solitude, this is a nice change, and I begin to feel that my home is more than just the Residence.

I imagine this feeling must be something like what my VP of Marketing, Stella Lujan, once described in a meeting about corporate identity. As a member of the Tiwa group of Native Americans from Taos Pueblo in New Mexico, Stella had a deep sense of place. For her, people, places, and all living things in that place were naturally linked. Our little encampment under the noisy freeway is a far cry from the natural beauty of Taos, and our home has existed for an eye's blink compared to the Pueblo's millennium. And yet, in the midst of America's fierce individualism, here we are, learning interdependence. Relearning it, actually, if we look back even a short time into our species' history.

I glance at our tiny community gathered around Mary's camp stove: Carlos distributing our shares of today's income, Mary opening her book and preparing to read to us, me supplying the food, and Jimmy . . . I'm not sure how to think about Jimmy. As a dyed-in-the-wool capitalist, I'm feeling conflicted about our little arrangement that's beginning to smell suspiciously like socialism. But our situation, and Jimmy's in particular, is pushing me toward a more flexible mindset; not a radical one, just more nuanced. It's a visceral thing now, far from theoretical or ideological. These are real people. *We* are real people.

This is our second reading night, and Mary opens *Sweet Thursday* to Chapter 3. She reads the first sentence, and I'm immediately taken in by what I hear.

"Looking back, you can usually find the moment of the birth of a new era, whereas, when it happened, it was one day hooked on to the tail of another."

The next few pages fade away like background music as I think about this simple but profound statement. We're such linear thinkers. When we're in the middle of something, all we can see is more of the same, stretching out in a straight line before us. Maybe slightly bigger, slightly smaller, a little better or worse, but basically just the next step along the same old line. But then later, when we find ourselves in a completely new and different situation, we can often identify the exact point in time when things went nonlinear.

Usually, this perspective seems to require a lot of travel down the timeline, and that was certainly true in my corporate life. But tonight, I think maybe I've identified one of those inflection points in my very recent past. I think it was the moment at the donut shop when I tried to save face by calling myself a volunteer. It wasn't just an attempt to avoid embarrassment and recover a little pride. Sure, it was that too, but it was also an unconscious shift in identity from passive victim to active agent. Then it was reinforced today, when I lied about a new nonprofit organization at the bookshop.

Like me, that lie needs to reinvent itself. It needs to become a truth.

~

As I drift toward sleep back at the Residence, I'm thinking about an equally important inflection point in the history of Deep Learning Systems. I was on the cusp of removing Stan Gorman from his obstructive position on the board and had settled on the basic strategy but wanted to get Claire's perspective on the plan before implementing it. I always looked forward to meeting with her, because she helped me think about problems like no one else could. She challenged me when I couldn't see my own mistakes or was too stuck to see alternative solutions. She encouraged me when things looked bleak. And her mere presence energized me.

But it wasn't one-sided either. Claire was enjoying an unusually high level of influence in the company, considering her official role, and I could see her drawing energy from that. Even so, I knew I was pushing the edge of ethical and professional acceptability. Neither Claire's title nor her compensation reflected the actual value she was providing.

And then there was the other edge, the one we vowed never to cross. But approach it we did—within epsilon— intensely and often. We both fed off the sexual tension and used it as a powerful energy source in our work together, despite the distraction it sometimes created. We often treated that distraction as a game, subtly challenging each other to stay focused on business while simultaneously working to do just the opposite. By never quite consummating our relationship, we kept it fresh, alive, and dangerously electric. Was there still an ethical issue in all this—a potential HR violation? Of course there was, but we chose to handle it as a gray area to be managed carefully. In retrospect, it was a clear case of dopamine-clouded judgment.

Claire and I had agreed to meet in my office at six-thirty in the morning to refine the plan to remove Stan as chairman of the board. We chose the early time because I wanted to try calling Stan that morning at eight before the rest of my busy schedule took over. And yes, also because we'd likely be alone at that hour. We had agreed on six-thirty with intimate smiles that would certainly have betrayed our dual purpose had anyone been watching.

I had chosen a gray suit that morning and was wearing everything but the shirt and tie. Those were tucked away in a desk drawer, awaiting the end of our meeting. Claire walked in without knocking, smiled at my wardrobe choice, turned slowly, bent slightly, and locked the door. She was wearing the short green skirt I'd noticed at the West End Tavern but now without the black leggings, or anything else, as far as I could tell. A sheer white top finished her minimal outfit—I mean, finished it, completely—and she carried a small bag, presumably with other items of clothing usually considered essential in a normal business environment, or really any public place.

"So, let's get to work on the Stan plan," I said, casually removing my suit jacket and hanging it on the back of my desk chair. I was proud of my shirtless rock-climbing physique and could see that Claire was enjoying the view. I moved over to the small conference table, pulled a couple of chairs away from it, and motioned for her to sit across from me, in the middle of the room. "You think it's warm in here?" I asked.

"Apparently *you* do, but I'm fine, thank you." Claire was clearly enjoying the tension she was creating. She retrieved the iPad from her bag and placed it on her lap.

"Just a *little* warm?" I said.

"Oh, maybe a tad." Claire reached up and slowly released the top two buttons on her blouse.

"I'd like to call Stan at eight," I said. "Will Annie be ready to restore his international calling option?"

Claire folded her hands across the iPad on her upper lap, and that short green skirt slid up to mid-thigh as she recrossed her legs. "I've got it covered. She's on alert and ready to act when you are."

I almost lost it. "Okay . . . Uh, excellent. So let's talk through a couple of scenarios."

"Yes. Scenarios." Claire's skirt was now barely functional, as was her blouse. She looked up at me, eyebrows raised, and her pursed-lip smile dared me to keep my eyes focused on hers. I failed.

"Scenario one," I said, working to regain control. "Stan answers the call and I describe his predicament and our intent to remove him from the board. He reacts badly and hangs up before I can invite him to the emergency board meeting."

"A likely outcome," Claire said, "given his past behavior." She released one more button.

"In that case, I'll follow up with an email or text summarizing everything," I said.

"Not everything."

"I'm sorry?"

"I don't think you should put anything in writing except the meeting invitation," Claire said. "It's too risky to have the other stuff out there where he or someone else could use it against us later."

"Yes, of course. How do you manage to be right all the time?"

Claire released all but her last button while trying to hold my eyes on hers. "It's hard sometimes. And for you? Is it hard sometimes? Like right now?"

Twenty-Two

Claire and I managed to work through two other potential scenarios while simultaneously driving each other to the edge of exquisite distraction. As always, we deliberately danced around our hot fire without getting burned.

At seven-fifty, Annie re-enabled Stan's international calling option at Claire's direction, and at eight o'clock I made the call, putting it on speaker. Claire sat in my office, now professionally dressed, and listened in.

"Hello?" Stan's voice sounded groggy.

"Stan, it's Roger Carrington."

"Who?"

"Roger, from the company."

"Oh, right, sorry. Kind of a rough night."

"I can imagine. Listen, Stan, let me get right to the point. There's no way to sugarcoat this. The board and I are asking for your resignation as chair and member at large. You'll lose all voting rights along with your equity position, but your initial investment will be returned to you with interest."

"What? That's insane! You can't do that."

"Actually, yes, we can, and we are."

"On what basis?"

"We clearly have irreconcilable strategic differences."

"I won't resign. I refuse, for the good of the company."

Claire quickly scrawled a note and passed it to me with a smile: *The good of the company, my ass!*

I recovered quickly and continued. "Well, that is certainly your prerogative, but resignation will look much better on your résumé than termination for cause. We're offering you a decent way out."

Stan did not reply, and I could hear the unmistakable sound of a cork being removed in the background.

"Are you still there?" I asked, now hearing liquid being poured.

"I'll fight you all the way on this, you bastard. I should never have allowed the board to hire you, and now you're trying to lead the company down a failing path that was flat-out invalidated by an expert independent consultant."

"Expert, maybe. Independent? Definitely not."

"What the hell are you talking about?"

"You know exactly what I'm talking about. When we did our internal due diligence on Cliff Hutzinger, we came across the public record of his tenure bid at the university."

"Okay, so . . ." Stan seemed unable to find the next words.

"So we know you deliberately held up his widely anticipated tenure approval for weeks with no explanation, while everyone else on the committee voted for it—something no one would do if they regarded a candidate as highly as you clearly do. And then we checked the record again, immediately after Cliff's heavily biased board presentation. That's when you granted him tenure. That was an obvious quid pro quo. Some might even call it extortion."

"Bullshit! And besides, you could never prove that."

"Actually, I'm quite certain we can, and not just from the tenure committee minutes, which should be enough by themselves. If it came down to a legal battle, we would subpoena records of all communication between you and Cliff. It's a good bet we'd find direct evidence that way. At the very least, you'd lose your own tenure and probably your entire academic career."

Stan went silent again, so I continued. "Look, even though the board agrees with me on this—we had a meeting a few days ago—they want to give you an opportunity to defend yourself at another meeting next week on Thursday at three, in the boardroom. So if you want to take advantage of that, you're welcome to do so. At the end of the meeting, whether you're present or not, there'll be a formal vote on your termination. But my advice, Stan—not that you asked for it—is to get a letter of resignation to the board before the meeting. That would be better for everyone, yourself very much included."

"You son of a bitch."

"When I need to be, yes."

The phone went dead.

~

I saw no value in trying to contact Stan again before the meeting. He could make his own decision, but the outcome for the company would be the same either way. Wednesday came and went without any word from Stan—no call, no email, and certainly no resignation letter. It seemed we were in for a nasty fight, possibly even a costly legal battle.

On Thursday morning, Claire contacted the board members, confirming they would all be present for our meeting that afternoon. Then, at three o'clock, Claire and I walked into the boardroom to find all members gathered around the table and looking somber. Claire opened her iPad, ready to take the formal minutes. I stood at the head of the table and started the meeting.

"Thank you all for interrupting your busy schedules to be here this afternoon. I know we would all rather be somewhere else, doing almost anything other than what we're faced with today. This is a critical moment in our company's life, and I assure you I don't take it lightly.

"As you all know by now, and at your direction during our last meeting, I contacted Stan in Mexico on Friday asking for his resignation. He refused. I then informed him of the evidence we have of his extortion attempt and advised him again to resign, suggesting that the consequences would be far less personally damaging than a termination. I invited him to this meeting today, if he wished to defend himself against our claims before a formal vote. He dropped the call, and I haven't heard from him since. Have any of you?"

Heads shook around the table.

"Okay then. We'll discuss nominations to replace Stan as chair of this board after we hold a formal vote to terminate him for cause. As you vote, please remember our agreement to return Stan's original investment plus interest to date as the only expedient means of removing his future voting power. That total will come to two million, one hundred sixty thousand dollars divided equally among the five of us so as not to affect the company's cash reserve. Each of our equity positions will be increased accordingly. But painful as this is right now, I believe it's a small price to pay for our company's ultimate success and a much greater future return for each of us."

Seeing no objections around the table, I continued.

"I therefore move that we—"

The door to the boardroom slammed open. Stan staggered in, clearly inebriated. He smashed a document down on the conference table and then took great pains folding it into something resembling a paper airplane while a visible tremor racked his hands. Seeming to be satisfied with his attempt, he stood back and tossed it into the air. It did a quick loop then crashed nose-down on the floor at the back of the room. Claire rose from her chair, picked it up, and handed it to me. I scanned it quickly, verifying it was a signed resignation letter.

"That what you're looking for?" Stan asked as he steadied himself with one shaking hand on the table. Strands of gray hair that were normally combed across the top of his balding head hung down his forehead. "I was gonna come here and tell you what an honor it's been to serve as your chair. You know, keep channels open, don't burn bridges, shit like that. That was this morning."

Stan pulled a flask from his suit jacket pocket, took a hit, and continued. "But then this afternoon, I thought, wait a minute. I got this company started with my own damn funds, did everything I could to make it a success, and now you have the gall to toss me out on the fucking street."

Two point one six million isn't exactly the street, I thought, but stayed quiet.

"So I'll just say goodbye, assholes, but don't think I'll ever forget this." Stan gave me and the entire board a prolonged middle-finger salute, then staggered out of the room. I declared a break in the meeting and asked Claire to call a car for our ex-chair.

When we reconvened twenty minutes later, we unanimously agreed to accept Stan's resignation and then moved on to the last business of the day: replacing him.

"And now I would like to nominate Dr. Kavi Singh to fill the role of chairman of the board," I said. "Are there any other nominations from the floor?"

The room was silent.

"Having heard no others, I'd like to ask Dr. Singh if he will accept this nomination."

"I will," he said, "with gratitude and humility."

"Excellent. Then I move that we elect Dr. Singh as our new chairman of the board. Is there a second?"

A hand went up.

"We have a second. All in favor?"

The vote was unanimous.

"Congratulations, Kavi. I yield the floor to you."

Twenty-Three

I'm jolted awake in the middle of the night by loud voices coming from the direction of Jimmy's shack. One voice is clearly Jimmy's; the other, unrecognizable. Then silence. I'm tempted to close my eyes, write this off as a dream, and drift back to sleep. But then the second voice continues, yelling this time, threatening. I throw off my rag covers, put on my shoes, and crawl out of the Residence to investigate.

A shadowy figure stands outside Jimmy's hovel, now screaming and slashing at the cardboard structure with what looks like a knife. "Get outta there, you little retard! This place is mine!"

I run toward the chaos, then slow my pace as the man notices me. I worry he's under the influence of something, or psychotic, or both, and I want to defuse the situation, not aggravate it.

"Hey there, my name's Roger. What's yours?"

"None of your fucking business."

"Okay, look, this place belongs to my friend, Jimmy.

Maybe you're confusing it with another lean-to. Maybe at the next overpass north of here?"

The man glares at me, then reaches into Jimmy's shack and yanks him out by an arm. Even in the dim light I can see that Jimmy's eyes are wide with fear as he breaks free. The attacker stumbles back toward Jimmy, knife out. I block his way.

⁓

I wake again, but this time to bright lights and the repetitive beep of something I slowly come to perceive as a heart monitor. I'm lying on my back, and there is pain—sharp, stinging pain—in my right side and arm. An IV line is taped to my left wrist. A doctor appears above me, shines a light in my eyes, and turns to someone else—a nurse, I think.

"Another 2.5 milligrams morphine," he says. "Let's get a chest X-ray and tox screen. He'll also need antibiotics. Must have been an awfully dirty knife."

"Do you know where you are, Roger?" I hear the doctor through a gradually clearing mental haze.

"Hospital? How do you know my name?"

"Right. You're at Harborview Medical Center. Your friend here rode in with you. You're a lucky guy."

I slowly turn my head to see Carlos sitting on my other side.

"Hey, old man," he says. "Close call, but the doc says you're gonna be okay."

"Thank you," I manage to say before drifting away again.

⁓

I'm back and see that Carlos is still here. The doctor and nurse are gone. I'm starting to remember.

"Jimmy? Is he okay?"

"He's fine. Mary and I heard the noise and came running. You were down. Jimmy was standing there, staring. There was a lot of blood, man, but Mary stopped it with her blanket."

"The guy with the knife?" I ask.

"He ran. Prob'ly thought you were a goner and got scared."

"So how did . . . how did you get me here?"

"Flagged down a cop while Mary stayed with you. She saved your life, man."

"No, you both did. I'll never be able to thank you enough."

"Hey, it's what friends do."

Twenty-Four

I'm back at the Residence after a night in the hospital. They tell me the knife missed my right lung by just a few millimeters, but except for a broken rib, it didn't do any other internal damage. I'm a very lucky and grateful guy, but a sore one. The pain is manageable, unless I try to sit up or roll over, and then it strikes in searing flashes. I have fifteen visible stitches in my side—I don't know how many internal ones— and eight in my arm. Harborview wants me back in three weeks for a checkup and to get the sutures out, and in the meantime, my bandages must be changed every other day, with an antibiotic applied. Mary has volunteered to help with all this, and I appreciate it but hate being a patient.

Maslow is outside making gull noises, but I have nothing to give him this morning. In fact, I realize, I'll have nothing to give anyone for a while. I've become one of those people I used to despise for leaning on others and getting healthcare at the expense of "hardworking taxpayers."

The hospital's unopened prescription bottle of OxyContin

sits alone on a rock in a back corner of the Residence and wants to hold a conversation with me. "Just a quick word," it says.

"Right, a quick word. Uh-huh."

"You're bored, you're hurting, and you can barely move. I can help with all that. That's what I'm here for. It's my raison d'être."

"So you're saying I should affirm your purpose, make you feel better about yourself?"

"Something like that, but I'm not being selfish. I'm here to help."

"No, Oxy, you're a trap."

"Okay, sure, maybe for some folks. But not you. You're strong. You're a CEO!"

"*Was* a CEO."

"Splitting hairs, Roger, splitting hairs. You are who you are."

"Thanks, I guess."

"You bet. See, I'm helping already."

"Still, Oxy, I'm going to throw you away today. Can't have you around here. No offense."

"There's that strength I'm talking about! But that would be a huge waste. I can be helpful in other ways, you know."

"What the hell are you talking about now?"

"Monetize me."

"What?"

"Sure! You could use fifty bucks, right? Maybe more. I'm clearly genuine stuff."

"How many pills are you?"

"Wait, hold on, let me count them out into this plastic bag . . . Wow, twenty. More than I thought. They must have doubled me up by mistake."

"Hmm, some of the folks on their way to Goldman Sachs,

or Amazon, or anywhere else downtown would probably fork over a hundred bucks for you. Pocket change for them."

"Now you're talking, Roger."

"I don't know. Do I really want to be responsible for somebody else getting hooked?"

"Whoa, now. It's not your responsibility to take care of them. And besides, nobody's getting hooked. You know exactly what high-stress careers are like. Those folks just need something to take the edge off now and then."

"Maybe, yeah."

"It's just business, Roger. Nothing personal."

Our conversation is interrupted by the sound of footsteps outside the Residence. They approach, then stop. No one speaks. I quickly tuck the bag of Oxy into my pack, toss the prescription bottle back in the corner, and crawl toward my entrance, trying to avoid aggravating my wounds or tearing out a stitch. I peer through a small hole in the cardboard. It's Jimmy, standing there staring at my home, holding a steaming paper cup in both hands. I push out the flap and attempt a smile. Jimmy takes a step back.

"Jimmy, hi. What you got there?"

"It's for you. Tea. Mary made it and told me to bring it over."

"Well, that was nice of her, and you. Want to come in for a minute? There's just room enough."

"Jay-Jay says no."

"Okay, no problem." I reach out, wincing at the pain, and take the cup. "Thanks."

Jimmy nods and turns to leave. He walks a few steps away, then stops and looks back over a shoulder. "Thanks for making that man go away. I'm sorry you got hurt."

"Hey, it's what friends do."

Twenty-Five

The next few days are a blur. I rest most of the time, read a little, eat a little, get up to use my freeway pillar now and then. Today, Mary is here to change my dressings.

"Looking better there, Roger," she says while placing new bandages on my side and arm.

"Thanks. Feeling better too. I'm even thinking about making the trek down to SoDo for a pizza pickup today. And maybe a shower at the shelter."

Mary looks at me sideways with squinty eyes.

"I'll be fine," I say.

More squinty eyes.

"I'll just take it slow and enjoy the good weather."

"How 'bout I come with?" she asks.

"I can manage," I say, looking away.

"Come on, don't be such a stubborn old shithead," Mary says. "I was gonna head on down that way for a shower today, anyway. Might as well go together, right?"

"Hmm, guess that makes sense. Just give me a few minutes

to get my stuff together and I'll meet you at your tent."

Mary and I walk together through the park on our way downtown, me with my pack, my old jacket, cowboy hat and tattered jeans, Mary with a canvas shopping bag sporting the green Starbucks logo, her new jacket, a black T-shirt, and jeans.

We stop to fill up our water bottles at the park and I allow myself a glance at the empty bench that was Tex's home not long ago. Mary follows my eyes with hers.

"I guess you miss him."

I nod and tip my hat to the bench as we walk on through the park.

Mary continues. "Sad that he's gone, but at least he's free of all this." She waves a hand around as she does a slow pirouette.

"Hmm, but what good's freedom if you're too dead to enjoy it?" I say.

"Yeah, I guess."

"They say 'rest in peace,' but what does that actually mean? You can't experience that peace. You can't experience *anything*. But okay, maybe that's the ultimate peace."

"Guess you don't believe in an afterlife," Mary says.

"Who knows? But no, I don't. Would you really want one?"

"Depends on what it is. If it's more of the same, then no."

"Okay, but to play devil's advocate, or maybe God's advocate, this one isn't over yet. At least, not for us." I look back over my shoulder toward the bench. "There's still time to make it worth another go-round if you think there might be another shot, or even if you just want this life to mean something on its own. I'm just saying we don't know what 'more of the same' is yet."

"I'll be right back," Mary says as she ignores me and takes

a detour toward the park restroom. "Don't die while I'm gone. That would totally piss me off."

I smile, sit down under a tree and wait, grateful for the rest. My wounds are reminding me of their presence this morning.

When Mary returns, she offers me a hand to get up. "I'm hungry from too much philosophizing," she says. "Let's go find something to eat."

"So, Mary," I say as we head toward the breakfast place down on Pike, "here's an easy question for you. It's crazy after all this time, but I still don't know your last name. Care to tell me?"

"Parker."

"Well, Mary Parker, it's good to meet you." I offer a hand to shake, and she takes it. "Anything else you can tell me?"

"Like what?"

"Like how you ended up here, for starters."

"It's boring. You wouldn't want to hear about it."

"I doubt if it's boring, and how can you know what I would or wouldn't want to hear, anyway? Kind of presumptive, I'd say."

"Now you *are* starting to piss me off," Mary says with a crooked smile.

"Good!"

"Okay, but only if you promise to tell me more about the stupid-ass decisions that got you here. Deal?"

"Soon, I promise."

We arrive at the restaurant at about ten, and it occurs to me that, between the two of us, Mary and I probably have more than enough cash to actually buy breakfast. Inside. Like regular people. I mention this and she agrees.

We're seated at a table near the window looking out onto a busy and sunny Seattle street. People are everywhere, milling around, looking in shop windows and generally taking advantage of the treasured phenomenon we Northwesterners call a "sunbreak."

Our waiter approaches the table, and I'm surprised to see that it's Ernie, the busboy who's helped me at the dumpster before.

"Ernie! Hey, looks like you've been promoted. Congratulations."

"Uh, thanks. Roger, right?"

"Yep, it's me. And this is my friend, Mary."

"Good to meet you," Ernie says. "You know, though, I can't serve you free food here in the dining room, but if you meet me out back in about fifteen minutes, I'm sure I can come up with something."

"Won't be necessary, Ernie, at least not today. We're paying customers. Is your boss around? Kenny? I'd like him to see this."

"He got fired."

"Ah, so there *is* fairness somewhere in the far reaches of the universe!"

Ernie smiles, pours coffee, and takes our orders. Mary is smiling too, and I can tell she's enjoying the whole experience.

"So, Mary Parker, you mentioned some time at UW before. What happened there?"

Mary's smile fades. "Do we really need to talk about that right now?"

"No, of course not. It's your call."

Mary sips at her coffee, blows steam off the top, and stares out the window. "Look at all those people out there, living their perfect lives."

"Yeah, but we both know everyone's got a story. And most of those stories aren't perfect little fairy tales, even if they look that way through a window at a distance. We hide shit, right? I know I do."

Mary nods and takes another sip. "Yeah, but why? Why do we do that?"

"You tell me. You're the psychologist."

"Ha! Never made it that far. And besides, what I meant was why do *we* do that—people on the street, like us? We've got fuck-all to lose, right? We're about as far down the basement as you can get. So what's the point in hiding our shit?"

"I guess we still have some old ideas of who we are, or were. Maybe we're protecting those, hoping to go back somehow."

"Maybe, but those old ideas—they're stale. You can't go back."

"What do you mean?" I ask.

"Everything's changed. Life goes on without us. You can't just go back and pick up where you left off. I think that's why I don't like talking about it."

Our omelets arrive and we dig in. I'd almost forgotten how fresh hot food tastes, and the experience is overwhelming. Food has only been fuel for a while now, but this is pure pleasure. It silences me.

"But I guess we can go somewhere else," I hear from beyond my culinary haze.

"Beg your pardon?"

"I guess if we can't exactly go back to our old lives, that doesn't mean we're totally screwed, right?"

"Right, and—"

Mary holds up a hand to stop me. "Okay, okay. It was the end of my sophomore year," she says, staring into her coffee cup for a moment before looking up and resuming. "And I was doing okay—actually killing it in the lower-division psych courses. I loved that stuff. But if you want to get a psych degree, you have to take some math too. Just basic calculus, then probability and statistics. I sucked at that. I mean, really sucked. Mostly, I just hated that shit and didn't study, but looking back, I think it was also because I'd always been told girls just aren't good at it, so why should I even try? I guess I just traded math study time for party time. I thought I could kind of slide by, but then I flunked Stats 101."

"Damn, I think I get where you're—"

Mary cuts me off with another raised hand, closed eyes, and a frown. "Let me finish. This is hard enough as it is."

"Of course. I'm sorry."

"So that F grade was kind of a double whammy because I had to deal with both the shame of it and the dread of having to take the damn class again with no idea how I'd pass it. And on top of that, my older brother I've told you about, Tim? He was paying for my tuition, so there was that pressure too. But you know what really got to me?"

"What?"

"It finally dawned on me that the other girls in the same class were doing just fine. So I had to ditch the excuse that my gender had anything to do with my failure. It was just me."

"But you're not alone. Lots of us went through stuff like—" Another raised hand.

"There's more. The summer was starting at the end of that semester, and I wasn't sure I wanted to come back in the fall, but my adviser called me in and told me about a tutoring program I could get into for free. The idea was to spend part of the summer getting smart on stats so I could pass the course in the fall. I didn't have any better ideas, so I went for it.

"My tutor turned out to be a grad student named Tanner, a good-looking blond-haired guy about six feet tall, athletic,

158

and of course, good at math. Weirdly, I was never actually attracted to Tanner—never understood exactly why until later—but I found I could learn stuff from him, and that gave me a new confidence. But he also introduced me to speed— said it would help me stay up to study longer. It worked, and I thought, well, more is better, so I started to spend the little cash I got from working in the cafeteria on amphetamines. Then, late in the summer, Tanner and I started doing cocaine whenever I would pass one of his quizzes—a kind of reward, you know. I thought he was my friend. Then one night he bought us some meth. I'm not sure he even used any, but he made sure I did. He raped me that night."

"Oh God, I'm so sorry, Mary."

"Thanks, yeah. I was so stupid. Never saw it coming. I didn't report it, I guess because I felt it was somehow my fault, and I didn't want to go through the humiliation of an exam, the legal shit, all the rest of it. I just wanted to hide out, so that's pretty much what I did. I never went back to school, leaving Tim with the bills."

"So where'd you go?"

"At first I bummed my way into staying in the dorm with some friends who stuck around for the summer semester, but that didn't last long. They tried to be nice about it for a while, but they eventually kicked me out because I was bringing heavy stuff into the room and staying high all the time. After that, my memory is mostly hazy. I tried other friends around town, then ended up roaming the streets, begging for food and money, spending almost everything I got on whatever cheap drugs I could find, staying as high as possible, hiding out from everyone, including myself. Tim tracked me down and got me into rehab. Paid for everything. But I left before I was done. That was probably the last straw for his wife. The money dried up."

"Then back to the street?"

"Yeah, and the only reason I'm alive is Carlos. He found me passed out down at Pier 52 one night, about a year and a half ago, and dragged my ass back to the overpass. He even set me up with that old army tent and blanket. The next morning, he came around and gave me the harshest damn lecture I've ever had. He must have yelled at me for a good twenty minutes before I dissolved into tears, and I hardly ever cry. I guess that and the partial rehab shocked me onto a new path. Still, the next couple of weeks were pure hell coming off the drugs, while Carlos kept me in something between captivity and care. It turned out he had had a friend who overdosed, and I think he kind of projected all that onto me. So, bottom line? I'm still fucked up, just not on drugs."

"Thank you," is all I can say.

"What the hell for?"

"For trusting me with your story. I feel honored."

"I call bullshit on that last part," Mary says with a scrunched-up smile.

"Okay, call it as you see it, but it's true. Look, let's get out of here. There're a couple of people I'd like you to meet."

Twenty-Six

After showers at the shelter, we arrive at Home Team Pizza around one in the afternoon. The place now has the look of a real sports bar—two giant ultra-hi-res screens, new tables and booths, large Seahawks and Mariners photos on one wall, an actual bar, and happy-looking customers. Bart spots me.

"Hey, Roger! Haven't seen you in a while. How've you been?"

"Not too bad, all considered," I say, preferring to sidestep any discussion of my absence and the stabbing. "Bart, I want you to meet my friend Mary. Mary, this is Bart, owner of this fine establishment."

Mary smiles and shakes Bart's outstretched hand. "The pizza's been great. Thanks."

"Well, your friend here earned it. I don't know if he's told you, but I probably wouldn't be in business today if he hadn't walked through that door a while back."

"Come on, Bart," I say. "Giving a little advice is one thing; acting on it is something else entirely. You've done a great job with this place."

We chat for a few more minutes before Bart loads us up with pies and salads—a little extra this time. Mary and I divide the food between her bag and my pack, and we're on our way again.

"What was that about Bart not being in business if you hadn't come along?" Mary asks as we walk.

"Oh, nothing really. He's just being kind. Next stop, Rain City Books."

"Where you got my paperbacks?" Mary asks.

"That's the one."

Thirty minutes later, we walk into the little bookshop in Pioneer Square, and I introduce Mary to Denise.

"So you're the Steinbeck lover!" she says. "I hear you're reading his books to other folks as a part of Roger's new Stairway organization. What a wonderful thing to do!"

Mary shoots me a confused look but recovers quickly. "Thanks, yeah. It's been good. Hey, I love your shop. It feels like old Seattle. You mind if I browse around a little?"

"Oh, gosh, of course not. Make yourself at home." Mary heads toward the back of the long, narrow space and I can see her scanning the shelves as she goes.

I turn back to Denise. "So how're things with the shop?"

"Fine. Well, no. To be honest, not so great. Barnes and Noble has been eating our lunch, and now it looks like Amazon is well on the way to eating theirs. We're at the bottom of the food chain, Roger."

"The bottom, yeah, I get it."

"Yes, of course you do, working with the homeless and all."

"Right. Wish there was some way I could help. You've got something very special here."

"Actually, I've been thinking a lot about that—"

"I bet you have."

"—and you know how little fish survive by banding together in schools, confusing the big predators?"

"Sure."

"Well, some get eaten, I know, but I still like the metaphor. The school survives, even thrives. Maybe some of us at the bottom of the food chain need to school together."

"So what did you have in mind?"

"I was thinking about your nonprofit."

Oh shit. I should've known that would come back around to bite me sooner or later.

"And I was wondering, do you have any office space yet?"

"Uh, no, not yet. Why?"

"Well, behind that door in the back, I've got another five hundred square feet that I'd love to rent to you. There's a separate entrance from the alley, too, and a small restroom you could share with the shop. It wouldn't cost you much and would help me stay afloat while I figure out my next moves. There's even a computer with a good internet connection, a desk, and a couple of extra chairs back there."

"Well, uh, that sounds amazing, but I haven't even gotten our funding sorted out yet. I couldn't imagine doing anything for, I don't know, maybe another three or four months."

"Oh." Denise's eyes fall. "I could probably hold out for two months, but the way things are going, I think three or four might be stretching it."

"How much do you need for the space, per month?" I ask, knowing I'm digging myself a deeper hole by the second. I've handled multimillion-dollar budgets with less stress.

"I'm almost certain I can get over a thousand," Denise says. "But I'd love to see your good work go forward, so I could probably do with eight hundred, and that would include electricity and internet."

"That's very generous but I still don't think—"

"What if I let you use the space now but don't start your rent for another two months? You could use the place to pursue your funding. Do you think you could make that work?"

What am I doing? "Denise, are you sure you'd be okay with that? I mean, you barely know me."

"Honestly? If renting the space was your idea—something you proposed to me—then I'd probably be a little wary. But it wasn't your idea. It was mine. And I think what you're trying to do with your nonprofit is outstanding. Those first couple of months would be like my little investment in Stairway. So think about it, will you? This could help both of us."

Maybe there's something to this. It would give me a mailing address. I could get a new email address, too, and then a checking account. And after that, who knows? Maybe I could actually land some funding and do something with this crazy fiction I've created.

"Okay, yes, I will. Can I get back to you in a few days?"

"That would be great, Roger. How about we meet here on Thursday to discuss it?"

"Deal."

Mary walks up with a thin paperback and places it on the counter in front of Denise.

"Ah," says Denise. "Viktor Frankl's *Man's Search for Meaning*. Excellent choice."

~

"What the hell was *that*?" Mary says as we begin our walk home. "You're full of surprises today."

"Oh, you mean the Stairway thing?"

Mary rolls her eyes. "What else would I mean? Yes, the Stairway thing. What the hell are you up to?"

"Oh, it's just an idea I came up with, kind of on the spot the other day."

"On the spot. So in other words, just something you made up to cover your ass."

"Maybe. At the time. But the more I think about it, the more I like it."

"But what the hell *is* it? You kind of blindsided me back there."

"Actually, it's all about something you said a while ago—that we're stuck down here in Maslow's basement, just surviving, not really living. So what if we could build a kind of stairway for folks up to the first floor, maybe even higher?"

"We?"

"Sure. You, me, Carlos. Maybe even Jimmy, somehow. There's more of us out there all the time. Have you seen those rows of dirty tents popping up all over the streets downtown? It's getting worse by the day."

"We can't save the world, Roger, not even just Seattle, maybe not even ourselves. And why would we even want to try?"

"Why did you buy that Viktor Frankl book?"

"Huh?"

"*Man's Search for Meaning.* Why did you buy it?"

"Just a whim. I was supposed to read it in college but never did. I just saw it on the shelf and picked it up. No big deal."

"Well, I think it *is* a big deal. I read it years ago, and I still remember the basic point, not that I ever took it to heart. He argues that happiness isn't something we can go after directly.

He says it's a natural side effect of having a purpose in life. Purpose brings meaning, and meaning brings happiness. Something like that."

"Sounds like happy horseshit."

"So why did you buy the book?"

"Okay, okay, I admit it. I read the back cover. That guy had it a hell of a lot worse than we do. You know the old saying about finding a pony hidden under all the horseshit? Well, I figured if a holocaust survivor thinks there's a pony down there, I owe it to him and myself to spend a little time digging for it."

"There you go. When you plopped that book down on the counter back at the shop, I thought, yeah, that's perfect. Stairway could be my purpose. It could be *our* purpose, if you want to be part of it."

As we continue along First Avenue on our way home, Mary is quiet, and I decide to let the whole Stairway thing just hang in the air for now. I mean, I don't even know what it really is, or could be. I know we're not qualified to provide the kinds of services that doctors, psychologists, or certified social workers do. But I understand at least two things: how business works, and what it's like to live on the street. I understand why people get hired and why they don't. I know how to sell a venture that's not much more than a PowerPoint. And now I understand—in my gut—how to relate to people who could become our clientele. I understand how bad decisions or bad luck can do more than just bring us down a notch or two. They can send us all the way to the basement.

I'll probably never be able to climb all the way back to the kind of life I had before—my past choices almost certainly preclude that. But that doesn't mean I can't climb back up Maslow's famous pyramid, and find some meaning along the way, by building a stairway for others. We wouldn't even pretend to try assisting people with serious addictions or debilitating mental illnesses—somewhere around 40 percent of us, from what I've read. We don't have the skills or qualifications. No, we'd focus on those we could actually help: people who've been through perfect storms of bad luck, lousy decisions, or both—those who just need help getting their confidence back, writing résumés, prepping for job interviews, getting rides to interviews, dealing with local agencies to find temporary housing or to sort out legal messes. We'd be one tiny piece of a solution to a gigantic systemic problem, but a piece nonetheless.

Lost in these thoughts, I step off a curb and hear Mary yell, "Look out!" I feel her grab my pack and yank me back to safety just as a car screeches to a halt, coming within inches of hitting me. The pack falls to the ground, spilling its contents onto the sidewalk.

I look up, dazed, feeling pain from the stab wound in my side, and see that the stopped car now has a flashing blue light. A cop steps out of the car and walks toward me. Another one comes from the other side of the car and moves toward Mary and the spilled pack.

"Step over here please, sir," I hear the first officer say. "Did you not notice the red light?"

"I'm sorry, officer. No, I wasn't paying attention. It was a mistake."

"Well, you need to be a lot more careful. You're lucky it was me driving and not someone as distracted as you were just now. I'm going to issue you a warning this time, but if—"

"Sergeant, there's something here you need to see," interrupts the second officer, pointing toward the sidewalk near my pack. "Looks like a baggie full of Oxy."

Twenty-Seven

"What the hell were you thinking?"

I look up to see a familiar face through the bars of my cell at the King County jail. The scar extending from the left eye and the disheveled clothes give the man away immediately.

"Charlie? Charlie Duncan? Man, it's good to see you!"

"You're a lucky bastard, Roger. When I saw your name on the roster, it rang a bell, and I took your case. You look like shit. How're you holding up?"

"Could be worse. There's food here, and it's warm."

"So when we met at Starbucks, before I got my law license back, I had the impression you were a lot smarter than this. What the fuck, man? Schedule 2 drug possession? They're even trying to prove you had intent to sell. Is that true? You've got to be straight with me if I'm going to be your public defender."

"No, I wasn't planning to sell it."

"Then what the hell were you doing with it?"

"I got stabbed and ended up at Harborview. They sent me home with OxyContin for the pain."

"I've seen the evidence. No prescription bottle, and looks like a lot more pills than they'd normally give you on discharge. Not a good thing for our case."

"I know."

"You didn't use any?"

"No."

"Also not good. Gives the prosecution more reason to believe you intended to sell."

"Shit. So what do we do from here?"

"I'll head over to Harborview this afternoon and dig into this a little. Again, you're a lucky bastard. No other public defender would take the time. You'd basically be screwed. Do you remember the name of the doctor who treated you?"

"Sorry, no. I was kind of out of it with all the morphine they gave me. I don't remember much of anything about that day. Oh, but the prescription bottle is still in my shelter. That should have the name on it."

"Okay, good. Tell me where your shelter is and let me see what I can do. I'll be back tonight. In the meantime, unless you can somehow come up with fifty grand for bail, settle in. Enjoy the ambiance. Take a nap."

~

It isn't easy to sleep in a county jail, even without a cellmate. There's always something going on: new inmates arriving, others leaving to face whatever awaits on the outside, clanging doors, crazies shouting unintelligible shit. But I must have managed somehow, because I wake up to the sound of a guard unlocking my door. Charlie walks in.

169

I sit up on the bunk and rub my eyes. Charlie is smiling, the lines in his face hiding most of his scar.

"You look like you've got news," I say. "I hope it's good."

"Yeah, it is. Mostly. I managed to find both the doc and the nurse who saw you that day and put the fear of God into them about supplying you with all that OxyContin. I kind of promised them and the hospital immunity from legal action if they wrote a formal statement acknowledging that they mistakenly gave you twenty pills and apologizing for their error."

"You *kind of* promised them? Do you have the authority to do that on your own?"

"Let's just say I was very convincing."

"You actually got the statement?"

"Yeah, right here." Charlie smiles and pats his jacket pocket. "I know, I'm amazing. But full disclosure: it didn't hurt that they had a friggin' legal neanderthal dealing with me. Their real lawyers must have been tied up with something much bigger."

"Thanks, Charlie. You *are* amazing. So what now?"

"I've already spoken with the prosecutor, and I've got an appointment with her in the morning to formally get the drug charges dropped. You'll be out of here by noon at the latest."

"Outstanding. But you said the news was 'mostly' good. What's the bad news?"

Charlie throws his head back and laughs. "I couldn't believe it, but those assholes are still gonna charge you with 'crossing against a light,' a minor misdemeanor. We'll just plead guilty and pay the fine. It won't amount to much, but if you don't have the cash, I'll front you. You can buy me coffee a few times at Starbucks. I'm usually there on Wednesday mornings around nine. Just sayin'."

Twenty-Eight

Sleep is elusive, at best. Cell doors clang and guards joke loudly throughout the night, as if the rest of us were just caged animals or not here at all. A few inmates—who would be under psychiatric care in any effective and well-funded social system—rant sporadically. My brain automatically tries to make sense of their words each time I'm jolted back to consciousness by their fearful or angry outbursts. Memories of federal prison come flooding back.

As always, the past is my refuge, and I go there as quickly and deeply as I can while covering my ears with the edges of a flat, yellowing pillow.

It was nine months post-Stan at DLS, and things were going well. Better than well. I had landed a second round of venture capital, the product was performing even better than expected, and several customers were reporting much earlier progress with their patients than normally expected. Our product was literally improving lives, and this was driving some very positive media attention from the *Wall Street*

Journal, Forbes, Psychology Today, and the *Denver Post.* And most important for my exit strategy, we were only two or three quarters away from profitability.

I was just finishing a round of yearly performance reviews and felt that everyone who mattered was happy and sufficiently motivated to take us to the next major milestone, an initial public offering. Three people who didn't matter had been fired—two in Engineering and one in Sales—but that was a very small percentage of our current two hundred fifty headcount, and a necessary part of maintaining excellence.

Claire's was the last review on my list, and I was looking forward to it with both pleasure and dread. I had gotten approval for a new comp package after discussing her key contributions with the board, minus some details of her sleuthing at CU.

After reviewing her excellent progress against the past year's written objectives, I came to the compensation part. It was difficult to maintain a formal manner with Claire during the discussion, but I felt it was important, given the significance of her achievements.

"Claire, the board and I want to show our appreciation in a very tangible way. You've been working under the title of 'Administrative Assistant,' but you've consistently operated at a much higher level, so I'm pleased to move you up several steps to 'Senior Executive Assistant.' And with that promotion, you'll be getting a completely new compensation package. You'll be receiving a twenty percent raise plus a yearly performance-based bonus, the first of which you'll see in your check today. But probably the most important part, longer-term, is the equity component. You've been granted two thousand shares of common stock in the company as well as five thousand more in options vesting over three years.

Depending upon how well we do after our IPO, this could make a big financial difference for you. So congratulations, Claire. You're now a part owner of DLS!"

"I'm stunned. Thank you so much! I don't know what to say. I'll do my very best to help us move forward."

"I know you will. It's just who you are."

Claire smiled at me, her pretty eyes sparkling with what I took to be tears of joy. I loved seeing this, but it also made my next move that much harder.

"There's something else, Claire, but it's not anything to do with your job performance."

"I think I know what it is, and it makes me sad."

"Makes me sad too. It's been wonderful, Claire, our times together, our play, if you can call it that. It was much more than that, at least for me. I love how we've been with each other, right up to the edge. But we can't continue. It isn't right for you, for me, or for the company. We need to get on with our personal and business lives, and I think that aspect of our relationship might stand in the way of both."

"I understand, and even agree, as much as I hate to," Claire said, her eyes still wet but probably now for a different reason. "I saw this coming a while back, because, at least for me, it's getting nearly impossible to stay on this side of the edge."

"Yes, damn near impossible."

We sat together, silent, in a strange new place, until Claire finally looked up with sad, soft eyes, reflecting my own feelings, and spoke again.

"Could I ask one question?"

"Of course, Claire, always. I want us to be as open with each other as we've always been. Just without the . . ."

"Are you seeing someone?"

"No, absolutely not. I'd be afraid of *any* relationship getting in the way of business right now, of taking the company public. That's going to take more focus than I've ever had to muster. Are you?"

"Am I what?"

"Seeing anyone."

"No, not right now. But I guess I wouldn't rule it out down the line somewhere."

"Of course not."

Twenty-Nine

Living on the street definitely has some redeeming qualities compared to life behind bars. Don't get me wrong, though. Both are miserable, and I wouldn't wish either on my worst enemy, except maybe if he happened to be named Stan. They're just miserable in different ways. It's a relative thing. Freedom is the obvious difference, I suppose, and it's top-of-mind as I make my way down toward the Pike Place Market on this drizzly, cool Wednesday morning. At first glance, street life offers a very high degree of that valued commodity. We aren't caged, and we can roam almost anywhere we wish, at any time. And money is no object, literally. But without basic resources and little hope of obtaining any, it's like Janis Joplin sang in 1970: "Freedom's just another word for nothing left to lose."

I walk past several of my tented brethren along the trash-strewn street decorated with discarded needles and wonder how many of these folks are about to follow Joplin down the deadly path she took only months after recording that

Kris Kristofferson song. I can tell that some are nearly there, and there's little hope for them now, but I wonder if there might have been hope when they first arrived here, before they ended up flat on the basement floor. Are their addictions a cause or an effect? I think it's probably a mix. I guess I really am a lucky bastard. At least I'm standing on the floor, not lying on it.

My Starbucks card, still holding some decent value, is a reminder of that as I walk through the door of the iconic coffeehouse by the market. That thin little card is one of the few things that separate me from the floor, but it's far from sustainable. Especially now that Charlie will be helping me deplete it faster. I scan the room and find him at a small table in the back, looking intently at something on his phone, no coffee yet in front of him.

"Mr. Duncan," I say as I approach the table. "I'm Roger, and I'll be your barista today. What can I get started for you?"

"Ah! You showed up. I was getting thirsty for a Grande Americano."

When I return to the table with our drinks, Charlie is smiling.

"Hey, you don't stink this morning. Nice."

"Yeah, they let me take a shower at the jail before they realized I'd be leaving that same day. Waste of taxpayer money, right? I'm not complaining, though, and seriously, I'm more than grateful to you for getting me out of there. Thank you again."

"I'm glad it all worked out. Kind of gave me a boost too, you know. Made me think I can really do this lawyer thing out here in Seattle."

"Of course you can. You proved it."

Charlie waves off my compliment. "That brings me

back to a question you never answered when we first met," he says. "What's next for you? A guy like you—there's gotta be something."

"There might be, actually. I've got this wild-ass idea about homeless folks helping each other get off the street. We don't have much of a chance with the serious drug addicts or the mentally ill, but there're a bunch of us who are reasonably healthy—just shot ourselves in the feet with bad decisions and fell so far down the food chain that we can't get back, or at least *think* we can't. Folks like that might respond better to me and my little group than to the city or state, even if there was enough funding there to make a difference. But only if we can show them we're on our way up and out too."

"Sounds like a fucking pipe dream."

"Thanks for the encouragement."

Charlie grins and takes a long draw on his Americano. "Pipe dreams aren't all dead ends, Roger, just most of them. What do you call yours? Got a name for it?"

"Stairway. It's meant to describe a path up and out of the basement of homelessness."

"Hmm. Doesn't actually suck too badly."

"A New Jersey compliment if I've ever heard one."

"So how can I help?"

"Seriously?"

"I wouldn't ask if I thought you were totally full of shit. Half full—I can handle that."

"Well, there is one thing."

I seem to have Charlie's attention, so I describe my dilemma about setting up a nonprofit organization: no address, no phone, no credibility, no expertise about the process.

Charlie nods his head, takes another long sip of coffee, and renders his opinion. "Sounds like you're screwed."

"Yeah, well, I *do* have some hope of getting an address."

"Oh?"

I describe the opportunity at Rain City Books—the two months of free rent, the free internet access, the supportive bookshop owner and potential landlord.

"Hmm, not a terrible start," Charlie says. "I know that place. Been in there once."

"But I have no idea how to deal with the legal and bureaucratic process of setting up a nonprofit," I say.

"I've got a guy," says Charlie with gangster eyes.

"Really?"

"No, dipshit, I'm just fuckin' with you. You think everyone from Jersey's got a guy?"

"No, I just—"

"And besides, you don't need a guy for this. I've made a few contacts around town, and I know some people who do that kind of boring shit for a living. And they're in a big firm that might have some budget for pro bono work."

"Do you think you could . . . ?"

"No problem. I'll try to set up a meeting. In the meantime, take that deal at the bookshop. Worst case, you'll just have to back out after a month or so. Oh, and get yourself a decent shirt, okay?"

Thirty

The next morning, I head for Rain City Books after picking up food a day late at Home Team Pizza and getting assorted pastries from Susie at the donut shop. It's a rainy Thursday in Seattle, but I'm hoping it'll also be a sweet one in the Steinbeck sense.

"Morning, Denise!" I say with a broad smile as I walk through the bookshop door and remove my hat. "What's all the noise back there?"

"Good morning, Roger. Oh, just a little fix-up for the new renter."

My heart drops. "Oh."

"Why the long face?" Denise asks.

"I, uh . . . I was kind of hoping that could be me."

"Who said it isn't?"

I'm confused, and silent.

"Well?" Denise asks. "What do you say? Are you in?"

"Definitely, yes. Thank you so much!"

We shake hands on the deal before I've even seen the space,

something I would never have done in my past life. But any space is infinitely better than none right now, especially as it's rent-free for a while. I want to hug Denise with gratitude, but refrain.

"How about some coffee, and then I'll give you a little tour," she says. "*Little* being the operative word here. There's not a lot to see, but I think you'll be happy with it."

We walk to the back of the shop and open the door to my new office. I'm expecting something with a dusty plywood floor, cracked plaster walls, no windows, maybe a couple of folding chairs, and a single bare lightbulb hanging from the ceiling over a dented, gray, WWII-vintage metal desk with a jammed file drawer—all reminiscent of a B-grade 1950s detective movie. And I'd be completely happy with that.

Instead, the only thing I'm right about is the lack of windows. Everything else is a complete surprise: a short hallway with a small storeroom and bathroom; a restored dark cherry hardwood floor in the main room beyond; a line of matching built-in bookcases along one wall; a perfectly functional, if old, wooden desk facing out from the opposing wall, with a side extension and a computer; freshly painted taupe walls; and four chairs around a small, circular wooden table. Two workers are installing new baseboard trim and overhead lighting. I'm speechless.

"Well, what do you think? Is it workable for you?"

"Workable? Are you kidding? It's perfect, Denise. Just perfect." Then I notice one more thing. There's a phone on the desk next to the computer.

"There's a phone?" I ask, staring right at it.

"Oh, yes, I forgot to mention that. It's a holdover from the old dial-up internet days. When we switched to broadband years ago, I just never canceled that old voice line. I'm not the world's best businessperson, as I'm sure you can tell by now. So what the heck, it's yours if you want it. The computer's on the new broadband connection via Wi-Fi from the bookstore, so don't worry about that."

"Worry? I'm anything but worried, Denise." I pick up the phone and the ancient dial tone sounds like the future. "This is all just incredible. Thank you."

"It's my pleasure, Roger. I can't wait to see what you do with Stairway."

I nod and wonder if Denise detects my doubts, but her smile tells me otherwise. I want to tap into her optimism, and this office is making that much easier.

Denise places a simple two-page rental agreement on my new desk, along with a key for the back door. She tears off a page from a small notepad in my top drawer and jots down my new phone number. "Take your time, read through the agreement, and if everything's okay, I'll make a copy of it after you sign. I'll be in the shop."

It takes only a minute to study the simple document, and everything matches our discussion from earlier in the week: two free months, then month-to-month at eight hundred, electricity and internet included. The phone isn't mentioned, and I'm tempted to ask Denise to write it in, but then think better of it.

I return the signed agreement to Denise; she makes a copy and hands it to me with a warm smile. "Congratulations," she says. "The first document for your file drawer."

I'd almost forgotten about physical file folders, having dealt almost exclusively with digital files for several years. My assistants handled any paper documents. And scheduling. And travel. And event planning. And interdepartmental coordination. And virtually all other aspects of office life. But of all the assistants I worked with in my career, only Claire helped me think. I miss her now more than ever.

I thank Denise again and return to my new office.

"I'll be out of your way in a few minutes," I say to the workers. "Just have a couple of quick things to get done today." They ignore me and keep working.

I label a file folder "Legal," drop my new rental agreement into it, then turn on the computer. It's still running Windows 7 with no password, so I add one and decide to ignore the way-out-of-date operating system for now. I'd love to get a real domain name and a website for Stairway, but there's less than fifty dollars in cash left in my pack and no way to pay for anything online anyway. Not wanting to associate Stairway with anything from my past, I decide not to use my old Hotmail account and turn to Microsoft for a new email address. After a few tries, I hit upon an available name and claim it: Roger.Stairway@outlook.com. *Odd*, I think, *how that little piece of the virtual world makes the rest suddenly feel real.*

~

Food in pack, hat on head, new key in pocket, I say goodbye to Denise for the day and exit via the back door into the alley. I've got two more stops today: the Umpqua Bank branch on 22nd Avenue and the Goodwill store down on 6th.

I decide to deal with the bank first, not knowing how long it might take and how much bureaucratic hassle I might need to deal with. As it turns out, the process is much easier than expected, and my anxiety level drops with each new question. Name? Address? Phone number? Email address? Minimum deposit, twenty-five dollars (I deposit thirty-five). No monthly fees. A debit card included. I answer all questions, feeling oddly proud that I actually can. Twenty minutes and I'm out the door as a new account holder.

My next stop is Goodwill. Chatter on the street says this particular store is one of the best, but never having been inside one before, I don't know how to compare it. Still, I'm immediately impressed. There's an amazing variety of merchandise, from electronics to clothing and everything in between, and it all seems clean and well organized. I head for the electronics section and find an old telephone answering machine for three dollars. At least it's digital, no tape to deal with. I pick it up and move to the men's clothing section, where I find a blue oxford button-down shirt, a pair of khakis, a brown belt, and a pair of socks. Shoes would exceed the budget, so I forgo them for now.

My total comes to less than twenty dollars, and I hand over my new debit card, trying to suppress an overly large smile at something that would be routine for most people but is an enormous source of pride for me right now.

The woman at the register takes a quick look at my card and then scans it. I enter my new PIN.

"Thank you, Mr. Carrington, and have a nice day."

"You too." I tip my hat to her, walk out the door, and start back to the overpass. It's been a good day. A Sweet Thursday.

Thirty-One

Back at the overpass, Carlos is busy making money for us at his intersection and I certainly don't want to interrupt that, so I offload pizza, a salad, and a couple of donuts at his place. Then I notice Mary over at Jimmy's and wonder what's going on; he's usually such a loner. As I approach, it's obvious that Jimmy is agitated, and Mary seems to be trying to calm him down, in her own way.

"It's okay, Jimmy. A little frickin' nuts maybe, but what the hell. We'll figure out another way to get you fed," I hear her say as I walk up.

"Roger, glad you're here. Look." Mary points to a hole in the ground near Jimmy's hovel. I can see the pointy end of a partially buried pizza slice sticking out from under a layer of dirt and remember my earlier discussion with Jimmy about this same hole.

"Jimmy," I say. "I thought pizza was okay. It's just the burritos that were poisoned, right? Isn't that what Jay-Jay said?"

"That was before."

Mary throws me a confused look.

"Before what?" I ask, feeling only slightly less in the dark than Mary probably is.

"Before he discovered the whole truth," Jimmy replies.

"About?"

"About the Spokane people and the pills."

"Okay . . ."

"You know, the people from Spokane, over the mountains?" Jimmy tilts his head toward the east, as if some pernicious evil brewing on the other side of the Cascades should be obvious to anyone. "They're trying to take over Seattle, and they're starting with us."

"With us? Homeless people?"

"Yeah."

"But why would they start with . . . Never mind. You know that Mary, Carlos, and I have all been eating the same pizza, and we're doing just fine."

"Sure. That's because you're in the control group."

"I'm sorry—the control group? Like in an experiment?"

Jimmy turns toward Mary. "See? Roger gets it."

"I'm trying Jimmy, but no, I still don't understand," I say.

Jimmy shrugs and doesn't respond. I'm afraid this discussion isn't likely to continue, or to follow anything resembling a rational path if it does, but I'm looking for clues—anything I can use to help get some food into this guy.

"You said something about pills, Jimmy. What was that all about?"

"The ones they gave me when I was a teenager, when I wasn't right. It seemed like they were helping, but all they really did was change my genetics. Jay-Jay knew it all along."

"Your genetics?"

"Right. It's why I get sick and you don't. My new genes

make certain foods poisonous for me. Their experiment is working."

"But why just you?"

"Oh, it's not just me. There're others too. Once the Spokane people know this works, they'll start giving the pills to everyone they need out of the way. They've got doctors who're in on this. The whole thing will just look like some weird food problem, and before anybody figures it out like Jay-Jay did, almost everybody in Seattle will be dead. Then the Spokane people will just move in. Easy."

"When did you stop taking these pills?" Mary asks.

"I don't know. Sometime when I was working, before I came here."

"Working? Where were you working? You've never mentioned anything about work before," Mary says.

"That's because I don't want to talk about it."

I nod to Mary and try to rescue the conversation. "Yeah, I get that. I don't like talking about my old work either. Makes me feel lousy."

"Why?" Jimmy asks.

"I guess because I screwed up so badly."

"He was kind of a shithead," Mary adds.

"Thank you, Mary," I say, glaring in her direction. "Very helpful." But in fact, it *is* helpful, because Jimmy laughs. It's just two small chuckles, but something I've never heard from him before.

"Maybe I still am, but I'm trying," I say.

"Jay-Jay says you are. It's not your fault. You didn't know about the burritos, or the pizza, or the pills."

"Well, tell him thank you for me. I appreciate that." I've never received a compliment from a hallucination before, but I'll take it. It feels genuine.

"You can tell him yourself. He's right over there." Jimmy glances over his left shoulder.

I look at the empty space in that direction. "Thank you, Jay-Jay. I really appreciate it."

"What did you do that was so bad?" Jimmy asks.

"Well, the short version is that while I was running a company in Colorado, I made a selfish and stupid decision that resulted in over half the employees losing their jobs and investors losing a ton of money. It was also illegal, so I went to prison for a while."

"Wow. So it was all your fault?" Jimmy asks.

"Well, not all of it, I guess. Something bad happened that spooked me into making that decision, and that thing alone would have been enough to cause trouble for the company, but not nearly as much, or for so long. I made it a lot worse. A good CEO would never have done what I did."

"What did you do?"

"I made a selfish financial move."

"Why?" Jimmy asks.

"I was scared I'd lose everything if I didn't."

"But you lost it all anyway, right?" Mary says.

"Yeah. Well, not everything. I have you guys and my shack over there."

Jimmy nods slowly. "I did something bad at work too."

"Oh?" I say, hoping to keep the channel open.

"I hacked into the company's network. But it was just to show them I could. You know, so they could fix it."

"Did they fire you for that?" Mary asks.

"Uh-huh."

"Assholes. You were just trying to help. Was that when you stopped taking those pills?" Mary asks.

"Yeah. I couldn't afford them anymore. Probably a good

thing anyway, right? Now that I know what they really are."

"You didn't get another job?" I ask.

"No, I only got that one because a high school teacher talked them into it. I was just like a paid intern or something."

"You never went to college?" Mary asks.

"No money for that."

"What about your parents? Couldn't they have—"

"I was a foster kid. One place after another. I don't think any of them liked me very much, probably because I was, I don't know, difficult? Then, when I turned eighteen, I was out on my own and ended up here."

Mary looks at me, then back at Jimmy. "Do you still have any of those stupid pills lying around somewhere?"

"Maybe in the bag with the rest of my old stuff. Why?"

"Could I see one for a second? I just want to know what they look like so the rest of us don't get conned into taking them. I'll give it right back," Mary says.

"I guess. Just a minute."

Jimmy disappears into his hovel, and I whisper to Mary. "Antipsychotics, you think?" She nods. Jimmy reappears, placing a small yellow pill in Mary's hand.

She examines both sides and hands it back. "Thanks, Jimmy." She nods to me again.

"So, Jimmy, you're gonna need some other food," I say. "I've got one more salad and a couple of donuts in my pack. Better than nothing, right? And not poison, I'm sure. Promise you'll eat?"

"Yeah. Jay-Jay says it's okay. Thanks."

I dig the food out of my pack and give it to Jimmy, who smiles and ducks back into his shelter.

I turn to Mary. "Let me walk you back to your tent."

We take a few steps away from Jimmy's place and continue

in low voices. "So," I say. "What was it?"

"Clozapine. I know someone who was on it for years. We've got to find a way to get Jimmy back on meds. Maybe a newer drug, something that'll work for him. And he'll need some therapy to go along with it."

"Not gonna be an easy task, the way he's thinking about pills and strangers right now," I say.

"No shit."

"Did you know about Jimmy's computer work before?" I ask.

"Not really. I just remember him saying something about website design or social media or something like that."

"Hmm, interesting. If we can get him some help, I might have a job for him."

"A job? What are you talking about?"

"It might be nothing."

"Does this have something to do with that Stairway thing you were going on about the other day?"

"Maybe. Let's talk about it tomorrow—all four of us."

Thirty-Two

The next morning, Maslow is waiting for me outside the Residence with an open beak. I duck back in to find an old pizza crust despite common wisdom telling me I shouldn't continue this habit. Maslow's a wild bird, and I should let him find his own way, to live or die in his own ecosystem, for his own good and the good of his species. *If we interfere, they'll just multiply to the point where they're both unmanageable and unhealthy.* But wait—I and my fellow humans became part of the Seattle seagull ecosystem long ago, so now there's not much point in resisting. Okay, that's the extent of my rationalizing. And then there's the guilt.

"Here you go, buddy."

As I watch Maslow pick apart the crust and raise his head to gobble down the pieces, I can't help but wonder, is this how we think about our unhoused population? If we feed them, they'll just multiply? And get sicker—or addicted—in the process? We still do it anyway, mostly out of guilt. But some of us, like my former self, become experts at suppressing guilt through another rationalization: *Don't give them money. They'll just spend it on drugs and alcohol.* Then we make the problem worse by quietly extending this reasoning to food and other essentials. And if we're being totally honest, this insidious and often unspoken thought process sometimes goes further: *If we give them free food and a place to camp, then they're going to be content with that and never try to change. Instead, if we just let them starve and make sure law enforcement is tough enough to prevent crime in the area, then the homeless will be forced to figure it out on their own and take a little initiative for a change. If some don't make it, then it's just natural selection and the population goes down. Either way, problem solved.*

I remember thinking something like that long ago, as my BMW comfortably cruised by a line of people with signs claiming they would work for food, or that they had three children to feed, or that anything would help. It didn't take long to drive by, and the scrawled signs weren't that hard to ignore. Most of them were just lies anyway, right? Sure, some, but probably not most. Not as I see things now.

Maslow finishes his high-carb breakfast and takes to the air. He looks happy, best I can tell. For him, it doesn't take much. Unlike his namesake's pyramid-shaped hierarchy of needs, my seagull's pyramid doesn't include the top levels leading to self-esteem and self-actualization. It's more like a short, flat-topped thing—just covering basic physical needs and a bit of safety and security. Unlike us, he's quite happy hovering at or near basement level.

I walk toward Carlos's corner, my thoughts clarifying with each step. Abraham Maslow's model is all about the *what*. Viktor Frankl's book—the one Mary bought the other day— is about the *why* and *how*. Stairway could be about all of that. Food, medicine, and basic shelter are essential for survival, and we can't ignore those needs, but by themselves they're rarely enough to get us permanently off the street and back into society. Frankl's notion of *purpose* is necessary for that. It's necessary for moving up the pyramid and staying there.

"Buenos días, amigo!" I shout, as Carlos anticipates the next slug of cars about to arrive at his corner.

"Buenos días. Como estas, viejo?" Carlos says with a smile and one eye on the traffic light.

"Bastante bien. Sigo vivo. Y tu?"

"Lo mismo, supongo."

"Uh . . . okay, that's about the extent of my Spanish," I say.

"Not too bad, amigo. Your accent could use a little work, but not bad. What's up with you today?"

"I was just thinking, would you like to come along on my foraging trip this morning? There's someone I want you to meet. Maybe two someones."

"I don't know, Mr. CEO. It wouldn't help our bottom line."

"Hey, I'm not the CEO here. But yeah, you're right, it wouldn't. Still, we might want to take a loss today. This could be worth it."

"Okay, if you think so. I could use a walk, and anyway, you're makin' me curious." Carlos folds up his sign, and I pay attention to it for the first time. *Why haven't I read it before?*

His sign simply says, "Please invest in my future, our future."

"Has your sign always said that?" I ask.

"Yep."

"Impressive. No wonder you make the big bucks."

We continue our easy banter on the way down to SoDo, but all the time I'm thinking about introducing Carlos to Bart at Home Team Pizza. There's something I want to discuss with him before that meeting, but I'm struggling with a way to start. Finally, I just dive in sideways.

"So I'm curious. How've you managed to stay ahead of the immigration people all this time?"

"What?"

"I mean, it's got to be tough being an undocumented person on the street, right?"

"I'm not undocumented, Roger. I'm a US citizen."

That stops me dead in the middle of the sidewalk. Carlos stops too, but faces away from me. People walk around us like a river flowing around an island.

"I'm sorry, man. I just assumed . . ."

Carlos still isn't looking at me. "Uh-huh, just like everybody else: 'Oh, a Latino. An invader taking our jobs. Probably a rapist.'"

"Carlos, I am so very sorry. That came right out of my past life. No, wait. I can't blame it on that guy. It's me, right now, being a shithead, like Mary reminds me all the time."

That brings a small smile as Carlos turns back toward me. "Apology accepted, shithead."

"What can I do to make things better, my friend?"

Carlos moves off the sidewalk to a nearby bus stop bench and pats the empty space next to him. "Well, you could start by finding out more about me, an actual person. Just ask."

There's no bus in sight, so I sit down next to Carlos. "Right, I'm really sorry about that. So, uh, were you born here in Seattle?"

"Okay, not a terrible start, viejo. No. It was Salinas, California. My mother was a farm worker, and no, she wasn't legal. She got deported back to Honduras when I was nineteen."

"And your father?"

"He died trying to hide my mom and me. I got away. He didn't."

"Did they . . . ?"

"I don't think they meant to, but yeah, they killed him."

I stare at my shoes. "What about you? Where did you go after that?"

"I hitchhiked up north, spent a year bumming around Portland, working odd jobs when I could find 'em. Then finally made it up here where I got lucky with a full-time job at a nursery in Highland Park, selling plants and stuff. I had a small apartment nearby and started making friends. I sent money back to my mom when I could."

"All sounds good, considering."

"It was. I even got a year into studying business at South Seattle Community College at night."

"That's great. What happened?"

"Long story."

"No problem. Let's get up and keep walking. You can tell me on the way, if you want."

As we make our way south toward SoDo, Carlos describes his job as a young salesperson on the greenhouse floor at the nursery, and I can tell he loved it. He had grown up around plants and had learned a lot about their cultivation and care firsthand. And now, in this job, he was able to share that knowledge with his customers and make a living at the same time.

"Then one day," he says, "everything changed."

But Carlos backtracks before he elaborates. He tells me he'd been getting some of his business ideas in front of the nursery's management team. He suggested grouping compatible plants together to form a kind of package for customers and showing those combinations on the nursery floor like attractive little mini-landscapes, with pricing slightly lower than if each plant was purchased separately. The result? Higher sales volume. Apparently, management loved it. But someone else didn't.

"Who was that?" I ask.

"Steve. Steve Mandrel. I'll prob'ly never forget that name. He was this white guy—tall, skinny, shaved head. He had the same job as me and we also traded off shifts at the cash register. Steve was friendly with customers but always had it in for me, and I knew it was my brown skin when I saw the ink on the guy's upper arm—a swastika. Even then, I tried to be cool about it, I guess because our manager started giving me the best shifts right about that same time. I think she really liked my ideas. I even got a raise. I don't know if Steve did, but I don't think so. Anyway, he was pissed. He framed me."

"Framed you? How?"

"Some money went missing from the register, like seven hundred bucks. And Steve said he saw me walk out with it one night, like I would really be that stupid. Thing is, the owner of the place believed Steve's story and called the cops. The manager stood up for me, but it didn't matter. She got fired too."

"Damn."

"Yeah. So you can guess the rest. They hauled my ass off to jail, I got convicted and couldn't pay the fine or give the money back 'cause, you know, I didn't have it in the first place. So back I went to jail. I got out after a few months, but now I've got a record and can't get work that'll pay anything close to my street corner."

"Yeah, I get it," I say. "But the difference is, I deserved my sentence. You didn't."

"So I guess you really believe me."

"Come on, Carlos, I've been around you for a while now. Of course I believe you."

Carlos nods and we walk on together in silence. By the time we get to Home Team Pizza, I've completely changed my plans for the day.

I pull Carlos aside before opening the door. "There's something I need to tell you. You know my thoughtless assumption about you and citizenship?"

Carlos doesn't reply, just tilts his head to one side and looks at me with squinted eyes.

"Well, I said something about that to the owner of this place a while back. I was asking if he might be willing to take you on as a part-time employee despite, you know, your immigration status."

"You did that?"

"I know. It was terrible. Stupid. I'm sorry."

"No, it wasn't so bad. Prejudiced, yeah, but still . . . Thanks, man. So what'd he say?"

I'm surprised at Carlos's response, and it takes me a moment to answer. "He said it might be possible, but he didn't have anything right then."

"And now?"

"I don't know. Probably the same, but I just thought it might help if he met you." We walk into the busy dining room and pick up our pizza allotment from Jeffrey, then spend a few awkward minutes in Bart's office where I introduce Carlos and apologize for my mistake about his citizenship. When I finish, Bart is looking sheepish.

"I've got a confession of my own," he says. "Did you know Chicago Pies went out of business last week?"

"No. Wow, that was fast. Congratulations."

"Thanks, I guess, but I feel like crap. Some good people lost their jobs."

"That happens," I say, immediately regretting it and painfully aware of the irony.

"Okay, but here's the thing: I hired their dishwasher and a waiter. I'm sorry, Carlos. I told Roger I'd consider you for one of those jobs."

"Don't worry about it, man. You did what you needed to do," Carlos says. "It was a good thing."

Bart smiles thinly and shakes Carlos's hand. "You'll be the first to know if another opportunity comes up. And if I hear about anything else nearby, I'll pass that along, too."

"Thanks," Carlos and I say together.

"Oh, and I don't know if this is anything," Bart says as we turn to leave, "but there's a rumor floating around about a new organization starting up somewhere in town that might be able to help. I think it's called Staircase or Stepwise or something like that. You guys might want to check it out."

Astonished, I stay silent.

Thirty-Three

"Thanks, viejo," Carlos says as we leave Home Team Pizza and head north to Pioneer Square. "Thanks for trying to help. We should prob'ly get back, though. My investors are cruisin' by without a chance to do their thing this morning. Gotta help 'em get rid of those pesky small bills and that nasty guilt, right?"

"Right, but one more stop? I think it'll be worth it."

"Sure. I guess it can't hurt. Much."

On the way I learn another surprising thing about Carlos, and it occurs to me that I'm surprised only because I continue to see him through a sadly stereotypical lens. For his sixteenth birthday, his father had given him an old point-and-shoot digital camera he'd found at a secondhand store, and Carlos took to photography immediately. He snapped pictures of his parents, friends, workers in the field, the local landscape, and anything else that caught his eye. He loved it. It became a passion and a welcome diversion from school and field work.

"Do you still have that camera today?" I ask.

"Yeah. I still have it, but it stopped working just before I went to jail. I can't believe I lost all those old pics, my old life."

"Do you have it with you, in your pack?"

Carlos nods. "I never leave it alone."

"Hmm, I've got an idea," I say as we turn into the alley behind Rain City Books.

We stop at a doorway and Carlos stares at me while I search my pockets for keys. I resist the urge to tell him anything before opening the door to my new office.

"What *is* this?" he asks, scanning the dark interior. I flip on the lights and usher him in. "Welcome to Stairway."

"What the . . ." Carlos says, glancing around the newly renovated space. "Is this that thing Bart was talking about?"

"Well, sort of. It's the office for what I hope can become that thing. It isn't even off the ground yet."

"And you are the . . . ?"

"The founder, I guess you'd say."

"Damn, viejo! Why didn't you say anything about this?"

"Because I don't even know if we can make it work."

"We? Who's we?"

"Me, you, Mary, and maybe even Jimmy, if you all want to be part of this. I wanted to get us all together tonight to talk about it, but I think maybe tomorrow would be better, right here in the office. There are a ton of loose ends. But for now, can I see that camera of yours?"

"Sure." Carlos is still shaking his head as he digs through his pack and hands me the device.

I pop out the ancient memory card and hope that my equally ancient computer has a card reader slot for it. It does, and I plug the card in, full of hope. Nothing. I use the Windows File Explorer to examine the card, and there is a deep hierarchy of folders. Drilling down, I finally see a few hundred JPEG files and try to open one. Carlos stands over my shoulder, staring.

"Shit," I say.

"The files are corrupted, right?" Carlos asks.

"You knew that already?"

"I tried this on a computer at the library a while ago."

"You could have said."

Carlos's eyes are laughing. "I just thought, you know, that a guy with a computer science PhD would be a lot smarter than me about this."

"Sorry to disappoint, but having a degree like that doesn't really have much to do with knowing specific shit about some image file format. And anyway, how did you find out I have a PhD?"

"I googled you at the library. So no ideas?"

"Nope, but I know a guy who might have some." I hand the memory card back to Carlos. "There's one other quick thing I need to do here before we head back."

I pull the old Goodwill answering machine out of my pack, hook it up to the phone line, and record a simple greeting.

"We need to test this," I say. "Come on. I'll introduce you to our landlord."

I knock on the door leading to the back of the bookshop and wait. Finally, I hear, "Who is it?"

"Hi, Denise. It's me, Roger. There's someone here I'd like you to meet." Denise unlocks the door from her side and opens it.

"Roger! Great to see you. And . . . ?" She holds her hand out to Carlos.

"Carlos. Carlos Rivera. Good to meet you."

"So," I say to Denise, with a hand on Carlos's shoulder, "I'm trying to talk my friend here into joining me at Stairway, to help me get it off the ground." Then, turning back to Carlos, "Denise's generosity is the main reason we have a shot at this in the first place."

After asking if I can use the bookshop's phone to test my answering machine, I leave Denise and Carlos to talk. I dial my new phone number and wait. After three rings, I smile at what I'm hearing: *You've reached Roger Carrington at Stairway, investing in the future of Seattle's unhoused people. Please leave a message and I'll get back to you.*

I leave the inaugural message: "Hi, it's Roger. Let's do this."

Thirty-Four

My night slips by without a visit to the past. I need to return soon, to confront what I did at DLS, but I'm not ready yet. Today I need to focus on the present. I want to convince everyone here, especially Jimmy, to go with me to the office for what I hope will be the first official Stairway meeting.

Mary and Carlos readily agree to come with me, but as we approach Jimmy's lean-to, I'm skeptical. I've never seen him more than ten or twenty feet away from his little shelter, let alone miles away downtown. He probably uses the restroom at the nearby park, but I've never seen him heading that way. Maybe he makes a run late at night or early in the morning when no one is around. His paranoia is so obvious, so clearly painful, that I'm doubtful I can pry him away. But I do have one idea, a long shot.

"Jimmy?" I say, already knowing the answer to my next question. "You home?"

The bill of Jimmy's baseball cap pokes through a cardboard flap, then his face with his long, stringy hair falling out the sides of the cap, then the rest of him.

"What's wrong?" he says. "Why're you all here at the same time?"

"Nothing's wrong," Carlos replies. "We're all going for a walk and want you to come with us. Roger's got something he wants to talk about."

"I can't do that. Jay-Jay says definitely not. Too dangerous."

"Not if we all go together, Jay-Jay included," I say.

"I don't know. Can't we just talk here?"

"Jimmy, this is important. There's something only you can help us with, and it involves a computer. The rest of us have no idea how to deal with it."

"A computer? Where?"

"Down in Pioneer Square."

"No. Jay-Jay says that's way too far."

"Could I just have a quick word with Jay-Jay?" I ask.

"I guess. Sure." Jimmy steps away from his shelter and looks to his right.

I turn toward that empty space, feeling foolish, trying to find the right words. "So, Jay-Jay, we're all grateful to you for keeping Jimmy safe. He's our friend, and we always want the best for him. We also need his help right now. We've got a computer problem, some corrupted files, and we just don't have the skills to repair them. But I think Jimmy does. He might be our only hope. Do you think he could go with us today to check this out? We'd all be there to keep him safe, and of course you can go too."

Jimmy looks from side to side, as if searching for his adviser who was there just seconds ago, then turns back toward me. "What operating system?" he asks.

"Windows 7."

"Really old. Okay though. What file type?"

"JPEG."

"There's already software out there to repair JPEGs," Jimmy replies, and backs toward his shelter.

I think I've lost him, but then a little white lie occurs to me. "I know. It's just that all those programs cost money, and we don't have any way to pay."

"Some are free."

Damn. He's right, of course. How can I turn this around? "Okay, yes, you're right, but I just don't trust free software. Do you?"

"No. It's full of adware. Sometimes malware. It's dangerous."

"Exactly. We've got to avoid that stuff. So will you come help us?"

Jimmy once again looks side to side, then back at me. "Okay. I think it's okay," he says. "But I can't stay long."

"No problem. We'll be back here before you know it."

"I don't think that's possible," Jimmy says, and I detect the hint of a smile.

Our trip to Pioneer Square is uneventful, if a bit uncomfortable. We're obviously out of place among the businesspeople and tourists, and I think our presence as a group accentuates that—especially with Jimmy looking wide-eyed and afraid in the protective center of our little cohort. I'm tempted to think of myself as separate, even superior, but one look at my torn and waterlogged shoes brings me back to the humbling reality of our shared situation. I recall the many times I've heard politicians or celebrities say they are "humbled" by an election result or an award. Such bullshit. They can't possibly understand the deep and gritty meaning of that word.

The first thing I notice after opening the door to our

new office is the flashing red light on my answering machine. I hurry toward it while Carlos—proudly, I think—gives the others a quick tour of the space and a summary of his conversation with Denise yesterday.

I play back the two messages on the machine: my test message and one from Charlie Duncan.

"Hey Roger, I got your number from a woman named Denise at the bookshop you mentioned. I hope you found a new shirt and took a hot shower, my fragrant friend, 'cause I got you a meeting with a lawyer named Paula Griffith from Anderson, Gibbs, and Larson in Seattle. It's set for this Thursday at ten in her office."

Charlie goes on to provide the address and phone number for the firm, leaves his own number, and finishes with a pep talk: "This is a great opportunity. Don't fuck it up."

I think the others in the room are almost as surprised at this message as I am, but for different reasons. I wasn't at all sure I'd get a meeting, but this is the first time my little group has even heard of the possibility.

"What was that all about?" asks Mary.

"I'm trying to officially form a nonprofit organization. But before we talk about that, Jimmy, could you take a look at those files?"

Carlos hands his camera's memory card to Jimmy, who then examines the files using my computer. I watch over his shoulder as he digs into the internal structure of one file, then several more. Finally, he looks up.

"Good news, sort of. They're all corrupted in the same way—segment marker damage. I could fix them one at a time, but that would take forever. I need to write some code to automate the process. Is there a C# compiler on this thing, or even just a plain old C compiler?"

"Uh, I really don't know," I say, marveling at Jimmy's knowledge and the clarity he now seems to be showing. He sounds like a different person.

"No problem. I can get one online. It's free, but I know it's okay. I've used it before."

Jimmy gets to work while I return Charlie's call. He doesn't answer, so I leave a message thanking him for the meeting setup and giving him my new email address.

The rest of us head to the bookstore for some browsing while we wait for Jimmy to finish. During periods when no other customers are in the shop, I share my thoughts about Stairway with Carlos and Mary. Denise listens in.

"I spent some time the other day here browsing the web for organizations that are focused on helping people like us. There are several in the area, but most of them seem underfunded, most only help with urgent things like food, shelter, and overdose treatment, and there doesn't seem to be a lot of coordination between the different groups. On top of that, not very many people on the street can access the internet or know how to. So unless these various groups actually reach out—which only a few do—people don't even know what's available to them. I didn't, until I had the chance to look online.

"Here's how I see Stairway working. We're not in competition with these other services. Far from it. Instead, we work *with them* to try and bring our homeless brothers and sisters up from defeat, through basic survival, through discovery of purpose, to jobs and exit from the street. We become a kind of personalized consulting service, helping people find and use existing resources, helping them climb up the tiers of Maslow's pyramid."

"Whose pyramid?" Carlos asks.

"I'll fill you in later," Mary says to Carlos, then turns to me. "Roger, count me in. I finished Viktor Frankl's book last night, and this whole thing fits. It feels right, but it still smells a little bullshitty."

"Yeah, I know. It kind of does to me too, when I try and put it into words," I say. "We need to work on that, if we're ever gonna get any funding."

"Funding?" Carlos says.

"Sure. We need money to pay for things like Ubers, Lyfts, or scooters. Different ways to get clients to the hospital, legal appointments, job interviews, things like that. And we need to pay for rent." I glance toward Denise. "And our own salaries."

"Salaries?" Carlos says.

"Yes, salaries. We should be paid something for our work, even if it isn't much. Besides, how can we help our clients get off the street if we can't begin to do that ourselves? We need to show them it's possible."

"I'm in too," Carlos says. "But I don't know what I can really do."

"We'll figure it all out. I can easily see roles for both you and Mary: Finance and Client Selection, for starters. And if Jimmy can resurrect your old photos, he just aced his interview for the IT job. Let's go see how he's doing."

We say goodbye to Denise and return to the office. Carlos's restored photos are clearly visible on the computer screen, but Jimmy is nowhere to be seen.

Thirty-Five

We rush out the back door and quickly search up and down the alley. No sign of Jimmy. I move to the street in front of the bookshop. Not there either. Then inside the bookshop, where I notify Denise. Finally, back on the street with Carlos and Mary. *I never should have left him alone! I can't even take care of one person, let alone a bunch of Stairway clients. I'm an idiot. What was I thinking?*

In the middle of my self-centered mental beating, I hear Carlos take charge.

"He's gotta be close by. Let's split up and search the area. Mary, you go east toward the freeway. Roger, you've got the north end. I'll take south and west. If anybody finds him, bring him home, okay? We'll meet back there before dark."

I start my search, trying to imagine a grid covering all the streets and alleys between Pioneer Square and the overpass. I know I'm missing a ton of places, because there's way too much territory, and down among the labyrinth of buildings it's hard to keep track of where I've been. On top of that,

Jimmy is probably moving at the same time. Or he might have ducked into a building somewhere. I could easily be within ten yards of him and never know it.

But over the next several hours, I keep moving, keep looking, keep asking if anyone's seen him. Some say no, some look at me with suspicion and move on without answering, some just shake their heads. I keep searching, a deepening sense of futility gnawing away at me. Finally, as dusk begins to settle over Seattle, I give up and head back to the overpass, defeated and exhausted but hoping one of the others has had better luck.

As I approach the overpass, I can see Carlos and Mary seated together outside Mary's tent around her camp stove. They're eating something, no thanks to me today, and I can't read their faces from this distance. Jimmy is not with them, so I can't imagine the news is good.

But as I join them, they're smiling. I'm confused. "Any luck?" I ask.

"Mary found him," Carlos says as he hands me a burrito.

"Wow, that's great news! So where is he?"

"Tell him, Mary," Carlos says.

"Okay, well, when I got to the freeway with no luck and more time on my hands, I thought what the hell, keep going. So I crossed under and headed up the hill. Then it finally hit me as I was staring right at it—the hospital. Long story short, that's where he was. A cop found him hunched down in the middle of 4th Avenue and hauled his ass off to Harborview. He's on a psych hold there."

"Whew! So what do we do now?" I ask.

"Well, the good news is they've got him on some new meds, and they'll discharge him day after tomorrow as long as he's stable and I'm there to pick him up. Thing is, though, we've got to keep him on those meds and get him to therapy twice a week for a couple of months. That's all the time they'll pay for."

"Sounds tough, right? But we can do it," says Carlos. "The kid's got a chance now."

"Yeah," Mary says. "If the new meds keep those wild conspiracy theories and delusions away so we don't have to force the damn pills down his throat. The doc seemed to think so when I asked."

"You know what's weird?" I say. "I think I'm gonna miss Jay-Jay." But as I head back to the Residence for the night, I know I'm just using humor to cover a deepening sense of doubt. *Jay-Jay was Jimmy's delusion. Maybe mine is Stairway. What makes me think that a little band of misfits like us has any chance of doing something like that? Sure, I've got an office, a computer, and three people who are probably just as deluded as I am, but that's not Stairway. Not even close. And two months from now, I'm going to have to start paying for all this. What the hell am I doing?*

In this dark frame of mind as I slide toward sleep, I find myself drawn back to the halcyon days at Deep Learning Systems just before the company's downfall. We were two years into our status as a publicly traded company, our stock was flying high, our product was on its way to becoming an enormous success, and employee morale was soaring. Everyone felt as good about the product they'd created as they did about their personal stock positions. And of course, that was true for me as well. It now seemed obvious that my financial future was secure. If all went as expected, I would retire in a year with more money than I'd ever dreamed of, all my debts would be erased, and life's possibilities would be endless.

But then the first call came in.

"Roger, Dr. Chou from the Wichita Mental Health Center is on line one," Claire announced. "He sounds agitated."

"Dr. Chou. What a nice surprise. How are you?"

"I'm fine, Roger, but I've got some very concerning news."

"Oh?"

"Yes, we've had great success with the DLS product so far, and our therapists are enthusiastic, but then something came up this morning that changed everything, and I wanted you to know about it right away. I got an email from someone claiming to have unredacted patient information for several of our clients: names, phone numbers, addresses, entire session transcripts. At first I thought, well, this is just some idiot faking it with a phishing scam, because I know how well your anonymizer software works. I've seen the results and it's thorough, to say the least. But then I got a second email from the same person with a link to the unredacted files."

"Shit."

"Yeah, shit. I got my IT guy involved at that point, and he followed the link on an isolated system."

"And?"

"And there it was. All the patients' information, including some very private session content. A major HIPAA violation. And if I had to guess, there's more coming. We could be sued, Roger, and so could you, not to mention serious damage to both of our companies' reputations. Needless to say, I've stopped all use of the DLS product, at least until we get this all sorted out. I'm sure you understand."

"Of course, absolutely. I'll schedule a meeting this morning with my engineering team to dig into this right away. You didn't mention any demand for money, but this sounds like ransomware."

"I know. That was my first thought too. But there was nothing. No demand for a Bitcoin payment or anything else, at least not yet. Just an announcement that the sensitive information will be published, and then proof they have it."

"Strange. Can you send me any other data you have on this? IP addresses, anything."

Dr. Chou promised more information within an hour, and I set up a meeting at noon with Jake. The rest of the morning crawled by as I worried my way through all the implications. How could this have happened? Our anonymizer software had been used successfully for years and there'd never been any evidence of patient information exposure, either inadvertent or intentional. We never retained any original patient information, and even the final redacted files were encrypted. And obviously, anything that seriously undermined confidence in our product could easily lead to our own demise. I needed to deal with this immediately.

Jake and Wade walked into my office at noon, lunches in hand, and I filled them in. They seemed stunned by the news and had several questions. *Was this the first case we'd seen like this?* Yes. *Do we have the relevant data?* Yes. *Could this have been the result of user error?* Doubtful.

Jake turned to Wade. "Have we ever detected any form of security breach in our system? Any malware found, even if it was removed?"

"None. Never."

"How often do we run that system integrity check we designed at the beginning—the one that checks for software corruption or modifications that didn't come via our protected code management system?"

"I'd have to check with IT, but I believe it runs automatically at midnight every day."

"Okay, double-check that and have them run it again right now," I said. "I'll get in touch with the Azure security folks to see if anything unusual is going on at the Microsoft end.

"Okay, guys," I concluded. "No one else needs to hear about any of this until we know what we're dealing with and have a plan to address it. Not a single word. Let's meet back here in an hour and see where we are then."

~

Thirty minutes later, the second call came in. This one was from a large psychotherapy practice in New York, and the news was much worse. In this case, over fifty separate patient transcripts had been exposed, and one of the patients had been contacted directly. That patient reacted by taking her own life.

Looking back, I'm deeply ashamed of what I did and didn't do next.

I panicked.

I didn't inform our own legal team or the board until much too late. I *did* begin a series of personal stock sales right away, selfishly and ignorantly reasoning that I could fly under the radar and save my own financial future if I just sold a few thousand DLS shares at a time, repeating the process over the next few days. Those shares were my only real hope for a decent retirement, and I was damned if I was just going to let it all go. I told myself I needed to do this in order to calm my fears enough to be able to concentrate on rescuing the company. That, of course, was pure bullshit. I put myself ahead of my employees, ahead of our investors, and ahead of

Claire—which I have to say, right or wrong, caused me the most grief.

But in keeping with that self-deception, I managed to compartmentalize my life and continue working with Jake and Wade to diagnose the digital cancer at the heart of our product. I swore them to secrecy throughout the whole process, concerned that any leak of our product's failure would get to the press before we had a plan to recover.

Then, two days into our work, the deeply disturbing cause of that failure came to light.

Thirty-Six

I will never forget the day. It was June 17, a warm Wednesday morning in Boulder. Claire and I were just finishing our usual planning session, but my mind was an hour ahead, anticipating a meeting with Jake and Wade.

"You seem preoccupied this morning," Claire said. "And you've been that way for a few days now. You okay?"

"Yeah, I'm fine," I lied. "Just dealing with a couple of customer issues. No big deal."

"Roger, I think I know you better than that by now. But okay, I'll leave it alone. Just know I'm here if you need to talk."

"Thanks, Claire. Appreciate that."

At nine o'clock sharp, Jake and Wade walked in with grim looks. Jake opened his laptop, and we all sat around my small conference table. He dove in without preamble.

"Wade and I found the source of the problem. It's been hiding in our system for over two years just waiting to strike. And the bitch of it is that it was put there by someone with administrative credentials inside the company, using our own protected software release tools. It all happened about the time we fired those two software developers almost three years ago. It's a program that runs at the highest permission level and waits until we either have two hundred customers or three years elapse. We hit the two hundred customer mark last month."

"What does it do, and why the hell didn't we know about it? We do thorough source code reviews, right?" I asked.

"Yes, of course. I personally sit in on all those review sessions. This software was actually disguised as data in a large array within a legitimate part of our system and was copied into executable code space by a small process embedded deep in our system integrity check, of all things. Embarrassing, to say the very least."

"So what does this damn stuff do?" I asked.

"It watches all incoming patient transcript traffic, intercepts it prior to the anonymizer, sends it to a site on the dark web, then removes all traces of its execution before terminating, only to wake up the next day and repeat the whole process. This was sabotage."

"How? Who? Why?"

"We think someone used old administrator login credentials to gain access," Jake said. "I have to take the blame for that. Two years ago, after we fired those two engineers, I didn't check with my team to be sure we had removed their accounts and invalidated their passwords. That was a major oversight on my part, and I'm incredibly sorry. As for who, it could have been one of those guys, but not necessarily. It could have been anyone using their credentials. We really have no idea right now. Same with the question of why."

I tried to control my anger, most of which was directed inward. "How do we contain the damage and keep any other customers from running into this now?"

Wade jumped in. "This morning at three o'clock, I took the liberty of shutting down all access to the system for four hours while we rebuilt everything, invalidated all admin logins, created new ones, set up a second level of authentication, and ran a full battery of system tests. Luckily, we were also able to access the dark web database and delete all the exposed patient data."

"So now it's down to customer damage control and PR work," added Jake. "But it's probably only a matter of hours before the press gets wind of this. I think it's time to loop in Jenny, Stella, and Bob. I'll coordinate that, if you agree."

"Yes, and I'll handle the board," I said. "I hope no other customers have been affected."

But they had been.

Claire opened the door and apologized for the interruption. "Roger, you've got customers holding on lines two and three, and the *Wall Street Journal* is on one. How would you like me to handle this?"

"Shit. Sorry, just get their info and tell them I'll call back." Claire disappeared and I turned back to Jake and Wade. "Do whatever you can to determine the hacker's identity. Then get anything you find to the FBI. Jake, I might need you in on a couple of these calls, so stick around."

One of the customer calls was a simple request for information. They had heard a rumor about exposed patient data, and Jake was able to assure them that we had found and fixed the problem. The other customer call was much more serious. They reported ten exposures and threatened legal action despite the liability protection clause in our license agreement.

I brought Stella in on the *Wall Street Journal* conversation after briefing her on the situation. She did a masterful job of answering the reporter's questions honestly and stressing our rapid technical response while avoiding any specific admission of guilt. After the call, I asked Stella to prepare a press release and arrange individual calls with everyone on our customer list to get ahead of any further damage.

Stella and Bob worked together to notify and reassure all customers, I had a painful teleconference with the board, and at the end of a very long day, Stella issued her press release. But before any of that, I swallowed hard and put in a sell order for my remaining shares while the DLS stock price remained near record highs.

By ten-thirty the next morning, my money was safe, but the company's stock had lost 60 percent of its value. And the slide didn't stop there. Over the next few days, the stock price fell to about 20 percent of its historical high and stabilized there, but other carnage continued. Nearly half of our customers put their subscriptions on hold, and ten of the remaining ones flat-out canceled. The press, always hungry for business drama, continued its onslaught. The Cleveland Clinic backed out as a major customer, citing the need to maintain its stellar reputation, and UCSD was heading in that direction before I was able to pull it out of the fire by flying to San Diego for a personal meeting with Sheryl Davidson.

Dr. Davidson had been our first significant supporter and had funded her involvement with us as part of a research grant. As it turned out, this was probably a key factor in our company's ultimate recovery, such as it was, because she and three of her graduate students were writing a paper on AI-assisted therapy, and I think they saw us more as an experiment than a commercial venture. Even so, she and her team needed assurance that we would at least survive long enough to deliver some useful data. My trip accomplished that goal and kept UCSD in the fold as a major source of credibility.

As I flew back to Denver the next day, I counted the UCSD meeting as an important win but knew it was only one of many we would need in the coming months. Fortunately, our cash position was good, and I was confident it would allow us to avoid layoffs for several months while working hard to restore our reputation and rebuild our customer base.

What I *didn't* know was that I would never have a chance to be part of that process. Instead, I would soon become the sole reason for a much worse decline and a massive layoff.

When I arrived back at DLS that afternoon, two federal agents were waiting for me. I was arrested, charged with insider trading, and marched, handcuffed, out of my office in full view of my management team. Even worse than that, worse than anything, was seeing the deeply hurt and confused look on Claire's face as I was escorted out of the building.

Thirty-Seven

Kavi Singh took over as CEO of Deep Learning Systems and tried to manage a rapidly dwindling set of customers as they reacted to my ignominious departure. Claire remained with the company as Kavi's Executive Assistant. Jake and his direct reports also survived, as did Stella, but two-thirds of the other employees lost their jobs as DLS bled cash.

Had I kept my head and not been so blindly selfish, I'm quite sure the company would have weathered the catastrophe and retained most of its customers. Our stock would have steadily recovered to pre-disaster levels, and the lives of over a hundred employees would not have been so terribly disrupted. As it was, the company limped forward into an uncertain future. As did I.

According to my lawyer, if I pleaded not guilty and went to trial, we would need to convince a jury that I had no intent to defraud the company and that my stock trades had been made in good faith without any foreknowledge of corporate disaster. Since the financial evidence itself was well documented and incontrovertible, my case would have revolved around a simple claim of ignorance about the state of the company I was supposed to have been leading. Aside from being a lie and a very weak defense, that would also have implied an appalling lack of awareness on my part, and I couldn't face being seen that way. But beyond everything else, the prospect of Claire testifying against me in court was unthinkable.

As a white-collar first-time offender, I expected a degree of leniency if I pleaded guilty, so all things considered, that's what I did. I expected a stiff fine and hoped for immediate parole with community service but was only partially right about the former and completely wrong about the latter. My sentence included a large fine and a corporate payback agreement that not only wiped out my retirement portfolio but also required the sale of every tangible asset I owned, including my treasured boat, *Independence.*

That alone rocked me to the core. But what I didn't expect—and I blame my lawyer for not preparing me—was actual prison time. I learned later that even relatively low-level corporate fraud cases like mine often result in a couple of years in a minimum-security prison "camp"—a cushy environment compared to a low-security federal prison, but incarceration nonetheless. These camps have no guard towers, no fencing, no violent inmates, no traditional barred cells, and amenities not found in the main prison system.

But at the time of my sentencing, all minimum-security camps were severely overcrowded, and unfortunately for me, this had also become a political hot-button. So, as an expedient alternative, the court sentenced me to a reduced term of ten months in FCI Englewood, the Federal Correctional Institution located in Littleton, Colorado. FCI Englewood is officially designated as a low-security federal prison, but it is still a traditional prison in every sense. Inmates at Englewood are typically serving multiyear to multidecade sentences for a variety of nonviolent and violent crimes.

The day I reported for prison was a jarring transition like no other in my memory. In under an hour, I went from freedom to captivity, from wide-open Colorado vistas to an eight-by-ten holding cell. Other than an unexpected terminal diagnosis, slavery, or death itself, I can't think of anything more existentially challenging or personally devastating than incarceration—especially for someone who has lived a privileged life in the driver's seat. Prison takes control of an inmate, removes them from society, strips them down to the bones of identity, and forces them to confront what's left. What they discover there, if they can bear to look at it, can either save them or destroy them.

I quickly learned that identity destruction—or at least realignment—is an intentional part of the process, under the theory that salvation cannot be had without it. An inmate must first be broken down—made to deeply understand their new status as a criminal—before they can begin the rebuilding process. I wondered if ten months was only enough time to experience the destruction phase. Not that I wished for a second longer.

Arriving by bus with eleven other new convicts, I got my first look at our new home: a sandstone-colored fortress with barred windows and tall razor-wire fences, all ensuring that the facility could not be mistaken for anything but what it truly was. Fear leaked from the eyes of a young man sitting across the aisle next to me as he turned to look out my window, while others—probably not first-timers—projected a stony indifference that made me shiver with a cold nausea.

This was not a world I understood or controlled in any way.

Armed guards opened a large gate in the perimeter fence, inspected our bus, waved it through, and locked the gate behind us. From there we entered a dimly lit underground concrete garage through a heavy steel door that clanged loudly as it closed, doubly ensuring our captivity. As if in direct response to the finality of that sound, another wave of panic-induced nausea hit me, and I struggled to maintain control. What had been an abstract and distant idea of confinement became immediately real and overwhelmingly threatening. Even though my rational mind knew my stay would last only ten months, my amygdalae did their best to project a hellish eternity. In a few seconds, my world changed radically, and the privileged life I had known for nearly sixty years ended.

~

The formal phase of my personal deconstruction began twenty minutes later, at Receiving and Discharge, or R&D—initials which had meant something familiar and positive in my former life. The carefully prescribed process demanded my attention, and I suppose that helped calm my nausea, but other sensations replaced it. I was unprepared for the identification I suddenly began to feel with the other inmates and how quickly I began to adopt an us-versus-them attitude toward the guards. Only minutes before, the guards had seemed more like protectors and the inmates more like threats, but now the situation felt reversed. I found myself blindly obeying orders while simultaneously harboring a growing desire to assert myself, to attempt even a minor degree of control. I had no idea that over my ten-month term, and even within the next few minutes, I would flip-flop many times between identification with one group and the other.

As detached and professional as the prison guards tried to appear, it was impossible for me to avoid a sense of personal violation during the next few minutes. Six of us were taken into a small room and told to remove all clothing and put it with all other belongings in large brown bags. Relieved of my backpack and stripped of my jacket, shirt, and pants, I stood naked on a cold concrete floor with a grated drain in the center. Then we were each medically examined and searched in the most invasive of ways. I suppose it was in a desperate attempt to recapture a shred of dignity or autonomy that I quipped, "What did you think I had up there, a flash drive holding cryptocurrency?"

"No talking," the guard said as he handed me my first set of prison clothes and pushed me and my brown bag toward an exit door. "Get dressed and wait for your name to be called."

When my turn came, the bag holding my belongings was searched, inventoried, and stored, my fingerprints and photo were taken, and my Federal Registration Number was printed on an ID card which I was instructed to keep with me at all times. Several of us were placed in another cold, harshly lit holding cell where, once again, we waited to be called.

"Prisoner Carrington!" I heard a guard yell.

"Carrington? What kind of weak-ass name is that?" said a thoroughly tattooed inmate I recognized as one of the detached and stone-faced men on the bus.

I tried to ignore the taunt, looked away, and followed the guard to an interview room.

"Sit," he said.

I faced a panel of prison staff members who briefly introduced themselves as a psychologist, a health service provider, a classification officer, and a unit team member.

After several probing questions obviously geared toward assessing my mental and physical health, the classification officer glanced down at a folder full of forms and took over the meeting.

"It looks like you'll only be with us for ten months—very unusual in a place like this. You might think that's a good thing, but it also marks you as different from most other inmates here, and they'll find out soon enough. It can look like you're getting special treatment, and believe me, you don't want to be seen that way."

I nodded as if I fully understood, and the classification officer continued.

"So for your protection, we're going to classify you as an administrative detention inmate and will place you in the SHU, or Special Housing Unit, a restricted section of the prison away from the general population. But don't get your hopes up. This is not an upgrade. You'll actually face more restrictions than the regular inmates. You'll be assigned a single cellmate, and your time in the yard, library, dining facility, and commissary will be minimal and tightly controlled. To the extent possible, you'll be segregated from the general population."

The officer went on to recite a mind-numbing summary of rules and regulations for the SHU, then issued me a copy of the fifty-eight-page Admission and Orientation handbook, suggesting I read it carefully and soon.

The unit team member spoke up last. "I'll be the UTM you deal with while you're here, and there's one more topic we need to cover before I take you to your cell. You can submit an application for up to three visitors. We'll contact them and let you know within ninety days whether any will be allowed. All visits to SHU inmates are in the noncontact room and are carefully monitored. You'll also get one phone call per week to anyone of your choice."

The UTM handed me a visitor application form, which I completed immediately. Name? *Claire Daniels*. Relationship? I froze for a moment, then wrote *business associate*.

Thirty-Eight

As my UTM walked me down a row of occupied cells in the SHU on the way to my own, he tried to fill me in on other important details, most of which I had to relearn later, because I found it hard to focus on anything but the shouts, taunts, and hoots coming from my new peers. But the one thing that did register was the fact that most of the inmates in the SHU were there not for their *own* protection, as I was, but to protect the general population from *them*. They were there because they were assigned "disciplinary segregation status" as a result of threats or outright attacks against other inmates or staff. Some were in the SHU for short stints, others for their entire terms. I wondered, with much more than academic interest, what status my cellmate would have.

My UTM opened a cell door at the end of a row and made a quick introduction. "Clive, this is Roger. Roger, Clive." He locked the door and left.

As a rock climber and outdoor enthusiast, I considered myself in great physical shape for my age. But Clive, at about the same age, struck me as formidable. That was the word that immediately came to mind as I saw him standing next to the bunks. He and the prison gym were clearly well acquainted. He stood well over six feet tall, was bald, with an eagle tattooed on each side of his white skull—one perched on a branch with something in its beak and the other in flight—and his thick arms, even more heavily inked, were crossed against an expansive chest. Clive wasn't smiling.

"Top bunk's yours. Stow your shit over there," he said, nodding toward the floor at the foot of the lower bed. "I hope to hell you don't snore. Do you?"

"Not that I know of, no."

"Well, now if you do, you'll know. That's how the last guy found out."

I thought it best not to respond and quickly scanned the cell. In one back corner, diagonally from the bunks, was a toilet that looked as old and well-used as the prison itself. Next to that was a very small sink with an aluminum-faced mirror above it—cloudy with years of scratched-in graffiti. It was obviously failing at its only purpose. But the big surprise was a small shower stall in the back corner opposite the toilet.

"We have our own shower?" I couldn't help asking.

"Yeah. Some SHU cells have 'em. How did you rate one?"

"I really don't know."

I wanted to ask how *he* earned it but decided, once again, to censor myself until I knew more about him. I'd been advised not to immediately ask anyone about their crimes, sentences, or inmate status, being told that most people lie about it anyway. Some deny their crimes altogether. Others exaggerate or embellish their stories to help establish a reputation for toughness as part of a survival strategy.

But apparently Clive didn't feel at all bound by such

advice. And as far as I could tell, he felt plenty secure about his own survival.

"So, short-timer, what're you in for?" he asked with eyes squinted, arms still folded against his chest.

I paused for a moment, trying to weigh the pros and cons of answering. I ran out of reasonable pause time without a conclusion. "Insider trading."

The first smile crossed Clive's face as a short laugh escaped his lips and his arms relaxed. "Okay, we gotta fix that right now, or you're gonna be in deep shit around here. You stole a boatload of money from some big-ass company that was screwing over its factory workers. Rumor has it there was a knife involved too, and some corporate bigwig got killed. The murder charge didn't stick, but everyone knew that was just because of a technicality. Evidence tampering or something."

I didn't know what to say and didn't much like the idea of owning that particular fiction, but what came out of my mouth was, "Got it. Thanks."

Clive nodded.

I wondered if my cellmate's easily constructed story had anything to do with his own history, but decided there was nothing to gain and a lot to lose by asking. I was much better off just accepting the gift I was being handed, because it looked like I might have an ally if I was careful. At the same time, I was infused with a disturbing mix of shame at needing a protector at all, and relief that I might have just gained one.

Three weeks into my incarceration, I began to fall into a kind of rhythm, learning more about my surroundings and generally feeling more settled, or perhaps just more resigned to my fate. I had managed to wrangle an extra pack of chocolate chip cookies from the commissary by discovering some common rock-climbing ground with one of the attendants and swapping stories. I gave the cookies to Clive later that day and repeated the favor whenever I could.

A few days later, ten of us were taking advantage of a sunny, dry, but bone-chilling winter morning in the yard. Two of the men were shooting hoops in a serious one-on-one rivalry, while the rest of us jogged around the short peripheral track or lifted weights with Clive under a small shelter at one end of the brown, weedy space. As I scanned the sky directly above, longing for the wide-open Colorado views available only to outsiders, I noticed two guards keeping watch from a window in the building above. They seemed more interested in conversation and coffee-drinking than actually doing their jobs. I wondered how long it would take them to reach the yard if needed, or if they would even recognize a need if they saw one. Or if they cared at all.

I had just counted my seventh lap around the track when a stray basketball bounced my way. I stopped to pick it up and found that the two players, guys I'd heard calling themselves Jack and Marco, were standing ten feet away, each competing for my attention. Jack was a good foot taller than Marco, but Marco looked faster, and he was smiling. Then, as I made a move to pass the ball back between them, Jack shoved Marco aside, yelling, "My ball, little man."

I suppose I identified with the underdog, because at the last second I diverted the pass to Marco, who snagged it and ran back for a quick lay-up. I continued my lap but within seconds found myself tackled to the ground, my face planted in prickly weeds.

"Guess you didn't hear my call, asshole," Jack said, as his

weight pinned me to the frozen ground.

"Oh, I heard you."

I immediately regretted my words. Jack drove a knee into my groin and ground my face further into the weeds against the cold gravelly soil below. The pain was excruciating and most of it had nothing to do with my face.

Just as I braced for more, I saw a shadow on the ground approaching us. A guard, I hoped, once again finding myself psychologically aligning with the prison authorities.

"Jack, you looking for more time in the SHU or just some special attention from me? Get the fuck off him."

The voice was clearly authoritative but didn't come from a guard. Clive yanked my attacker away as if he were nothing more than a light blanket across my back and pushed him toward the basketball court, where his cronies stood staring.

I rolled over, wiped blood from one side of my face, and picked out small pieces of rock. Clive extended a hand and, as much as I wanted to lie still, waiting for the pain between my legs to subside, I took it and pulled myself up.

"Thanks," I said.

"Good lesson. Learn from it and don't make me do that again. Go get cleaned up." Clive put two fingers in his mouth, turned toward the guards above us, and produced the loudest whistle I had ever heard. One looked up, and I thought I saw annoyance in his face as he shook his head and slowly stood to come down.

~

Three months into my incarceration, I had my first and only visitor. In the no-contact visitation room, I watched from behind a thick plexiglass barrier with an unsettling mix of excitement and dread as Claire walked in and sat opposite me. She was dressed conservatively in a black business suit and smiled thinly, the conspiratorial, electric glint in her eyes I had always loved gone.

"Roger," she said.

"Claire."

We sat in uncomfortable silence. I stared down at my hands. Finally, unable to stand the tension, I looked up and spoke.

"I'm sorry, Claire. I am so very sorry."

She nodded.

I wanted more from her, even a single word, but knew I didn't deserve it.

"So . . . How . . . how are you doing?" I tried.

"Oh, you know. Betrayed, angry, deeply disappointed. I guess that about covers it."

It was my turn to nod. "Of course. I get it."

"Do you? Do you really? I trusted you, Roger. The whole company did, and you let us all down. You and I shared almost everything. Everything, that is, except the most important and impactful things you were dealing with. You never really trusted me."

"No, that's not—I wanted to—"

"Stop. Don't even try." That silenced me, and I watched Claire recompose herself before she spoke again. "I came here for one specific reason, and I didn't want to get into all this other stuff, but I guess it was unavoidable."

Unavoidable? This other stuff is the stuff. How can she just dismiss it—dismiss us—like this? Is there still an "us"? Was there ever really an "us," or was this all just a stupid fantasy wrapped in a shared corporate life?

"Okay, what did you come here to tell me?"

"We know who was behind the company's sabotage."

That snapped me back into the moment. "Who?"

"Three guesses."

I imagined the old glint in Claire's eyes, but it wasn't there.

"Stan," I said.

"Yes. Years ago, he blackmailed one of our former employees and got the login credentials he needed. But he didn't have the knowledge to finish the job, so he found a CS grad student who was drowning in student debt and paid him an exorbitant amount of money to do the technical dirty work online from his office at CU. Stan shorted the company's stock right after the deed was done, then just waited patiently for our demise."

"That greedy bastard!" I said, immediately wanting to swallow my obvious hypocrisy.

"Roger, he took his own life yesterday."

"Oh."

"Apparently it wasn't all greed that drove him," Claire continued. "We learned from his wife that he had Parkinson's—the kind that comes with dementia in the later stages. Stan had become convinced his wife would be left deep in medical debt after he died and said as much in a suicide note. It wasn't true, of course, but in his mind it was, and he was desperately trying to avoid it. I guess this had been his main goal for several years."

"Damn. That would explain a lot."

"Yes. A lot."

Stan had done a tremendous amount of damage but with arguably noble motives, however confused and delusional they were. I had done more damage—to my employees, to shareholders, to customers and their patients, to Claire—and with motives that lacked any semblance of nobility.

When Claire got up to leave, I begged her to stay. Could we just talk? Just for a few more minutes? But with a sad smile and a shake of her head, she refused. I missed her last words as she walked away.

Thirty-Nine

My last few months in the SHU passed slowly but with less drama, at least of the physical kind. Credit for that goes mostly to Clive, because after my first incident in the yard, everyone seemed to understand that I was off-limits. I can't say I made any real friends among the other inmates, but we got along, even having short conversations in the yard from time to time. Clive himself remained mostly an enigma. I learned he was serving out the final eighteen months of a ten-year sentence for armed robbery and had been placed in the SHU two years before my arrival for reasons he wouldn't discuss. He never offered more details, and I didn't ask.

When I was within thirty days of release, prison administration began to pay more attention to me, and I started to imagine a bright future beyond bars. If I could survive prison, I told myself, I could do just about anything.

My case manager, a rare female member of the unit staff, put together a release plan and provided reentry counseling. I listened with feigned interest, convinced that I, of all people, had no need for such advice. But at the same time, I didn't want to jeopardize my release by appearing unready or ungrateful. She also offered several post-release services related to employment and housing, and I thanked her politely. Privately, I had absolutely no intention of following through with any of it.

I was a seasoned business executive with a PhD after my name, for God's sake! Sure, I'd made some bad mistakes, but I'd learned from them and paid a heavy price in money, possessions, and time. I wasn't anything like the stereotypical ex-cons who end up as flagmen on road construction projects. I was more than capable of starting over.

My case manager granted me expanded phone privileges during my final two weeks, and I had full confidence that my old West Coast contacts would be more than happy to take my calls and help me find a fast path back to success. They would be far more useful than any post-release federal services could possibly be.

But my renewed confidence—my *hubris*, more accurately—was not to last. Conversations with former business associates in Seattle, San Diego, and the Bay Area ranged from coldly polite to downright hostile, and the best offer I got was a free week in someone's Maui timeshare to "get myself together," no airfare included. In the business and technology community, a murder conviction would probably have earned me more sympathy and assistance than insider trading did. It took about a week and fifteen phone calls for me to go from a state of confidence about my impending release and future life, to surprise, to anger, to resentment, to despair. My story was apparently well known on the outside. I had become a pariah.

~

Vacillating between despair and denial, I narrowed my goal down to release itself. I could concentrate on that and figure out the rest once I was out. The outside world, I assured myself, would still be infinitely better than prison in every conceivable way, and ex-associates be damned, I would find my own path once I had time to focus on it. I would finally be in control again.

But when that time came, I suddenly found myself utterly alone in a hostile world with a pack on my back, a bus ticket, and less than eight hundred dollars to my name. The release process had felt grindingly slow right up to the end, but then it was over in a flash. I had expected to bask in the warmth of freedom on that spring morning, to celebrate reentry to the world as I passed through the gate, but neither the weather nor society cooperated. A furious midspring snowstorm had blanketed the Front Range the night before, and the broad mountain-to-prairie view I had craved for weeks was now nothing more than a blinding sheet of white stretching to the horizon in all directions. My thin cotton jacket over my old shirt provided little protection from the cold as I waited outside the prison fence for the bus that would carry me to the central station in Denver, where I would decide on next steps.

Not long ago, I had expected those steps to be clear. Two or three decent requests for interviews would certainly be on the table, and one of them would determine my next destination. I knew that another CEO position was out of the question, at least for a while, and I'd resigned myself to a lowly Engineering VP role, or maybe even some kind of executive staff position as a temporary stepping stone.

But none of those choices materialized. And at the time, I

had no idea that almost all other options—even ones I would have considered miles beneath me—were off the table as well. I suppose I should be grateful for my level of ignorance at the time, because I don't know what I would have done had I fully understood my situation then.

When I arrived at the Denver Greyhound bus terminal, I bought a razor, found a restroom, and shaved off the beard I had allowed to grow for months. Not finding any cheap scissors for sale and not wanting to spend money on a barber, I left my long, unkempt hair as it was, telling myself that anyone who might judge me for my appearance wasn't worth my time. And in any case, I had come to like it that way. I think it reminded me of my youth and the vast potential I felt then.

I parked myself on a short, uncomfortable bench—one clearly designed to discourage people from sleeping there—and pondered my situation. For obvious reasons, I hadn't included anyone at my former company in Boulder in my recent phone calls, and I still couldn't face the shame of a conversation with Kavi or Jake, and especially not with Claire. But there was one person at DLS who seemed "safe." She had been on my mind a lot during the past few days, even though she was unlikely to be in any position to help. And yet, the urge to call her persisted.

I found one of the few remaining public phones in the bus terminal and made the call.

"Deep Learning Systems. How may I direct your call?"

"Stella Lujan, please."

"May I tell her who's calling?"

"Roger."

"Is there a last name, sir?"

How soon they forget. "Carrington."

"One moment."

"Marketing; this is Stella."

"Hello, Stella."

"Roger. Uh . . . hello. Surprised to get a call from you."

"Yes, I can imagine. I won't take more than a minute of your time, Stella. I know this must seem strange, but I just got out of prison this morning and felt compelled to call you. But before you say anything, I want to tell you how incredibly sorry I am. For everything."

Stella didn't respond right away, and I thought she might have hung up. I wouldn't have blamed her. But then she cleared her throat and spoke again.

"Okay, well, thank you for that. We're moving on here, slowly rebuilding the company, and we'll be okay in the long run. What will you do now?"

"I'm thinking about coming back to Boulder and trying to restart my life there."

"Hmm. Where were you born, Roger?"

"Seattle."

"Then that's where you should go. Seattle holds your past, and it will speak to your future. It's your place."

There was a powerful authority in Stella's voice that shocked me, and I made a feeble attempt to resist it.

"But there's nothing there for me now, Stella. Everything I owned was sold and everyone I knew has either moved away or won't talk to me."

"Still, it's your place. Maybe you have something to offer Seattle, not the other way around."

It took just under thirty-four hours and $230 for Greyhound to get me home.

Forty

Even today I don't fully understand what it was about that conversation with Stella that tipped the scales and put me on the bus to Seattle. Maybe it was simply the fact that there were no obvious alternatives. Or maybe it had more to do with Stella's wisdom about a person's "place" and obligations to that place—foreign concepts to me at the time but perhaps ones that registered somewhere deep in my subconscious.

Whatever the reason, I found myself back in downtown Seattle two days later, walking out of the bus station onto the street with a pack on my back and a thinning wallet in my pocket. I had been away for a few years and the changes in the city were almost as dramatic as my own. There were several new tall buildings and high-end hotels—the kind I would have insisted on booking not long ago—but alongside all the wealth were glaring new signs of poverty. The contrast was alarming. I walked past dirty tents and ignored panhandlers along the streets as I began the long hike north to a suburb where I thought I might find less squalor and a cheaper place to stay while I put a plan together.

Hours later, I settled on the Paradise Inn on Aurora Avenue for $88 a night—a two-star, 1960s-style two-level L-shaped motel with outside stairways; a place I would never have noticed in my previous life, let alone stayed at. Checking in, I was proudly told my room would have cable TV, free Wi-Fi, a microwave oven, and a queen bed. I had to admit, compared to my prison cell, the place was luxurious. But as I dropped onto the bed, exhausted, it hit me that even here my cash would last only three days, maybe four if I was able to feed myself for next to nothing. And, adding insult to injury, the little Wi-Fi password card on my nightstand reminded me that I had no phone, no computer, no way of accessing the internet even though it was free.

It was in this dark frame of mind, and with a kind of irrational rebellion against my painful financial situation, that I got back off the bed, ran a hand through my hair, and took a short walk down the street to a liquor store. I bought a cheap bottle of red wine with no vintage date or varietal description and brought it back to the room, telling myself it would calm my mind, reset my expectations, and help me formulate a realistic plan. I suppose the calming part of that story had a modicum of truth to it, but the rest was pure self-deceptive bullshit.

I found some paper and a pen in the small motel desk, pulled the window curtain closed, and settled into serious planning mode. The wine's screwcap came off easily, and I poured my first paper cupful of the elixir, which I found to be borderline tolerable. The second cup was better, and I told myself that the wine had been a good bargain and simply needed a little time to breathe. Forty minutes later, the third cup was tasting a bit like a fine Bordeaux blend, and I was beginning to feel downright optimistic about my future.

But the page in front of me didn't seem to be filling up with evidence of the outstanding ideas swirling around in my head. In fact, other than a large wine stain in the middle that looked a bit like a Canadian goose, it remained entirely blank, and I laughed out loud, thinking how incredibly funny this was. I realized in that moment, with astonishing clarity and a renewed sense of pride, how exceptionally intelligent and perceptive I was, and how lucky I was to be out of prison, having such a great time back in my hometown, and how I should make immediate plans to go shopping for a new BMW as a reward for everything I'd been through, and how surprisingly masterful the painting of the two-masted schooner on the wall above the bed was.

My paper cup seemed to have developed a leak in the bottom, which neatly explained the hilarious stain on my paper, so I decided that drinking directly from the bottle would be a much better way to finish it off. And I was right. Worked like a champ. No leaks.

I think it was somewhere around 2:30 in the morning that I began to understand two important things. One: the disgusting taste in my mouth was coming from the dirty shag carpet I was inhaling with each breath, and two: I needed to get to the bathroom immediately.

I tried to stand, but the room was spinning. Crawling was going to be my best and only option. The bathroom seemed miles away in the semidarkness, and I wasn't at all sure I'd reach it in time. Along the way, I thought of Stan and cursed myself.

I did finally make it through the bathroom door, but not quite to the toilet. The last few inches defeated me, and I discharged most of my stomach contents right there on the cold linoleum floor. Feeling immediately better, I took a moment to claim credit for not fouling the carpet. Then, after lying motionless for a few minutes, staring at the wine-colored mess—and worse, smelling it—I managed to clean up most of it and hang my head over the porcelain portal before the next round hit me. And the next. And the next. And the next. It was a lovely evening, all in all.

By sometime around seven in the morning, I'd been able to keep some water down and had managed to move from bathroom to bed. Early daylight was starting to leak in around the edges of the window curtain. It burned into my brain, so I buried myself deeper under the covers and fell into a dreamless stupor.

When I awoke, the clock on the nightstand said simply 11:58, with no AM or PM, but a glance toward the thin window curtain told me it was near noon, not midnight. Slowly, I got up and sat on the edge of the bed, rubbed my blurry eyes, and vowed never to touch red wine again. Last night's empty bottle still stood on the little desk beside the paper with the stain which now looked nothing like a goose, Canadian or otherwise, and the bottle begged to be thrown away, as if I could discard the entire wretched night with it. As I rose to do this, I noticed that the paper contained a scrawled note in my handwriting. It said simply: *Generate income by . . .*

Brilliant, if a bit lacking in detail.

After taking a shower and getting dressed, I felt about three-quarters human and tried to distinguish between something that was either resurgent nausea or extreme hunger. Remembering that my last meal had been over thirty-six hours earlier, I decided it had to be hunger and made my way out the door and over to the motel office, where I paid for another night and asked about nearby restaurants.

I was told that the motel had its own restaurant and that a continental breakfast was complementary and available all day. Even though it turned out that the "restaurant" was more like a tiny customer lounge in a discount tire store, I welcomed the coffee with powdered creamer and the prepackaged pastries. Sugar packets for the coffee were all used, but the overwhelming sweetness of the plastic-wrapped bear claws and heavily glazed donuts made them unnecessary anyway. I took full advantage of the free food, such as it was, even tucking two additional pastries into my pack when the only other guest in the room was looking down at his phone. *Was that stealing?* I quickly dismissed the thought. Of course not. My $88 per night would have been calculated to include the cost of a little loss here and there. I had paid for it, fair and square.

"Heading back out into the cruel world?" the other guest said as I got up to leave.

"Yep. Back to work," I said, surprising myself with such a quick and easy lie.

"Ah. What do you do, if you don't mind my asking? My name's Max, by the way." The man held out his hand and I shook it. He appeared to be middle-aged, had brown hair graying around the temples, and was wearing what struck me as a rather ill-fitting dark blue business suit.

"Roger," I said. "Engineering consulting. Software, mostly."

"Excellent. I'm kind of in the consulting game myself, but not anything quite as lucrative as your field."

"Oh?" I said.

"Yeah. Career counseling. Kind of a reverse headhunter, I guess you'd say. I work for the job seekers, not the hiring companies. I get paid a little up front, but most of my fee comes out of my clients' paychecks for a few months after they start work."

I'd worked with traditional headhunters many times when trying to hire people for high-level positions, but never had a need for someone like this. Besides, I didn't have enough money left for any kind of up-front fee and just couldn't admit that. I could find my own work anyway. Still . . .

"Hmm. I might know someone who could use your services," I said. "You gonna be around for a while?"

"Sure. I'll be here for a few more days." Max smiled and handed me a business card. I thanked him and walked out into the parking lot as if heading for my car, not wanting Max to think I didn't have one. *Why should I care what he thinks? Or anyone?* I stole out of the far end of the lot and onto the sidewalk.

I had no destination in mind and was wrestling with the humiliation of searching for work, almost any kind of work, just to replenish the coffers while I found my next real opportunity. I passed a coffee shop with a "Dishwasher Wanted" sign in the window. *Well, not* any *kind of work,* I decided.

Along the next ten or twelve blocks, I saw several similar signs. Some for waitstaff, one for retail sales, others less specific. I passed them all, picking up my pace as if I were running late for an important meeting. Then, a couple of miles into my trek, I noticed a neatly printed sign in a small law office window: "Wanted: Part-time IT Manager."

It was still a far cry from anything I really wanted, but there it was, right in front of me, and it wasn't a full-time commitment, so I'd still be able to pursue other opportunities while staying afloat financially. I walked in.

"Can I help you, sir?" said a smiling young receptionist

from behind a curved desk.

I swallowed hard. "Yes, I'm interested in applying for the IT position?"

The receptionist nodded and glanced at her computer screen. "Let's see here . . . Okay, Mr. Owen is in a client meeting right now but should be finishing up in just a few minutes. Would you care to wait?"

I told her I'd be happy to, and settled into a chair with a copy of *Car and Driver*. But about a half hour later, Mr. Owen had still not appeared, so I looked up at the receptionist with raised eyebrows and caught her attention.

"I'm sorry, Mr.—uh, I'm sorry. I didn't catch your name when you came in."

"Carrington," I said. "Roger."

"I'm sorry, Mr. Carrington, but that meeting is running a bit longer than I expected. Would you like to leave your contact information and check back later?"

But the decision was made for me when someone I imagined to be Mr. Owen appeared in the lobby with his client and ushered him out the front door.

The receptionist turned to her boss. "Bob, this is Roger Carrington. He's here about the IT job."

"Great. I've got about thirty minutes. Come on back and let's have a chat."

I sat across a large mahogany desk from Robert Owen, Attorney at Law, and thanked him for taking the time to see me.

"So let's get right to it, Roger. Tell me about your IT background."

"Well, I hold a PhD in Computer Science and have extensive experience in both large and small corporate environments."

"In their IT departments?"

"No, not exactly. Software development early in my career, then mid- to upper-level management."

"Okay . . . Are you at least Microsoft IT certified?"

I was fighting some serious annoyance and tried hard to hide it. "I was part of Microsoft Research when we began the Azure cloud-based architectural work. That ought to count for something, I would think."

"Right, well, that's very impressive, but unless you can dive right in and manage our local network and client database, I don't think this is a good fit for either of us."

"Really? I disagree. I have a solid grasp on the underlying technology and the rest is just details," I said.

"I'm sorry, Roger, but I don't get why someone with your background would want this kind of job in the first place. I wish you the best of luck." Mr. Owen stood and gestured toward his door. "Why don't you leave your contact information with Cindy at the front desk, and if we hear of anything more in line with your background, we'll give you a call. How's that sound?"

"Sounds condescending," I muttered on my way out, thoroughly burning the bridge behind me.

Forty-One

I had no contact information to give anyway, so at least I'd saved myself the embarrassment of admitting that, or the shame of creating a new lie on the spot. I walked the streets for the next few hours until hunger once again began to gnaw at my gut. It drew me into a McDonald's, where I checked my wallet and decided I could spare a few dollars if this was to be both lunch and dinner for the day. I bought a Quarter Pounder with cheese and filled up my water bottle at the drink dispenser under the watchful gaze of the young manager. He was clearly doing his best to prevent a serious Coke or Dr. Pepper theft on his watch.

The burger tasted better than any recent meal I could remember, and it was gone before I knew it. Refreshed and feeling a bit more hopeful, I continued my search for employment. As I was about to pass a library, it occurred to me that they would have public computers. How could I have been so stupid not to think of that before? But I hadn't been in a public library since before the internet became widely available, so I rationalized away my stupidity and walked in.

A few quick searches yielded several local possibilities, and I decided to pursue one of them in person, if only as a test of my ability to land something. There was a customer service specialist opening in the electronics department of a Target store less than a mile away, so I jotted down the address and headed back out to the street.

As I walked through the doors of Target, I gritted my teeth and reminded myself that lowering my standards was a temporary necessity. It helped to imagine myself as a kind of spy, concealing my high-level identity and my nefarious intentions as I entered foreign territory on an information-gathering mission.

I also imagined that I might be able to speak with an actual person, at least to learn more about the job and obtain an application. But no. I found myself in a room with several kiosks where people a third of my age were filling out online applications. I took the next available kiosk, realizing that I could probably have used the library computer to do the same thing an hour earlier.

I had anticipated the problem with contact information, so I used an address and phone number I remembered from childhood. I could update that information with something else if I got the job. My only real piece of contact information was an ancient Hotmail address I'd used for decades, not that I had any means of accessing it now. I made a mental note to find myself an old phone or tablet for use as a simple Wi-Fi device to check email at public hotspots, as my phone had been a corporate perk and was long gone.

Completing the sections on education and work history was straightforward but tedious. But then came the question I wasn't prepared for: *Have you ever been convicted of a felony?*

I had already provided my Social Security number, which would allow Target to verify my answer via the Federal Bureau of Prisons. So even if I had wanted to try, I knew I couldn't get away with a lie about this. A *Yes* answer took me to a page explaining that Target's hiring policies prohibited them from considering my application further. When I clicked "OK," which was the only option available, I was presented with a cheerful *Thank you for applying for a position at Target. Have a wonderful day.*

When I left the store, the sky was dark and starting to leak heavy drops. I trudged back to the motel in a matching mood.

The rain continued for the next two days, as did my depression. My only options now seemed to be ones that didn't involve actual companies or even individuals who might do background checks. I thought about the federal job assistance programs I'd been offered at the prison and kicked myself for ignoring them. I wondered if I could backtrack on that but immediately rejected the idea, still clinging to shreds of pride.

I even thought about scrounging for handyman jobs but foolishly rejected that idea as well, and for the same reason. As a result, money was getting critically short. I had barely enough for two more nights at the motel and a couple of cheap meals. After that, I'd be out on the street, brought down to the level of the tent people I'd recently passed by in Seattle. That was an intolerable thought, and I drove it deep underground.

By this time, my last remaining cash was beginning to feel like an essential part of my identity, and I decided

I'd rather keep it than spend another night at the motel. A Salvation Army shelter I'd recently passed on the street with disdain was now starting to look like a viable alternative for a few nights, if it meant I could keep my money. At least it wouldn't be like living on the street. Not exactly.

The morning I made that decision, I decided to take advantage of one last visit to the motel's "restaurant" before checking out. I had just settled down with a cup of coffee and pack of miniature powdered sugar donuts when Max came through the door.

"Roger, right?" he said. "Mind if I join you?"

"Be my guest."

"Thanks. I'll just grab a cup and be right back." Max returned with the same fine breakfast selection I was enjoying and sat across the small table from me. He tried to start a conversation about the Seahawks' prospects for the upcoming season, but that went nowhere. Football hadn't been on my mind since I pretended to enjoy the Broncos over a year before. A similar attempt with local politics died quickly.

"Roger, can I level with you about something?" Max asked.

"Sure."

"Look, I don't mean to pry, but I happened to see you out on the street yesterday, and, honestly, it didn't look like a lot of consulting work was happening. Are you okay?"

"Yeah, I'm fine. Just between jobs."

Max leaned in and lowered his voice as if there were others around to hear us. "Really? How long?"

I suppose I was more in need of empathy than I realized, because I opened up immediately, not only about my former professional life but also about my prison time and the problems that was now creating.

"Damn! You were a hi-tech CEO before?"

"Yeah, well, it just is what it is. I used to hate that expression."

"So what's the plan now?" Max asked.

"Honestly? I really don't know. But I've got to move on from this place."

"Short on cash, I'd guess."

"Uh-huh."

Max went silent, staring down at the table, slowly shaking his head. Lost in thought or embarrassed for me, I couldn't tell which.

Finally, he looked up and spoke. "Look, Roger, I get it. I've been there. It hurts like hell to admit it, but I've been there for months. Why else would I—why would either of us—be staying in a place like this, right? At least you've been honest about your situation. Now I guess it's my turn."

"Okay . . ."

"Clients stopped calling about a year ago. Work just dried up."

"Why? What happened?"

"A couple years ago, I placed a guy at a biotech start-up in Bothell. Turns out this guy lied about his background and just couldn't handle the job. He made some decisions that lost the company some serious money. They fired him, then sued me. I lost, and social media did the rest of the damage. End of story, pretty much. Nobody would touch me after that. Until yesterday, that is."

"Oh?"

"Yeah. I guess I've still got a friend or two out there. One of them runs a small contracting company called Software Solutions in Seattle, and he called yesterday. Normally, I don't work for the hiring companies, like I said. But he wanted me to know that if I ran across anyone who was looking, he might have something. I thought of you but figured you were already busy."

"What kind of something?"

"This friend, Jim Mason, owns Software Solutions, and he recently landed a nice software development contract with Amazon. But his project manager disappeared, leaving a real mess behind. He's afraid if Amazon discovers this before he can find a competent new manager, they'll revoke the contract. Frankly, he's desperate. If you can do the job and get his project back under control, I'm almost certain he'd be willing to bring you on board, at least temporarily. I know it would be well below what you're used to, but would you be willing to step in and help out? It could be a real win-win."

I didn't hesitate. What I was thinking was, *Are you frickin' kidding me? Thank you, thank you, thank you!* But what I actually said was, "Sure. I'd be happy to help."

"Excellent! I'll just make a quick call. Can you stick around for a few more minutes? I'll be right back."

Max breezed out the door while punching a number into his phone. He looked back over his shoulder and smiled. Minutes later, he was back with an even bigger smile.

"Jim heard of your great work at Microsoft a few years back and was impressed by your willingness to step in for a while. He also knows about the whole Colorado thing—I guess he read about you in the news—but he's totally happy to ignore all that if you'll fly under the radar and deal with him on a cash basis. So as long as that's okay with you, the job is yours. No interview necessary. I guess fame helps. All we have to do is get downtown this afternoon, and you can start right away."

"I really don't know how to thank you, Max."

"Well, there is the small matter of my fee, but seeing as

how you're kind of in a spot right now, I'm happy to bring it way down. How does five hundred up front sound, with another thousand due after you've been on the job for three months?"

I don't think I'd been so embarrassed or ashamed since being marched out of DLS in handcuffs.

"I . . . I don't have five hundred. I'm sorry."

"Oh, okay. Well, what do you think you could afford?"

"A little less than half that, I'm afraid."

"I can make that work, my friend. I'll pick you up in thirty minutes out front, and we'll get you on your way. Jim's office is near the freeway on Pine."

I went back to the room, took a shower, and dressed as professionally as my limited wardrobe would allow. I checked out of the motel and met Max in the parking lot. He was quiet on the ride downtown, and I spent the time mentally rehearsing how I would introduce myself to Jim Mason, and how I'd request an immediate project status briefing. I was eager to dig in.

When we arrived at our destination, it was still raining and the only parking available on the street outside the building was a loading-zone, so Max suggested we settle up on the fee before he went to park the car in a nearby lot. He would drop me off and then walk back to Jim's office to make introductions and formalize the deal. I told him there was no need to drop me off, and that I'd be happy to walk back with him, but he insisted.

"I wouldn't want you soaked to the skin for the first meeting with your new boss. Besides, I hate to admit it, but I don't have any cash on hand for parking."

I handed over all but five dollars of my remaining money.

"Right there under that green awning," Max said, pointing

to the building entrance. "I'll be back in a few minutes."

I ran through the rain and ducked under the awning, looking for a Software Solutions sign. There was none, so I opened the door, thinking there were probably several businesses in the building and that I'd find a helpful directory pointing me to the right floor. There was a directory, but not a helpful one. Three businesses were listed: an accounting firm, an insurance agency, and a law office.

I stepped back outside and scanned the street, hoping to find another green awning nearby. There was none. The rain had become heavier, and the sound of it nearly drowned out the wet rush of the freeway above the street across from me. A Hispanic-looking man in a yellow poncho stood on the corner with a sign I couldn't read, probably asking for money.

I stepped back under the green awning, waiting for Max to return, still unwilling to admit I'd been scammed. It took me over a half hour to decide he wouldn't, and I had been. The sky was getting dark, I had a wet pack on my back, five dollars in my wallet, and only one viable option.

The freeway overpass across the street promised protection from the rain, so that's where I headed. I made my way past the man on the corner and over to the far side of the overpass, away from an old army tent and a couple of makeshift shelters. There was some heavy equipment stored nearby, along with a large, empty cardboard box. I dragged the box over toward one of the massive concrete pillars supporting the noisy road above and stowed my pack inside. There was just enough room for me as well, and the air was getting colder by the minute, so basic survival instincts overrode my last vestiges of self-esteem. I crawled inside, curled up, and closed a flap against the world.

Forty-Two

Those first hours at the overpass were my darkest, in every imaginable sense of that word. How had I allowed myself to reach such a point? How had I, a seasoned businessperson, fallen for such an obvious scam? I had not understood the depth of my own despair—a depth from which an implausible offer looked like a ray of light filtering down from above. How had I become so gullible, so isolated, so alone?

For longer than a day but something less than two, I left my box only to pee. I suppose I had enough sense left—I don't think it was even pride—to avoid fouling the nest. Eventually, hunger and thirst forced a decision. I would either need to reenter the world or die, and the best choice wasn't obvious.

But after a while, a strange settling came over me. I had reached the bottom and, short of death itself, I couldn't sink any lower. I had found the basement floor and, as hard and cold as it was, it felt like a limit.

It might have been simple hunger and thirst, or the fact

that my cardboard box began collapsing around me as the material picked up moisture from the air. Or perhaps it was the slightest rekindling of self-respect. Whatever it was, I eventually left the box in the darkness of early morning and took my last five dollars to a nearby 7-Eleven. I filled up my water bottle and bought a breakfast sandwich.

Not having anywhere else to go, I took the meal back to the overpass, sat down next to my collapsed shelter, and ate. As predawn light began to glow in the east, the objects around me slowly gained definition: a snowplow, a street sweeper, a small fenced-in area containing what looked like road maintenance materials, and a pile of old wooden shipping pallets outside the fence.

The calories from the sandwich provided much-needed energy, and the wooden pallets gave me an idea. I began to focus on it. There were two other shelters and a tent nearby, but I had yet to see anyone other than the man on the street corner in his yellow poncho. The other shelters were obviously thrown together with little thought—especially the one closest to me. It was more of a lean-to built against a concrete wall, and it seemed that the slightest wind would reduce it to trash. I could do better.

I walked over to the pile of wooden pallets and examined them. Yes, they would do. I searched the ground around the fenced-in area and found a few old, rusted nails. A rock would serve as a primitive hammer. Another discarded box, this one made of double-corrugated cardboard, lay nearby. I gathered everything together and hauled it over to my collapsed shelter.

It took less than three hours to frame a wooden rectangular structure about four feet high, eight feet long, and four feet wide. The new heavy cardboard became siding and a flat roof, and the old cardboard became a floor. The last piece served as my front door, bent into a kind of hinge on one side. I crawled in, stored my pack in a back corner, and let out a long breath. I had done something. I had created a decent shelter, and it needed a name worthy of its luxurious thirty-two square feet. I laughed for the first time in weeks as my shelter became the Residence.

~

Now, many months later, as the Seattle sky slowly begins its morning glow once again, that time seems distant and complete. It's an irrevocable part of me, to be sure, but now only a part, and my need to constantly revisit the past seems to have dissipated with the night.

For the first time in recent memory, I have an actual plan. It's not yet a detailed set of tactics and objectives based on a solid strategy, and my vision ahead is restricted to less than a day or two. It's barely worthy of a single PowerPoint slide, but it *is* a plan, and I take comfort from something I vaguely remember E. L. Doctorow writing—that we only need to see down the road as far as our headlights can shine.

I still don't know if Stairway will ever be more than a pipe dream, as Charlie Duncan once cynically described it, but I take some encouragement from the fact that he personally climbed out on a limb far enough to set up a meeting for me at Anderson, Gibbs, and Larson. That meeting is today at ten and is the only step currently visible in my headlights. But it's a big step.

The new pants and shirt I bought at Goodwill will have their debut today. They both fit reasonably well, and I try to clean up my old shoes to avoid a jarring contrast with the rest of the outfit. It's partly successful. I almost leave the cowboy hat behind but then decide, no, it's part of me now. I'm wearing it.

On my way past Mary's tent, she calls me over.

"Hey, looking good!"

"Thanks. I'm meeting with the nonprofit lawyer this morning and thought I'd better make an effort."

"Oh, right. I forgot that was today. I was going to ask if you'd go with me to break Jimmy out of Harborview this morning, but I guess that's not in the cards."

"Actually, you know what? The law office is up on First Hill, not far from the hospital, so if we leave now, I could go in with you to get him, then hit the meeting right after that. Do you think you'd have any trouble getting him home by yourself?"

"Nah, I can handle it. He trusts me."

When we arrive at the hospital, we conquer the pile of paperwork by dividing it up between us, and then a nurse takes us to a small room where Jimmy is waiting.

I see a difference in our friend right away. His eyes are clearer, more attentive, less anxious, and his long blond hair has obviously been washed. In his muted smile, I see both apology and gratitude.

"Thanks, guys. Thanks for coming for me."

"It's what friends do, right?" Mary says. "Couldn't just leave you here to rot. Well, we could've, but—"

"You're looking good, Jimmy," I interrupt, amused at Mary's style but also thinking Jimmy might not see the humor. "How're you feeling?"

"Different, I guess. Better. Sorry for everything."

"No problem, buddy," I say. "Feel ready to go home?"

"Yeah, mostly."

"Mostly?" the nurse asks, eyebrows raised.

"No, I'm ready," Jimmy tells her. "It's just that I don't know what I'll do now. I don't want to end up back how I was." He turns back to me. "You know what I mean?"

"Yeah, I know, Jimmy. Believe me, I do. But here's the thing: Mary, Carlos, and I need your help. We have an idea that might be good for all of us, but we can't make it work without someone who can manage our computer system, build us a website, get us onto social media, and basically handle all things digital. That could be you. We want it to be you. What do you say?"

Jimmy looks from me to Mary and back again. "Really?"

"Really. We can't do this without you. But you need to stay on your meds, for your own sake and for ours."

"Okay, yeah, I can do that."

"Good. That's great."

The nurse steps forward with the last piece of paper for Jimmy and us to sign. She hands Mary the clipboard and turns to Jimmy. "Sounds like you just got yourself a job. So please, don't just listen to me when I say you must take one of these pills each morning. Listen to your friends here, too. I think they really need you to be on your game. Can you do this?"

"I can do this," Jimmy says. He puts on his old Sonics ball cap and a new smile.

"There's one last important thing," the nurse says. "To really benefit from this medication, you're also going to need regular psychotherapy for a while. We've referred you to a practice in Seattle called Life Balance, which has had outstanding results in cases like yours using assistive AI technology. Can you commit to two visits a week for at least the next six weeks?"

I recognize the name of the practice immediately, as it

was one of the DLS customers that made the tough choice to stay with the company during its downturn. As Jimmy nods his assent, I jump in to reinforce his decision.

"That's great. Mary and I will help you get to those appointments."

During my time as CEO, I'd only visited the largest or most strategically valuable customers, and Life Balance had not been one of those. But now this customer feels critical for a completely different reason. For the briefest moment I imagine introducing myself in an effort to ensure the best possible care for Jimmy. But the moment passes quickly as I realize that my presence would be confusing at best, and a serious liability at worst. I'll need to remain on the sidelines as Jimmy's caregiver and nothing more. But that is enough.

~

The offices of Anderson, Gibbs, and Larson are less than a half mile from Harborview, and I arrive a few minutes early, remove my hat, and introduce myself to the receptionist, who offers coffee and promises that Ms. Griffith will be with me shortly. I've been in many law offices during my career, and from what I can see beyond the reception area, this one looks typical of a mid-tier firm serving an urban clientele: black metal-framed windows everywhere, desks and bookcases of an auburn-colored hardwood, black and chrome chairs, and modern offices behind floor-to-ceiling glass along a large open area of tastefully separated desk clusters housing paralegals and other staff. It looks like they can afford a little pro bono work.

In walks a tall, slim Black woman with a sincere smile. She's wearing a long red dress with a muted green floral print reminding me of the Caribbean. She offers a hand.

"Roger, great to meet you. I'm Paula Griffith."

"My pleasure, Paula. Thanks for agreeing to meet with me this morning. I really appreciate you taking the time."

"Glad to do it. So Charlie tells me you have grand plans for a nonprofit organization aiming to assist Seattle's homeless?"

"Well, I don't know about grand, but yes, that's the gist of it."

"Excellent. Come on back to my office and let's see what we can do about that. I see Clarice has you all set with coffee."

Paula leads me to one of the glass-enclosed offices and ushers me inside.

"Please, have a seat and tell me about your hopes for this organization."

I settle into a comfortable leather guest chair across from Paula's desk while she opens her laptop and looks up expectantly.

"It'll be called 'Stairway,'" I say, "and its mission will be to help homeless people like me climb up and out of poverty and despair, back into meaningful lives."

"That sounds commendable. It isn't really my job to evaluate the business itself, but I'm curious. This is a very general concept, one that's at the core of many different organizations, both governmental and private. So how would Stairway be any different?"

I describe how Stairway will develop highly personalized plans for each client, leveraging other agencies and organizations whenever possible to form the steps of a custom stairway, then monitoring and managing individual progress. I stress the credibility advantage of homeless working with homeless, of one-on-one attention. Stairway will not be a broad outreach program, I tell her. Instead, it will be a narrowly focused program designed to reach a relatively small number of people, but with the central goal of permanent change, not just temporary assistance.

"Okay, now I'm getting it," Paula says. "Sounds exciting. So let's talk about the legal process of setting up your company and applying for 501(c)(3) tax-exempt status."

Over the next half hour, Paula gives me a detailed description of the process she will follow to make all this happen, at what points along the way she'll need my participation, and how her firm will absorb all the cost.

"I can't tell you how grateful I am for your work on this, Paula," I say while shaking her hand at the end of our meeting. "If Stairway succeeds, you will have made a significant contribution. Thank you."

Paula nods as I don my cowboy hat and turn to leave.

"Nice hat," she says.

"Thanks. It belonged to someone on the street, a friend I couldn't help. Now it reminds me to do better."

~

During the next few weeks, I split my time between coordinating with Paula, talking with people on the street, getting Jimmy to therapy appointments, and performing my usual food foraging duties. Writing grant proposals is no fun, but I crank out twelve of them after registering for a Unique Entity ID with the federal government. I also reach out to local foundations. The bureaucracy is soul-crushing, but I try to think of it as a rock-climbing problem, always looking for the next handhold, making one move after another with the summit in mind.

Spending time on the streets with my fellow homeless

people is much more interesting and illuminating. It forces me to admit that I've been avoiding these folks, other than my own local clan, even though I've been part of their world for a while now. After learning names and sharing short versions of our own stories, Mary and I ask people questions like "What do you need most right now? Have you gotten any help from local agencies, and how is that working for you? Before life on the street, what were the things that got you out of bed each morning and made life worth living?"

The unhoused are surprisingly open with us, probably because we're so obviously part of their world. Each day I add to a log on my computer, noting everything significant that people tell us, refining my vision for Stairway, and working with Mary to develop a list of potential clients. Sadly, some of the people we meet are barely functional—physically, mentally, or both—and I fear they'll share Tex's fate before long. Some have fallen into deep addictions. A few seem oddly content with their lives on the street. But many have at least some motivation to move up Maslow's levels, and a few even have plans.

I'm beginning to understand more about our ongoing battle between social gravity and hope. Once we sink to a low enough level, the downward gravitational pull becomes exponentially stronger. It drags us down toward the basement. Hope, glimpses of the possible, can resist that pull and even reverse its direction. But that hope must be based on specifics, not just vague wishes. Stairway's main goal for each client must be to provide that kind of tangible, individualized hope. And we can't stop there. We must help each client turn those glimpses of the possible into a discovery of purpose, personal plans, and then action leading to jobs and housing.

Mary, Carlos, and I visit all the local food banks, shelters, and free clinics, the Y, and other relevant organizations, and Jimmy creates a database incorporating everything we learn. I ask myself why we—and many others around us—haven't taken more advantage of these resources before. I suppose we each have our own reasons. Mine have something to do with resisting dependence—needing to be the driver, not the passenger. But I think a common factor is the basement itself. There's nothing left to lose down there, and there's a perverse kind of safety in that. Trying to emerge and failing each time feels like dark hell. Eventually, the basement just seems safer, and gravity wins the battle.

But for now, my little team and I are fortunate. We've found a purpose, and we're finally looking down at the basement from a step or two above.

Forty-Three

Nearly two months have passed since we started in earnest, and Stairway is now an official nonprofit organization. We've refined our vision, we've got detailed plans, and we're almost ready to begin operation. But there's one big problem: we still have no money.

This weighs on me as I trek back to the overpass tonight, knowing it would be pointless trying to assist clients with transportation, food, and other practical necessities without funding as we help them navigate local resources. We could limp along, providing some basic services, but any tangible follow-up support would be impossible. Many small businesses fall prey to under-capitalization, and I'm painfully aware that Stairway could easily become one of them.

Our first rent payment is due in a week, and I've reassured Denise several times that we'll be handing her a check on the first of the month, but we're no closer to fulfilling that promise now than when I first signed the rental agreement. This is more than just a business obligation, because I know the bookstore is struggling, and Denise with it.

As I'm about to pass an enclosed bus stop, I notice a copy of *The Seattle Times* abandoned on the bench and pause to pick it up. A front-page article grabs my attention: *Mayor to Order Encampment Closures.* I stop to scan the article and continue to an inside page, where the writer describes the usual problem of clearing public spaces while providing few new resources for the displaced people. I understand the tension between local business owners and homeless advocates, but the so-called solutions always seem to address only one side or the other, as if this were a game to be won or lost by a competitor instead of a systemic problem to be addressed holistically. But the article continues with a description of a new organization called the King County Regional Homelessness Authority (KCRHA), which has plans to address the problem more systemically.

Then, just as I'm making a mental note to pay a visit to the KCRHA, my eye is drawn to a map on the third page of the article, where color-coded dots identify the specific camps to be cleared in thirty, sixty, and ninety days. Ours has a red dot: thirty days.

Great. The timing couldn't be much worse.

Mary, Carlos, and Jimmy are gathered under Mary's awning when I return under the darkening sky. Red tags attached to each of our dwellings have already spread the bad news.

"I know," I say as Jimmy points to the tag on Mary's tent. "I just read an article in the *Times.*"

"We're in deep shit," Mary observes.

I nod. "Feels a little deep, yeah. But if any funding comes through in the next few days, we might have a way out. I might be able to convince Denise to let us all stay in the office for a while even though it wouldn't be strictly legal. But I can't even think about asking her without paying our rent."

"Viejo, we all know you're not great with money," Carlos says. "I'm not sayin' you're not tryin'. No, you're tryin' real hard, and we all appreciate that. I even think we're gonna be okay down the line. But right now, Mary's nailed it. We've got what my business school called a cash flow problem."

I have to smile. Carlos is right, of course. It's the worst kind of cash flow problem, where there's a near-zero bank balance, large outstanding obligations, and no revenue in sight.

"Exactly, smart-ass. Got any constructive ideas?"

"Well, yeah, actually. I'm gonna invest in our future, just like my sign says." All eyes turn to Carlos. He's smiling broadly.

"You don't think I've been handing over all my street corner money to you fools, do you? I've been savin' up."

We're all silent, and it looks like Carlos is enjoying his moment. He continues. "So if Denise'll take lots of small bills, we've got the first month's rent covered. And there's more if we need it."

I'm stunned. "I, uh . . . I don't know what to say. That's amazing. That's fantastic!"

"De nada."

"It's not nada, Carlos. Stairway could easily have been dead in the water, and all of us with it. You just saved our collective asses!"

"To our collective asses!" Mary shouts, raising her coffee cup.

"Our asses!" Jimmy adds with a smile I'm seeing a lot more often now.

Forty-Four

The next morning, I emerge to sunshine and find my seagull in his puddle, looking to me for breakfast.

"Hey, Maslow. Looks like you're gonna have this place all to yourself soon. Not really what you were hoping to hear, is it?"

The bird ruffles his feathers, raises his beak to the overpass, and emits three piercing gull cries.

"Right. I didn't think so. But it might actually be good news for us humans. We don't operate as well down here. Gonna miss you, though."

I duck back into the Residence and return with a large pizza crust that I toss toward the gull. It nearly hits him, and he flaps upward before diving back down to snag it and fly away.

I finish getting ready for the day and meet the others at Mary's tent. Everyone seems eager to make the hike down to the office, but I want a word with them first.

"This morning is a big deal. Thanks to Carlos, we're going

to make our first rent payment, and it'll even be a couple of days early. But this is an office we're talking about, not a home. So we're going to have to ask Denise to bend the rules a little, and she might not agree. I wouldn't blame her. So we need to reassure her of two things: first, that this is temporary, and second, that we'll pick up everything each day and keep the place spotless. We need to make it look and function like an office during the day, every day, without exception. And we need to keep the bathroom cleaner than clean. Everybody on board with all this?"

There are enthusiastic nods all around, and we begin our trek to Pioneer Square. An hour later, I unlock the alley door, and we start our workday. I check voicemail and email first, looking for any hope of funding but finding only another rejection.

Jimmy discovers an old portable disk drive in one of the desk drawers and sets it up as a backup drive before upgrading the operating system. Mary stays with him and begins planning the living space while Carlos and I go next door to speak with Denise.

"Good morning, guys," she says. "Coffee?"

We both return the greeting and accept steaming cups of black morning salvation.

"Great news," I say, and look toward Carlos who counts out eight hundred dollars in twenties, tens, fives, and ones. Mostly ones. I can feel his pride as he carefully lays the bills down one by one on the counter in front of Denise.

"Carlos is our angel investor," I explain. "He stepped up to fill the gap from his personal savings while our main funding is still pending."

"Well, thank you, Carlos. I'm very impressed. I have to admit, I wasn't sure you'd all come through. I knew you'd try your best, but I just wasn't sure how you'd pull it off, and never guessed it would be this way."

Denise reaches across the counter to shake Carlos's hand and then gestures toward yesterday's *Seattle Times* laid out on a nearby table. "Did you guys see this? Does it affect you?"

I move to the table and point to our little red dot on the article's map. "Yep, that's us right there. Thirty days."

"I was afraid of that," Denise says. "What will you do now?"

"Well, I was kind of hoping that maybe . . ."

I look up to see Denise smiling, seeming to enjoy my discomfort.

"Just messing with you," she says. "Of course you can stay here until you get things sorted out."

"Thank you, Denise. That means the world to all of us. The place will be strictly an office during the daytime. Anyone who comes in will see it exactly that way. And of course we'll take charge of bathroom cleaning and anything else you might need."

"There *is* one thing," Denise says. "I'm trying to be better at the business part of life, so I'm sorry, but I'll need another fifty dollars a month to help cover extra water and electricity."

"You got it!" Carlos counts out another fifty before I can respond, not that I would have objected.

We bring two more coffees back to the office with us and join the others. After Jimmy finishes the system upgrade, Carlos puts together a spreadsheet to track our finances and then walks back to his corner at the overpass to replenish our capital base. Mary and Jimmy make a run to Home Team Pizza while I make calls to local foundations and track the status of our grant applications.

~

Back at the overpass for our last night, we gather at Mary's tent for dinner and a short meeting where we decide how to move our meager belongings in the morning. Mary finishes reading *The Pearl* to us, and I wish she had chosen a different Steinbeck story this week. The ending is incredibly sad, but maybe it's a useful cautionary tale for us. If all goes as planned, we'll be responsible for managing some serious money in the next few weeks and months—our pearl. Will we be able to resist its pull on our personal lives and deploy it responsibly, taking only what we need to live and using the bulk of it to help our clients climb up and out of the basement with us? My own track record is less than stellar, to put the best possible spin on it. Sometimes I trust my partners more than I do myself.

The next morning is bittersweet, and the bitter part is much more pronounced than I expected. As small, primitive, and uncomfortable as the Residence is, it has been my home long enough to become a part of me. I'm attached to this place in ways I couldn't have imagined a year ago. I've been houseless, yes, but not entirely homeless. The Residence offered basic privacy, community, and, not least, free rent. Now I'm about to join my partners in a more intimate form of one-room communal living, with the added stress of monthly rent, and I'm not at all sure I'm ready for either. Still, the hope of Stairway drives me forward.

Forty-Five

Three weeks later I'm alone in the office on a Monday morning, scrolling through emails, when the phone rings. It takes me a second to recognize the ringtone for what it is, because incoming calls are almost nonexistent here. I reach for the handset, hopeful that a funding agency might be looking for more information or might even have some good news.

"Stairway, Roger Carrington."

"Good morning, Mr. Carrington. This is Pamela Dixon, counsel for the King County Regional Homelessness Authority. How are you this morning?"

A lawyer? Damn. Not usually how good news is delivered. "Great. How can I help you?"

"I'll get right to the point, Mr. Carrington. We were contacted last week by the State of Washington regarding a grant proposal they received from you, and they reached out to us because the charter for your nonprofit so closely parallels ours. Naturally, they were concerned about needless duplication of effort and funding, so they asked our director for comment. He found the parallels encouraging and didn't want to see your efforts go to waste just because your plans and ours are so similar, so he wanted to explore some form of joint effort. That's when he asked me to do a bit of background checking."

I can't speak.

"Mr. Carrington, are you still there?"

"Yes, I'm here. Go ahead."

"I'm sorry, but your criminal record makes it impossible for us to consider bringing you on board."

"Impossible? Really? I've paid my debt, both to society and to my creditors. And Stairway is my best attempt to do more. That should be obvious."

"I'm not here to judge that, or you, Mr. Carrington. KCRHA simply can't afford the optics. Not while we're just starting up ourselves."

"Are you kidding? Screw the optics! This is a chance for your agency to tell a success story—a redemption tale about the rise, fall, and crawl-back of an unethical corporate executive who had no clue about homelessness but was brought face-to-face with it and is now working to defeat it. KCRHA could own that story, or at the very least, not stand in the way of it."

"I'm sorry. We just can't do that. There's a lot of financial tension between us and the County Council right now, and we can't risk making that worse. I also have a duty to report my findings to the state. Still, I wish you the best going forward."

"Wait. What about my three employees? They have no connection with my past, and they're working just as hard as I am to make Stairway a reality. Your website makes a big freakin' point about homeless helping homeless!"

"I'll mention that to the director."

I hang up the phone and stare at my computer screen as if its cold, algorithmic soul could provide the answers I need. As if it could change my situation as easily as it flips a bit from zero to one. As if it could at least offer a little digital empathy. But no.

I feel like an inmate in a debtor's prison. Another catch-22, another resource deadlock. Can't do something good because I did something bad. Can't leave captivity to do what it takes to get out. Shit!

The door from the alley opens, and Carlos walks in. I'm glad he wasn't here minutes earlier.

"Hey, viejo! How's it goin' this morning? Any news?"

"No, same old stuff," I lie. "More requests for information. No results yet. But we'll get there."

"Okay, if you say so. What's the plan today?"

"When they get here, Jimmy will be on website structure and Mary on content. I'll review it all. Could you set up a small petty cash account so we can easily pay little office expenses and reflect them in your spreadsheet? And then, I hate to ask, but we're getting close to the end of the month and rent will be due next week. Would you mind working your corner extra late this afternoon? I've got some work to do with a couple of funding agencies, and then I'll make a trip down to Home Team Pizza to pick up dinner."

"You got it."

~

There've been many times in the last few months when I wished I could sit down with Claire and hash through problems and opportunities, but today I'm feeling this with more intensity than ever. Until my phone conversation with the KCRHA attorney a few minutes ago, I knew exactly what to do next, and mostly how to do it. My headlights illuminated the road ahead enough to see the next turn. The opportunities were clearly visible. And the problems? Sure, there were lots of them, but they were just potholes in the road. They were tractable, solvable, sometimes even fun to tackle. Now they feel like concrete roadblocks. Not only is any opportunity to work with KCRHA gone but it seems they'll be actively turning other funding agencies against us, poisoning the well. This must be something like Jimmy felt when lost in one of his wild conspiracy theories.

I imagine Claire walking into my office, iPad in hand, a bright smile on her face, maybe even that sexy conspiratorial glint in her eye, and I consider picking up the phone to call her. Right now. To ask for forgiveness. To tell her all about my vision for Stairway. To hear her say what a positive, redemptive thing it could be. To welcome her advice and maybe even begin to heal our wounds.

But then the memory of our last encounter at the prison attacks me. That was the final reality. Her disappointment, her anger, my shame. I can't go through that again, and I'm sure she wouldn't want it either. So I force myself to put any thought of contact aside.

Instead, I revert to imagination. What would Claire say to me, what insights would she offer if I hadn't destroyed our relationship and she were here with me now? My mind goes blank, and I think I've lost even the ability to imagine a conversation with her. No, I've lost the privilege of doing that. I don't deserve it.

But now, what's this? An imaginary conversation between Claire and Mary forms in my head, and it feels almost like I'm eavesdropping. It begins with Mary answering some unheard question.

"I know, right? A real shithead. He's told me a little about it, but you know what? I think he loved you. He never said that exactly, but it's obvious from the way he talks about you."

"He had a strange way of showing it, then," Claire says. "I think it was always about him. Not me, not even the company. He even told me that directly once, and I remember his exact words: 'I'm not some perfect, altruistic angel. This is my ticket to a decent retirement.' At the time I thought that was just a moment of honest, shared reflection—a small part of his reality. Now I think it was nearly all of it."

"Maybe, yeah. But you should see what he's trying to do now. I think he's changed. Or at least chang*ing*."

"Hmm, I'd be careful if I were you. Have you ever been betrayed?" Claire asks.

"Actually, yeah, I have. Not by Roger, though."

"So you know what that feels like. It's not something you just get over."

"No, it's not. But I'm worried about Roger right now."

"Sorry, I know this sounds horrible, but why should I care?"

"I don't know. Maybe because you loved him too?"

"I admired him, I'll give you that. Okay, all right, it was more than that. I admit it."

"Then . . . can I just tell you something?" Mary asks.

"Sure, I guess."

"He's homeless. You know that, right?"

"I'd heard."

"But he's also started a nonprofit called Stairway to help other people get off the street and back to real life. Did you know that?"

"No. But I have to ask, what's in it for him? There's got

to be something."

"Okay, I get that you're still pissed at him. I do. I get that. But come on, Claire! Have you ever had to beg for food? Do you know what it's like to have somebody spit out their car window at you? Have you ever been so cold you couldn't sleep for nights on end? Have you ever had to ask for free tampons at a homeless shelter, from a man? I've known all this, and Roger has too—minus the tampons, I guess. The only thing he's hoping to get out of Stairway for himself is some purpose in life, the satisfaction of helping some of the rest of us, and maybe enough money to rent a shitty little studio apartment someday. So give him a fucking break!"

"Okay, okay. I'm sorry. I can see why you're worried about him."

"Yeah, but that's not even the worst of it. It's the depression. I don't think I've seen him quite like this before. He was almost ready to land some funding for Stairway, and now it looks like that won't ever happen because none of the agencies want to donate money to an organization run by a convicted felon. They could do it, but they just don't have the balls. Roger had everything lined up, including jobs for me and two others, and now it looks like all his work's been for shit."

"That's got to be frustrating. But what could I possibly do about it?"

"I don't know. I *do* know one of the things he loved about you was your knack for helping him find his way around tough problems, being honest with him. If he could brainstorm with you now, I think that would be it."

"I can't do that, Mary. I'm sorry, but I just can't. But one thought occurs to me. Something I'd probably tell him, if I could. Maybe you could pass it along to him?"

"Sure. What is it?"

"Well, this might sound a little harsh, but I think it's probably the only way forward. He left DLS—was fired, actually—because he put himself ahead of everyone and everything else. Now I think his best chance of saving Stairway is to leave it too, but this time by putting himself last."

"What the hell are you talking about? I don't get it."

"It sounds like he's got everything started and now, ironically, the only impediment to success is him. If he's as dedicated to this as you say, he should just step aside and let it all happen without him."

"Wow. Okay. But what would he do then?"

"I don't know. Take a vacation?"

"Don't be such an ass."

Forty-Six

I have to smile despite the pain. My imaginary Claire is right, as usual. And, luckily, I'm still smiling as Mary and Jimmy walk in the door after scrounging for breakfast. They can't know my plan, not yet, because it would spook them. But they need to be part of it anyway. And I need to hide my anxiety and do a little acting. I pull myself together.

"Hi, you guys. Change of plans. It's résumé day. We all need to get ourselves prepared for working with the money people. And that means making ourselves look great on paper."

"You mean lying?" Mary says with a smirk.

"No, just emphasizing the good stuff and not boring anyone with the rest. Not denying it. Just not dwelling on it. That means describing accomplishments—we've all got some—and ending with aspirations and goals. For example, Mary, how would you feel about going back to school part-time? Getting that psych degree."

"Yeah, sure, but I can't see that ever happening."

"Put it down on paper. That's often the beginning of

reality. There are scholarships, you know. And Jimmy, you've got some valuable skills right now. I'll help you describe those and explore where you could go from here. Same with Carlos when he gets back. We need to convince these funding agencies that we're examples other homeless folks can follow—that we can be most effective, not just because of our skills and ambitions but also because we're living lives just like theirs right now. We're not privileged people swooping down from on high to rescue them, making ourselves feel better and getting tax deductions. We *are* them."

"Okay, so how do we start?" Jimmy asks.

I ask each of them to jot down some notes about their past. Things they've done. Jobs they've had. Education, timeframes, goals for the future. I tell them I'll edit their work and help them put it into traditional résumé format. I warn them not to take my edits personally, that I'm going to be tough. Then I tell them I'll work on my résumé too, right alongside them. I don't tell them no one will ever see mine.

~

The next two days are a blur: résumés written, edited, and emailed to KCRHA along with an extensive description of the Stairway vision. I worry that my friends might not be able to manage a nonprofit strictly on their own, but I do think they could thrive within KCRHA, or even separately with active help and direction from the agency.

I've spent some extra time coaching Carlos, seeing him as the group's natural leader, but I haven't told him or anyone else that I'm the reason we can't be funded. I haven't told them I'm leaving because I don't know how to do that. Because it depresses the hell out of me, because I'm afraid I'll demoralize them, because it feels like another failure. I can think of a hundred more reasons to just slip out the door in the dead of night and let them succeed or fail on their own. Maybe my sudden departure would actually energize them, force them to follow through more urgently in my absence. I could see Carlos doing that. Mary, I don't know. Maybe. Jimmy? He might interpret my departure as some new government plot, sending him down another rathole. But maybe not, now that he's back on meds and has some new hope. Shit, I don't know what to do.

Thankfully, an opportunity for distraction pops into my head, and in a very un-CEO-like move, I lunge at it. It's Wednesday morning, and Charlie will probably be at Starbucks soon. I owe him another coffee, and the balance on my card is getting low. What if I'm tempted to spend it before I see him again? The situation is clearly urgent. What could possibly be more important? I grab my pack and head out the door.

I arrive, winded from jogging the last couple of blocks, just in time to find Charlie ordering a drink. I rush to the head of the line, probably annoying the hell out of everyone waiting, and toss my card down on the counter in front of him.

"This'll cover his, and could you add a double tall mocha onto that, please?" I say to the barista.

We carry our coffees to the back of the room and claim one of the few empty tables.

"So you look like shit this morning. What's up?"

"Thanks for the boost, Charlie. Just what I needed. And you're welcome for the coffee."

That earns me a smile, but Charlie's question still hangs in the air, so I attempt an answer. "What's up, you ask? Oh, not much. Just a major existential crisis, I guess. Nothing that a little suicide wouldn't fix."

"Not that funny, man. Seriously, what's going on?"

"Attorney–client privilege?"

"Sure."

I spill the whole situation—the KCRHA rejection, the résumé writing, my decision to leave the area, waffling about telling my Stairway friends, concerns about their futures.

When I finish, Charlie is silent, staring out the window beside our table, squinting. I can't tell if he's focused on something at the market across the street, if he's thinking about my situation, or just pondering something else altogether. I'm not sure he even heard much of what I said.

"Well?" I ask.

"Right, uh . . . What were you saying just now?"

"Shit, man! Really?"

"Hey, easy. I'm just yankin' your chain. I heard you."

"Okay, okay. So?"

"So the one thing I *didn't* hear was anything specific about *your* personal future. That tells me you actually *are* suicidal, or you think you're about to do something frickin' noble. Which is it?"

"It's not the former and I can't claim the latter."

Charlie nods and runs a finger around the rim of his coffee cup. "Okay. You wanna know what I think?"

"I'm not sure I do."

Charlie ignores my response and plows ahead. "Basically, you're screwed every which way from Sunday. If you just pick up and leave without telling your merry little band, thinking it's some kind of noble move on your part, it might feel like freedom at first, but then you'll spend your last miserable years on some other street beating yourself up about it.

Because they'll fail, almost guaranteed. But if you stay and try to remain the face of Stairway, that's not gonna work either. If there's one thing those funding agencies are allergic to, it's financial white-collar crime. You're poison as long as you hang around."

"Excellent. I'm encouraged."

"Hey, life's a bitch sometimes. But there's a third option: Getting the hell out of here and putting as much distance as possible between you and Stairway is probably the right thing to do. But at the same time, if you want your people to have a chance at success, you've gotta suck it up and level with them first. Tell them flat-out you're poison and that's why you need to go. Rip the damn bandage off and admit you're the problem. Then, before you go, give them what they need to have a shot at success. They need more than just nice résumés floating around out there. First, they need a new leader, and from what you've told me, Carlos might be it. They also need an advocate somewhere that matters, probably inside KCRHA. The higher up, the better. I might be able to help with that. Then they need a solid plan for how to proceed without you, and a plan B in case that doesn't work, and maybe even a C. Contingencies, man! When you finally go, they need to feel like they're equipped and in charge. Work yourself out of a job. Hell, you've been a CEO—you should know this shit!"

I feel like a kid getting a lecture from the principal about some basic social skill everyone learned in kindergarten that I'd somehow forgotten, or shamefully decided to ignore. Of course I know this shit! I guess I'm just looking for a less painful exit strategy, trying to convince myself I've already done enough.

Forty-Seven

Exit strategies are not my strong suit. Obviously. So now I'm faced with something my former self would have euphemistically called a "growth opportunity." It's just that I'm not at all sure I have any reason to grow. Or any motivation. I mean, really, what's next? I'm tired of being shut down at every turn, especially when I've been trying to do something most people would consider positive. It feels like some cosmic force is punishing me for past sins despite my recent attempts at atonement. It feels cruel. But I know it's just a simple case of self-inflicted natural consequences. That doesn't make it any easier, though. Just less mysterious.

If it was just me, I'd get out of town today and write the whole damn thing off. But it isn't just me. If I've learned anything in the past couple of years, it's that I'm not the center of the universe. Who knew? Certainly not me.

So today I'm sucking it up, hiding all my own crap, and meeting with Denise and the whole team. I begin by trying to put Charlie's advice into practice.

"I've got some bad news. I've told you all about my nefarious past. Well, it seems my criminal record has come back around to bite us. I got a call this morning from an attorney for KCRHA who told me that they and other agencies won't touch us because of my record. I've basically poisoned our well, and I'm more than sorry."

Looking around the room, I see stunned faces. No one speaks for what feels like minutes but is probably only seconds. Finally, Carlos breaks the silence.

"Viejo, we've all made mistakes. Okay, maybe yours was a little bigger and badder than most, but these assholes don't know you. *We* do, though. Right, everybody?"

I see nodding heads, then Carlos continues. "So we'll just do this on our own. We don't need their damn money. I can bring in enough to keep us going while we figure out what to do next. And Roger's got the food and general management covered."

"Definitely," Mary says. "We can do this."

"Sure," Jimmy adds.

"The bookstore had a surprisingly good month," Denise says. "I can probably reduce the rent for a while. I want to. I really do."

"Thanks for all the votes of confidence," I say. "But I've got to ask, if you had to do Stairway without me, would you still want to continue? Honestly, now. I really need you to think about that."

"What do you mean, without you?" Mary asks. "Stairway kind of *is* you. You'd still be here, right?"

"Well, that's item number two on the agenda. I think it's amazing that you all want to see Stairway succeed, but the reality is that it's not likely to happen without active cooperation, if not money, from KCRHA and some of the other organizations around here. I mean, that's how we all envisioned this thing, right? Custom individualized counseling leading to connections with the other agencies who can provide the right kind of services for each person? But as long as I'm involved, those agencies aren't going to partner with us, let alone fund us."

I'm surprised to see Mary blink back a tear. "So . . . what are you talking about here?"

"I'm talking about leaving Seattle."

More stunned silence, but this time I jump in to fill it. "Look, the fact is I've become a liability. We can either make Stairway work without me, or we can go back to life on the street with no purpose other than survival. And we all know how bad it's getting downtown."

"You keep saying 'we,'" Jimmy says.

"Right, because I'm not going anywhere right away. I'll work with you as long as it takes to put together a solid, detailed plan, and then we'll present it to KCRHA after telling them I'm leaving. I'll take responsibility for my past and fall on my own sword. They only need to know two things about me: one, that I'm dedicated to the success of Stairway, and two, that because of that, I'm removing myself from the picture."

"But why would they even agree to hear us out?" Mary asks.

"Because there is actually a little good news, like your pony hidden under all the horseshit. When the KCRHA lawyer called me, she said their director was impressed with our vision because it parallels theirs so closely. He didn't want to see needlessly duplicated effort and wanted to explore some kind of cooperation with us. That could mean either working alongside Stairway or bringing us on board to join some kind of internal Stairway-like team. Unfortunately, when his lawyer discovered my background, all that went out the window. But I think either of those things could still happen if they know I'm leaving."

"But what about you, viejo?" asks Carlos. "Where would you go? What would you do?"

"I haven't figured that out yet. Not really my focus right now. My focus is you guys. I need to know if you want to follow through with this, if you really have the guts and the will to do it, because it'll only work if you're driven enough to make it happen. And don't factor me into your decision, because I've made up my mind that it's time to go regardless."

"I'm a hundred percent in," Carlos says.

"It's the only thing that's made sense to me in years," Mary says. "Damn you. I *have to* do it."

"I can do this. I want to," Jimmy says.

To me, this all feels like a giant longshot, but I'll never say that—won't even hint at it. I know each person here has lots of raw potential, good intentions, and a desire to get off the street. But little else. Still, that's all it might take if they have the right support, and it's up to me to make that part happen.

But as Denise speaks up, I'm reminded I'm not the center of the support universe either.

"I believe in you and your vision," she says to the whole group. "As long as I can keep the bookstore afloat, I want to work with you. I'll keep the rent flexible as long as possible. I'm also willing to write letters of recommendation and help in any other way I can."

"Thank you," we say together.

"There's one more thing I want to get settled today," I say. "You need a new leader to work with me now and to take over when I leave."

To my relief, all eyes turn to Carlos.

"My thoughts exactly," I say to the group. "Carlos, you're the natural choice. Will you accept?"

"Con mucho gusto, viejo. I'm honored, and I'll give it everything I've got. Investing in our future, like my sign says."

Forty-Eight

I like to think my opening remarks at the KCRHA presentation two months later were the key, but I know better. Sure, my personal story and departure decision had an impact and were probably essential, but the deciding factors were clearly the honest, sometimes raw, but passionate contributions from the expanded Stairway team. Mary and Jimmy told their personal stories, from pre-homelessness to early life on the street, to despair, to discovery of purpose and hope. Carlos did the same and then very capably described our vision, first-year objectives, and proposed budget. Charlie and our new attorney, Paula Griffith, each gave very different but powerful arguments for the existence of Stairway. And Denise, as a Seattle small business representative, vouched for our reliability and spoke of the need for involving the homeless community in solutions—a core value of both Stairway and KCRHA.

The results came two weeks later: one year of funding with an option to absorb Stairway into the KCRHA organization if it proved successful during that time. Carlos negotiated the success metrics, and a check appeared in the mail the following day. He and I worked with the bank to create official business accounts for the newly funded organization, Jimmy obtained a domain for Stairway and acquired an email address for each person, and we modified the nonprofit filing to replace me with Carlos as Executive Director. In short, Stairway was off and running. And I was officially out.

But I don't think I really felt out until now. What I thought was going to be a final low-key lunch at the office has turned out to be a party. Along with Denise and the core team, both lawyers are here with the KCRHA director, and Bart has arrived with pizza and a keg of beer.

Charlie raises his glass. "To Roger and Stairway! Two things I never saw coming."

"To an ex-shithead!" adds Mary.

After other toasts and roasts along similar lines, Denise asks the question I knew was coming: "So, Roger, what's next for you?"

I don't have a specific answer, so I decide it's time for a pep talk instead.

"I guess the only thing I know for sure is that I'm not gonna sit around. I'm so proud of you guys, and I want to use your energy as a sort of personal springboard for whatever's next. Like I did with another springboard experience years ago from a famous and charismatic mountaineer named Scott Fischer. I only met him once, at Mountain Madness, his company here in Seattle, but he made a huge impression on me.

"He was giving a talk about his record-setting K2 ascent without supplemental oxygen, and was making a point about pushing personal boundaries, always moving forward, looking for the next big challenge. I remember him saying something like 'If you ain't cruisin', you're bummin'.' And when he said 'cruisin',' he didn't mean going along for the ride. He meant moving with focus and intentionality—fast and hard. I tried to take that to heart back then, and I'm gonna try again now. I hope you guys will do the same."

~

By three o'clock the party's over and more than a few tears have been shed, including some of my own. I'm out the door for the last time with a pack on my back, only the vaguest of plans in my head, and a hundred dollars from Carlos in my pocket. *Go west, viejo!* I imagine him saying. And so I do.

A fog begins to settle in as I walk down to Colman Dock and onto the ferry bound for Bainbridge Island. Once out on Elliott Bay, smelling the salt water and feeling the thrum of the diesel-electric engines beneath my feet, fond memories of my pilothouse aboard *Independence* come flooding back. But as I turn to watch the Seattle skyline recede behind the white churn of the ship's prop, I wonder if I would choose the same name for a boat, given the chance in some unlikely future. I think not.

As Seattle disappears behind the growing fog bank, I turn to face forward again, and Eagle Harbor emerges from the mist like a new beginning. *Is this freedom?* I wonder. Maybe, but only in the Joplin sense for now. Is this cruisin'? Literally, yes, but not quite as Fischer meant it. That requires a solid goal, a lofty destination, and now I have neither. I've left those things with my Stairway friends back on the mainland. Mary would probably say, *Well, that's something*, and I smile at the thought.

Epilogue

It *was* something, as it turned out. Stairway found some real success during its first year, lifting seven clients out of homelessness into jobs related to newfound interests or rekindled aspirations, two of them becoming direct contributors to Stairway itself and later to KCRHA. Carlos rose to the management challenge while also finding time to finish his two-year degree at community college, before transferring to UW. And Jimmy kept the digital heart of the organization beating securely, earning praise and encouragement from his coworkers. Last I heard, he'd even made a new friend outside of work—an actual person with a real name not beginning with J. But the most surprising success—and the most gratifying, to me—was Mary's.

Unknown to any of us during our time at the overpass, Mary was not only an avid reader but also a budding writer. Apparently, she had been spending rainy afternoons in her tent working on a gritty, brutally honest, sometimes heartbreaking, often witty memoir that she ultimately named

Down Town.

No one had seen her work—or even knew of its existence—until Mary dropped off the only copy of her handwritten manuscript at a small boutique publisher in Seattle one day, "almost as a joke." She had no literary agent in her corner and no expectations other than "getting rid of the damn thing," as she later admitted in a *Seattle Times* interview. The publisher picked up her work, and it quickly rose to number two on the *New York Times* bestseller list. She and the publisher were stunned. With the book's proceeds, Mary bought herself a small house on Queen Anne Hill and went back to school, finishing both her psychology degree and an MFA. She continues to work with the Stairway contingent at KCRHA while writing a novel and slowly paying off old debts to her brother.

As for me, life has been good, following a rough restart. After walking off the ferry onto Bainbridge Island, I spent two cold days and nights making my way out to the Olympic Peninsula, where I convinced a kind young farmer in Chimacum to let me stay in a primitive cabin in exchange for chores. That lasted a little over a year, until my aging bones began to rebel against the labor, and I started taking Social Security. Then I swapped chores for rent and saved the rest of my meager income until I had enough squirreled away to make my next move.

Now I'm living the dream, and I'm not being facetious when I say that. It might not be a conventional retirement dream, but it's mine and I'm cruisin' with it—yes, this time in the Scott Fischer sense of the word. West Marine in Port Townsend decided that my boating experience and former technology career outweighed any risks my old felony conviction might imply, so they hired me as a part-time floor salesman, specializing in marine electronics. And when I'm not working there, I'm managing the local food bank, where I'm slowly expanding its mission to include something I'm calling Stairway West.

I've also moved into a comfortable retirement home within easy walking distance of both jobs. Okay, it's not your typical retirement home. Not even close. It's a beautiful old Kadey-Krogen trawler in need of major work, side-tied to a dock in the marina where I can look over the breakwater from my pilothouse toward Whidbey Island at high tide. It's a place to permanently hang my hat too, quite literally, as I've created a little shrine to Tex in one corner of the large salon. I'm restoring the vessel little by little, hoping that one day before I die, she'll be ready to leave the dock and cruise again.

There's an ancient superstition against renaming a boat, but I think I'm immune to the curse, as I've probably used up my full allotment of bad luck and worse decisions. So now, written boldly across my trawler's transom in flowing script, is her new and forever name: *Claire*.

Acknowledgments

My wife, Donna, spent many hours reading all chapters of this book as they crawled off the keyboard, offering suggestions, flagging typos, and identifying grammatical issues. I'm so grateful for her, in every way.

My close friend and overall renaissance man, Bill Wood, provided excellent feedback on the business side of the plot. In fact, I completely changed the product of the fictional start-up company in direct response to his input, avoiding some serious timing and realism issues.

Scott Gunnison shared essential insights into the federal prison system gleaned from his professional experience in parole, probation, and pre-release work.

Bob Liepmann, Jackie Antoine, Ben Thompson, Grace Thompson, Katie Rose Fischer-Price, Leathia West, Linda Davis, and Barbara Regan were my beta readers, providing much-needed encouragement and valuable suggestions. Dean Wight and Susan Friend kept me going with questions about progress and frequent kind encouragement.

My editor, Katherine Kirk, exceeded all my expectations, and they were high to begin with. Her expertise, professionalism, command of the language, and friendly interactions worked together to improve the manuscript significantly. I'm grateful for her essential work.

My proofreader, Roberta Basarbolieva, found and fixed several remaining issues, and I'm thankful for her professional attention to detail.

Finally, I want to thank my publisher, Tahlia Newland of AIA Publishing, for her direction, her professional wisdom, and her decision to publish this book.

A Note From the Author

Maslow's Basement is a work of fiction about radical life changes and the personal choices that drive them—choices that sometimes have far deeper effects than we can foresee. It is about the astonishing nonlinearity of life, our tendency to focus inward to the detriment of ourselves and others, and the essential role of outward-looking purpose in our potential redemption.

I've used the pernicious problem of homelessness as a vehicle for the story as related by a very atypical victim—if Roger Carrington can be considered a victim at all. Many people fall into homelessness due to a corrosive mix of bad luck, unsupportive environments, and dubious choices. Often, people who are already living under the strains of economic uncertainty, mental or physical illness, or abuse of various kinds, are the ones we see pushed over the edge and onto the street, with addictions sometimes holding them there.

But Roger's situation, while rare, is not entirely unprecedented. He has all the advantages of education, wealth, and nearly limitless opportunity. So when he makes his serious mistakes and falls into homelessness, he does so from a great height. His case, along with similar ones I've discovered while doing research for this book, illustrates the point that homelessness can happen to anyone—not just those who appear to fit our stereotypes. As Roger himself says while observing businesspeople on their way to work from his new vantage point as a homeless person on the street, "They probably think they're impervious to ruin, infinitely distant from the likes of me, a different species. But they're wrong. We're all just two or three bad decisions or unfortunate events away from the edge."

That humbling realization ultimately serves Roger well. It leads him, albeit circuitously and often with less than pure altruism, to see people differently, to confront his prejudices, and to accept painful changes in his own life. Perhaps most importantly, he finds purpose—not so much despite adversity, but because of it.

Of course, this is fiction, but homelessness is painfully real and can strike anyone. Fortunately, we can all help. A quick internet search for "homelessness volunteering near me" will yield many opportunities to assist, either directly by donating time or indirectly via donations of material or money.

One way you've already made a difference is by buying this book, because all first-year proceeds go to a very special organization in Seattle called Mary's Place, which you can learn about at www.marysplaceseattle.org.

Thank you for reading *Maslow's Basement* and for doing what you can to help eradicate homelessness.

Please help the book be seen by as many people as possible by writing a review and publishing it at your point of purchase.

Other Books by the Author

Bending the Arc

When Luke Mason learns of his brother's white supremacist connections, he and his family are horrified. Initially they treat it as a thorny but manageable political difference between relatives – a private matter – but as shocking new information comes to light, Luke is forced to see the situation in broader terms. Tolerance and inaction are no longer options.

Bending the Arc is the story of the Mason family as they navigate a path of loss, confusion, and transformation. Ultimately, it's a story of love and hope.

Available from online bookstores or by order from your local store. worldwide.
Quote ISBN: 978-1-922329-06-6

www.ingramcontent.com/pod-product-compliance
Lightning Source LLC
LaVergne TN
LVHW092244191224
799569LV00005B/23